CROWN OF DANGER

THE HIDDEN MAGE SERIES

Crown of Secrets

Crown of Danger

Crown of Strength

Crown of Power

And set in the same world:

THE SPOKEN MAGE SERIES

Voice of Power

Voice of Command

Voice of Dominion

Voice of Life

Power of Pen and Voice:

A Spoken Mage Companion Novel

CROWN OF DANGER

THE HIDDEN MAGE BOOK 2

MELANIE CELLIER

CROWN OF DANGER

The Hidden Mage Book 2
First edition published in 2020 (v1.1)
by Luminant Publications

ISBN 978-1-925898-51-4

Luminant Publications
PO Box 201
Burnside, South Australia 5066

melaniecellier@internode.on.net
http://www.melaniecellier.com

Cover Design by Karri Klawiter
Editing by Mary Novak
Proofreading by Deborah Grace White
Map Illustration by Rebecca E Paavo

For Deborah—
sister, editor, fellow-author, friend

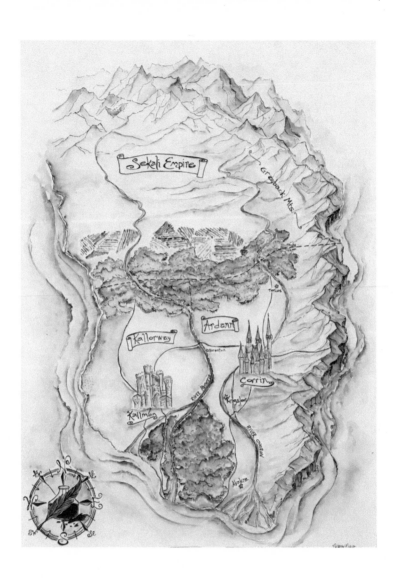

CHAPTER 1

"Come on, Verene. Hurry up! This is our last chance." Bryony urged me through the streets of Corrin, impatient with my sedate pace.

I gave her an amused look. "The shops aren't going anywhere."

"No." She sighed. "We're the ones going somewhere. Back to the Academy, and its awful, remote location." She looked longingly at the wall on the other side of the wide street which mostly concealed my own kingdom's Academy. "Why can't the Kallorwegian Academy be in the capital like your Ardannian one?"

I grimaced. "Would you really want to be in such easy reach of the Kallorwegian court? I, for one, have no such desire."

Bryony wrinkled her nose. "No, I suppose when you put it like that..."

The Kallorwegian court was poisonous, presided over by a cold, cruel king and full of deep rifts and divisions. It bore little resemblance to the court in Ardann which was ruled with the firm hand of my aunt, Queen Lucienne, a woman who had dedicated her life to ensuring peace and prosperity for her kingdom.

But I thrust thoughts of courts and politics aside. They

inevitably led to thoughts of Darius, and not even weeks of separation had managed to calm my conflicted feelings about the Kallorwegian crown prince.

We passed the Academy and University, our attendant guards walking two in front and two behind, keeping a clear bubble of space around us despite the busy traffic. Bryony practically danced in her impatience as we passed the railings that separated the grand houses of various mage families from the road. Bryony had no interest in the green grass, fountains, or elegant buildings we could glimpse behind the fences. As an energy mage from the Sekali Empire, she had little need to worry about the power games played by the Ardannian great families.

I had found myself with less interest in them over the summer as well, my mind full of the darker politics of the Kallorwegian court. I picked up my speed, suddenly as eager as Bryony to be past this section of the city and through to the shops. I glanced over my shoulder at the palace behind us, its tall towers of white marble dominating the capital from its place atop the hill that housed Corrin. It had been home for most of my sixteen years, and yet my thoughts about our imminent return to the Academy had a feeling of homecoming about them. My heart was in as much turmoil as my mind these days.

When we reached the section of road where the large homes usually gave way to elegant storefronts featuring wares designed to catch the eye of passing mages, I stopped.

"What's happening here?" I asked.

Captain Layna, who had been temporarily reassigned as my personal guard for the summer, stopped and looked back over her shoulder. She followed my gaze, her brow clearing when she saw I was looking at the construction to the side of the road.

"Who cares?" Bryony asked. "It's just a building." She threw a plaintive glance at the closest shop only a few steps further down the street.

"I can see that." I eyed the red sandstone blocks that lay in neat piles ready for the actual construction to commence, their color giving a clue as to the future purpose of the site. "It's some sort of public building. But why is it being built here?"

I looked inquiringly at Layna who shrugged, her focus flitting between me, the building crew and the street on my other side, her eyes alert for threats.

"I'm sorry, Your Highness, I haven't heard anything about it."

One of the royal guards behind me cleared his throat. "I believe it's a new office for the management of sealed affairs, Your Highness."

"Sealed affairs?" Bryony threw him a confused look before her face suddenly lightened. "Oh, you mean people who have had their power sealed. We don't have special offices for that in the Empire."

I grimaced slightly. I could imagine they would have no need for such special efforts in the Sekali Empire where every commonborn was sealed at age two. Here in Ardann, however, the sealed had become their own class of society—with a whole host of attendant complications. Allowing them access to reading and writing while keeping unsealed commonborns from having similar access was an ongoing struggle.

"But they already have an office." I frowned. "Has something happened to the old one?"

The number of sealed commonborns hadn't been expanding at a fast-enough rate to warrant a second office. In fact, one of the current complaints from the leading commonborn merchant families was that there was a shortage of mages completing sealing ceremonies. The crown might feel the lack of mages either failing the Academy or committing serious crimes to be a positive indication of the state of the kingdom, but those on the list to be sealed viewed the situation less favorably.

The commonborn guard who had spoken cleared his throat even more awkwardly than he had the first time. "I believe the current office in the lower city is still functioning, Your Highness. But certain interests requested the opening of a second building."

Ah. His careful choice of words clued me in to the likely motivation for this particular project. Twenty years ago, a derelict building near the outer wall of the city had been demolished and replaced with an office for the sealed. But in the years since then, the sealed had established their place in our newly reformed society, and I could only imagine some of their more influential members must have been complaining about having to make the trek all the way down to the lower city.

"Well that explains that, then." Bryony rolled her eyes, clearly still too focused on the shops to be interested in deciphering the layers of meaning behind his words. She gave me a pointed look. "Shopping? Remember?"

As I turned back to her, orange robes caught my eye, making me pause. Once the orange robes of creator mages would have dominated a scene like this, commonborn laborers scurrying around them only for the purpose of cleaning up debris and other such menial tasks deemed not worth the energy of mages. But I had already picked out the leaders of this team—two older, commonborn men, their wrists bare but for the elaborate pattern on their skin that marked them as sealed.

One of them held a small, intact scroll of parchment in his hand, clearly a composition that he was ready to work once his workers had the site prepared to his satisfaction. The other consulted a sheaf of parchments that I guessed contained plans for the new building. Had they prepared the plans in concert with a creator mage? Or had they drawn them up themselves, sending them off to a mage in some distant part of the kingdom and receiving them back along with all the necessary compositions for the work?

It wasn't unusual for a creator mage to be in attendance for the actual moments of creation, especially for such a significant building, but something in the manner of the two I now

4

spotted caught my attention. One was older, his hair entirely gray and his bearing stiff and confident. The other, by contrast, looked almost impossibly young and hunched in on himself, casting constant uncertain glances at the two sealed commonborns.

Instead of standing at the forefront of the scene, as I would have expected, they lurked to one side, almost out of sight. The older man pointed to something in the middle of the work site and said something to the younger man. His words were lost in the noise of the workers and the street beside us, but a faint look of frustration crossed his face at the answer he received.

Bryony appeared at my side. Looking first at me, and then following my gaze to the two mages, she heaved an enormous sigh.

"That mage looks uncannily like our discipline instructor, Amalia, considering he's male and must be two decades older. We'll be back in her not-so-loving care soon enough, I don't need reminding of her right now."

I chuckled although her words brought the scene into instant clarity. The creator discipline must be using the project as a chance to train one of their newer members. That would explain why there were two mages in attendance.

Sure enough, when the man with the building plans called a loud halt, sending the workers scurrying to the edges of the site, the older mage stepped forward, beckoning for the younger one to follow. When the second sealed man glanced at them, his hands poised about to rip his composition, the mage spoke loudly enough for me to hear.

"If you please, we will take care of the foundations."

The commonborn glanced at the man with the plans before shrugging and nodding his agreement, carefully placing his unworked composition into an internal pocket. The younger mage stepped forward, drawing a visible breath and pulling out a composition of his own.

"Verene," Bryony said by my side, lengthening my name into a plea.

I started to reply as the young mage tore his parchment, but the words died in my throat.

"Bree!" I hissed, and she stiffened, instantly alert to my change in tone.

Sliding closer, she whispered. "What is it?"

I didn't answer, my full focus on the scene now unfolding on the site in front of us. As an energy mage, Bryony couldn't feel power at all and only knew a working was being conducted because she had seen the composition torn. And while power mages like Captain Layna and the creator mages in front of us would be able to feel it, they would sense only a general, swelling rush of power released by the composition as it spread out to hover over the piles of stones around the edges of the site. For most of my life I had been like them, despite not being a power mage myself.

But everything was different now. I could sense the working in a way none of the rest of them could. At the end of my first year at the Kallorwegian Academy, I had stumbled on hidden powers I never suspected I possessed. And ever since then, my awareness had shifted, expanding from its old limits over the course of the summer. Now, if I concentrated on a specific working, I could feel the broad shape and purpose of it. And if I let down my guard, it called to me, a siren song inviting me to take charge of the power and shape it to my own will.

I didn't need my new ability to know the purpose of this composition—the creator mage had spoken it aloud. But something felt wrong. The power bucked and twisted, almost as if it fought against the shape it had been given. No one else reacted, but the sour note grew stronger as stones rose into the air and began to move around the site.

I hesitated, torn. I wanted to call a warning, but what could I say? No one but Bryony knew of my new ability, and I couldn't put my concern into words. I just knew something was very wrong.

An itching sensation, more mental than physical, urged me to reach out with my words and claim the power, but I held back. What would I do with it? I knew nothing of the expertise that must go into creating a building foundation.

And I had never tried to subvert a composition that felt so twisted before. While one part of me longed to reach out and control it, another part of me pulled away, repelled by the discordant note in the power.

The stones drew together, stacking on top of each other in an unnatural shape that could only be held in place by power.

Bryony frowned. "I'm no expert, but shouldn't a foundation lie flat on the ground?"

Almost as if he'd heard her, the older mage uttered a sharp exclamation, striding forward to pull the two torn halves of parchment from the hands of his student. He held them against each other and scanned their contents, his expression growing thunderous.

The stones piled higher and wider, forming the outline of the base of a large building...If the base of the building rose vertically into the air instead of lying against the ground.

Captain Layna stirred beside me. "Your Highness," she murmured, unease in her voice.

She didn't have to say more for me to know she wanted us to move away from whatever was developing here. But my feet had implanted themselves in the ground, and I couldn't have moved if I wanted to.

Other passersby lacked the instinctive caution of a trained guard, and a number of them stopped, drawn by their curiosity at the strange sight. The younger mage babbled at his mentor, but I didn't catch his stream of words, my attention too focused on the sensation of the power.

"Look, Mama!" A high-pitched voice broke through my

concentration as a young girl pressed in beside one of my guards, oblivious to our presence. Her full attention was on the stones still dancing through the air to stack ever higher.

Her mother gave us a wary look, but when no one remonstrated the girl, she moved to stand beside her daughter.

"They're building a new office for the sealed," she told the girl, apparently better informed than me.

But she frowned as she spoke the words. I was no longer the only one who could tell there was something awry with the composition.

"Princess Verene," my captain said, more sharply, but I continued to ignore her.

Bryony dropped her voice to the faintest whisper. "Can you…?"

"I don't know," I murmured back. "I don't know anything about creating."

All of the stones had now reached their place, although the structure they created was clearly unstable. A fresh surge of power fused them together, merging them into one solid block of stone more effectively than any mortar could do.

But now that they had formed a solid shape, the power holding them together loosed. If they had been spread out on the ground, it wouldn't have mattered. But they weren't. The tall, thin structure teetered.

"Take control!" I gasped.

If anyone heard me, they must have thought I was entreating the creator mages to take action. But my power responded instantly, free to do what it had been straining toward.

Reaching out, it grasped control of the working, and the hazy sense of a twisted composition became instantly clear. Without having to think about it, I knew immediately the full shape of the working and all its intricacies. I could feel the power trying to drive the footings deep into the ground, the effort muddied by the incorrect placement of the blocks. The power kicked and writhed as it fought against itself, torn by the two competing directions that had gone into its composing.

As the power attempted to drive the stone shape into the suddenly soft dirt, the whole structure swayed. For a moment it looked like it would fall onto the site, but then the momentum moved in the direction of the street.

The mother beside me screamed and snatched up her daughter as the solid stone shape fell toward us.

"Flat!" I gasped, as quietly as I could in my panic.

Power sprang to life around me, enclosing both Bryony and me in the comforting sensation of one of Captain Layna's shields. But it was tight and contained, offering only enough protection for the two of us—and only that because Bryony stood so close to me. I ignored it, my focus on the creator composition.

Its power, now under my control, quieted, no longer fighting itself as I asserted the correct image of flat footings driven into the dirt until they hit the solid stone beneath. Instantly the power caught the falling stone, pulling it away from the spectators and back upright into its original position. It teetered there for a single breath before crashing down in the opposite direction to lie flat on the work site. The structure slid, creaking slightly as it found the right position on the site, before pushing itself down into the already softened dirt.

I felt the moment it hit the more solid ground further down, the power instantly dissipating as the stone settled into place with several final groaning noises.

CHAPTER 2

or a single moment utter silence gripped the work site and the adjoining section of street. And then pandemonium broke out as Captain Layna, the two sealed commonborn builders, and half the gathered crowd called recriminations or demands for answers at the younger creator mage. He cast a panicked glance around before his attention was caught by the cutting voice of his mentor, rising above the hubbub of the crowd.

"Tell me exactly what went wrong there."

"I...I don't know. It worked." He shrunk in on himself at the withering glance he received from the older mage. "In the end."

Layna and the builders had fallen silent to hear the conversation, but the crowd continued to call out, making it hard to hear the mage's words. My captain nodded at her team, and they immediately began to move the bystanders on. Experts at their job, the guards soon had our side of the street clear and traffic flowing again, the more recalcitrant giving way before their red and gold uniforms and stern expressions, some throwing glances at me in response to barked words by the guards. Even the mages among them knew not to question royal guards on active protection duty.

Layna had drawn close, hovering over me in a threatening manner and glaring at everyone around us. She didn't try to make me move, though, obviously as anxious to hear the mage's explanation as I was.

"This composition reads perfectly," the older mage said. "If it didn't, I wouldn't have allowed you to work it. But a perfectly composed working would not have gone wrong in such a fashion."

His student gulped. "I've never done a foundation working for such a large building before. I was trying so hard to keep the whole image in my mind."

"You fool!" His mentor seemed to grow several inches until he towered over the younger man. "I told you that you weren't ready to layer your workings. Not for something like this. So you went and did the worst thing possible and overlaid it with a conflicting instruction!"

The young mage's face had drained of all color. "I didn't mean to."

"You're just fortunate your true intention turned out to be stronger," the older mage said darkly. "Or you'd be having a conversation with the Head of the Royal Guard right now. Or hadn't you noticed we have a royal audience?"

The student glanced in our direction and gulped, nearly toppling over as he hurried to bow deeply.

"What is he talking about?" Bryony asked, casting concerned glances at me, but knowing better than to attempt to question me on my own part in the drama. "What did he do wrong?"

I knew vaguely what the older mage meant by layering, but our first yearly composition studies hadn't extended that far, and Bryony wouldn't have been likely to hear about it from her energy mage parents. When I didn't attempt an explanation, Captain Layna spoke, her voice heavy with displeasure.

"Newer and weaker mages write long compositions, making every aspect and limitation of their working explicit with their words. More advanced compositions, however, can be shortened. Mages only achieve that level of control when they can place a secondary overlay of meaning over the words as they write them, shaping the power they force into their composition so it contains more complicated controls than outlined in the words themselves."

She shook her head. "None of your power mage year mates would be able to do that yet, but I can assure you they would all know better than to let their concentration slip while in the middle of a composition."

Layna was wrong about at least one of our year mates. I had no doubt that Prince Darius possessed the capability to overlay his compositions with deeper meaning. But I couldn't imagine him ever making the mistake of this new creator mage.

Bryony frowned at the two orange-robed mages. "So he did the layers wrong?"

"It sounds like he didn't mean to do an overlay of meaning at all," I said. "But he must have been picturing the image of the foundation from a different angle, and accidentally overlaid a competing instruction."

In fact, I knew that was what had happened because I felt it from inside the working, although I hadn't understood the reason behind it at the time. I couldn't say that in front of my guards, though.

"We're all fortunate the true intention ended up having the stronger direction," I added.

Bryony gave me a loaded look but didn't say anything.

"I would issue him an official reprimand," Captain Layna said, "except he had no idea you were here. There was clearly no harm intended for anyone, let alone you." Her voice calmed somewhat. "And while the threat to public safety is unacceptable, that isn't within my purview. Plus it looks like the creators have that well in hand themselves."

She sounded satisfied with the way the older mage was continuing to berate his student, threatening all sorts of dire punishments, including a year spent on the most basic and repetitive compositions needed by their discipline. I hid a smile at her pleasure, too distracted by my own unseen role in the near disaster to wish to join in castigating the mage involved.

"So only the most powerful mages can write short compositions?" Bryony asked, her mind obviously still on Layna's explanation.

I frowned at her, nervous about the direction of her thoughts since she seemed to be carefully not looking in my direction.

The captain nodded. "We have legends about a mighty mage of old who won a battle with a single word composition scratched in the dirt. But currently the Spoken Mage is the only one I'm aware of with the power and control for a single-word composition." She spoke my mother's popular title with respect. "I believe the instructors at the Academy are working with Crown Prince Lucien in the hope he might one day match the achievements of his mother."

I grimaced at her mention of my talented older brother, but her words didn't have the same sting they might once have carried. I was no longer the powerless sibling, constantly comparing myself to my gifted brother. It didn't matter if no one currently knew of my hidden abilities. I knew—and one day they would, too. I just had to work out how and when to make the truth known.

"Oh, I see," said Bryony, and this time she couldn't resist throwing a single glance at me.

I tried to glare at her without moving my features too noticeably, and either she received my message, or her own natural wisdom asserted itself, and she let the matter drop. No doubt she would be full of questions, but she could ask them later when we managed to find a moment alone.

"Shall we continue to the shops?" Captain Layna asked. "Somehow I imagine the creators will leave the poor work team to complete the rest of the foundation with their own compositions. And we can assume they sourced them from a more competent mage than that—" She cut off whatever insult she had been about to utter with a glance at me.

I grimaced but nodded, not having the heart to disappoint Bryony by saying I would prefer to return to the palace. But she spoke for me.

"You know, after being nearly squished like a pancake, I find I've somehow lost my enthusiasm for shopping. There's only one store I have to visit before we leave." She looked at me. "Do you mind one quick stop, Verene?"

"No, of course not." I gestured for her to lead the way, curious in spite of everything that had just happened.

She led us down the street, Captain Layna keeping pace beside her while the other three guards formed a close circle around me. The fence railings had disappeared, the buildings now standing close to the road so that passersby could admire the wares displayed behind the wide glass windows. We continued past most of them, however, Bryony ignoring her usual favorites such as the store she claimed made the best gowns in the kingdom or Empire.

When she finally stopped, it was in front of a smaller shop, one of the furthest from the palace. I could see further down South Road where homes once again replaced the shops, these ones tall and built close together in a uniform weathered gray stone. But the houses of the commonborn population, while crowded compared to the mage mansions, still looked bright and cheerful thanks to the many window boxes overflowing with color and life.

Bryony didn't glance down the street, though, pushing through the door of the store with vigor.

"There's only one thing I absolutely have to get," she said over her shoulder to me. "A gift for your mother for hosting me all summer. I know my parents brought all sorts of things from the Empire when they came to visit, but I want to give her something specifically from me."

"That's thoughtful," I said. "But you know she loves having you here. She considers you family, after all."

"All the more reason to give her a gift." Bryony smiled brightly.

The store owner hurried forward to greet us with a low bow. "Can I help you?" She looked eager as her eyes took me in, along with my four trailing guards.

"I'm looking for a gift," Bryony explained.

The lady started to point toward the display of intricate glass creations she had set up in her window, but Bryony continued.

"I'd like something made by a commonborn. Without the use of power."

"Oh?" The woman assumed a thoughtful expression as she surveyed the inside of her store. She must have been confused by the request, but she knew better than to question a customer.

"I would recommend having a look at that set of shelves over there." She pointed to the ones she meant. "All those works were made by a prominent master glassblower right here in Corrin." Her face turned proud. "He's considered the leading master on glassblowing, and he isn't even sealed."

"Thank you." Bryony moved over to examine the pieces which looked exquisite and startlingly detailed, even if they lacked some of the more impossible designs of the pieces displayed in the window.

"Are those made by mages?" I asked the storekeeper, pointing at the window. "Or by commonborns with mage compositions?"

"Both," she said. "I'll admit it's not a common practice, but

15

glass blowing is captivating for some. There are a few mages over the years who have fallen in love with the art form and create themselves. It's demanding physical work, though, and once they stop, some will form partnerships with commonborn glassblowers and provide them with compositions. Or sell them to a number of different glassblowers. We don't need the compositions to create the more basic, practical items, but they are incredibly useful for more artistic creations like these."

"What about this one?" Bryony asked, calling us both over to her side of the store. "Surely this wasn't created without power."

The storekeeper chuckled. "No, indeed, you're correct there."

I examined the striking piece which depicted two clear glass forearms rising vertically from the base of the piece and twining together, the two hands clasped. The entwined fingers gripped a long green stem, topped with a beautiful flower in vibrant red and orange. The base of the stem disappeared into the hands, long trails of green snaking down through the clear glass of the hands and arms as if the roots of the plant came from inside the people.

"Was this one not made by the master you mentioned?" I asked.

"Oh, no, it was," she said. "But he didn't make it alone. Last summer a retired grower sought him out. Apparently she had long appreciated his work. And since her retirement had relieved her of her duties to her discipline, she spent several months learning about glassblowing and experimenting with him before returning to her home estate. They created a number of stunning pieces together, but this is the only one I have left."

"It's perfect," Bryony said with decision.

"I thought you wanted something made without power," I said as the storekeeper hurried to securely wrap the piece.

"I did." Bryony watched her purchase being prepared. "But this is even better. Aunt Elena was telling us how she often feels disconnected from her commonborn origins these days, and I wanted something to remind her of the commonborns and her history with them. But this is absolutely perfect. A commonborn and a mage coming together to create new life and growth. It could be a sculpture of her own story."

I slipped my arm around Bryony's shoulder and squeezed, tears in my eyes. "She's going to love it."

"I hope so." Bryony paid the storekeeper, taking careful charge of the delicate parcel.

We exited the store together, starting back toward the palace. We walked in silence, my thoughts taking a darker turn. My mother possessed a unique gift, and she had used it to free her kingdom from war and bring new hope and voice to the commonborn people. Now I, too, had discovered I possessed a unique gift, but all I could do with it was subvert the workings of others.

My mood, buoyed up by the excitement of my success at the work site, crashed. If all I could do was fix others' mistakes—relying on happening to be in the right place at the right time—then my own legacy was likely to be insignificant. I had barely even managed to practice with my new ability over the summer, hampered by keeping it a secret. Bryony could only give others her energy, a useful skill but limited for my purposes—and not something I could ask of her more than occasionally.

I itched to experiment with a range of different power compositions, but I could hardly go around taking control of other mages' workings around the palace. My parents had noticed my frustration and strange moods but seemed to have decided not to ask me directly.

Their decision might have had something to do with Darius, fueled by my mother's intuition. Whether it was hints dropped by Bryony, or something I'd said while relaying Darius's request for support to my aunt, but somehow my mother had grasped the basic idea that I was far from indifferent to the Kallorwegian prince. And that we had not left our relationship in a positive place.

Whether she forbore from questioning me out of respect for what she no doubt considered my adolescent feelings or because she and my father were dismayed at the idea that I could possibly have romantic interest in a member of the Kallorwegian court, I wasn't sure. But I appreciated it all the same. I wasn't ready to talk about Darius to anyone, even my mother.

Forbearance was not one of Bryony's strengths, however, and as soon as we arrived back at the palace, she dragged me back to the guest suite she had been occupying for the weeks of our summer break. As soon as the door closed behind us, she carefully put down her new purchase and then pounced.

"It was you back there, wasn't it? Tell me everything."

CHAPTER 3

I flopped onto her bed while she remained standing, no doubt wanting the freedom to stride around and gesticulate wildly in response to whatever I said.

"I could feel there was something wrong with that composition from the beginning," I said. "It was fighting itself. But I was afraid to intervene."

"It's a good thing you did, though. Or who knows who might have been hurt?"

I nodded. "I should have taken control sooner, but I don't know anything about building foundations, and I knew there had to be a fair amount of power in that composition." I hesitated before admitting truthfully, "And I didn't know how easily I would be able to hide my involvement."

Bryony let out a sigh. "Yes, we were fortunate there, in the end. I don't think anyone suspected a thing. And I guess you didn't need to know anything about buildings after all."

I frowned, rubbing at my temples. "Well, that's actually the strange thing."

Bryony raised an eyebrow. "Really? That one thing?"

I rolled my eyes at her, pushing on with what I was trying to say. "I was worried because it was a composition that required a reasonable level of specialist knowledge, but as soon as I took control of it..."

"Don't tell me you gained all the knowledge of a master creator," Bryony exclaimed. "Because that's an ability I really would envy. Think how easy it would make study. Just claim a composition from each one of the instructors, and boom! You'd never have to study again."

I chuckled. "Yes, I can imagine you'd find that appealing. But I'm afraid I'm as ignorant about foundations and...and load bearings as I was before."

"Load bearings?" Bryony looked at me suspiciously. "What are load bearings? Maybe you did absorb some knowledge."

I threw up my hands. "I have no idea what they are. It's possible I just made that phrase up."

Bryony laughed. "Fine, then. I will accept you know nothing about constructing buildings." Her forehead creased. "Although you did more than stop that giant abomination from squashing everyone. It looked like it actually did what it was supposed to in the end. At least it sank into the dirt, which I'm assuming is what it was supposed to do. But I thought you'd taken control of the working at that point."

"That's the strange thing." I sat up straight, tucking my feet under me. "I don't know anything about building *now*, but the second I took control of the working, I understood it. Not just that its purpose was to create the footings for the foundation, but all the intricate details of how that was going to be achieved for that particular site. It all made sense to me. Right up until the working finished, and then the details just...slipped away."

"Well at least you knew it while you needed it. That seems like quite a helpful tool with an ability like yours."

I nodded, trying to keep frustration out of my voice. "I just wish it hadn't taken me all summer to discover it. I wish there was a way I could practice."

Bryony grimaced in sympathy. "I'm sorry. You know I'd help if I could."

I sighed and rubbed my hand over my face. "I know you would. Sorry to be so negative."

"I still think you should start stealing some of the compositions lying around this place," she muttered rebelliously. "You've told me the palace is practically coated in power."

"Yes, power that is doing something. All kinds of things, in fact. Things I can't identify properly until *after* I take control of the working. Who knows what might happen if those compositions suddenly disappear? Or who might start investigating why the palace compositions are failing?"

Bryony rolled her eyes at my practicality but didn't protest further. It wasn't the first time we'd had the same conversation. She strode restlessly up the room, collapsing into a chair on her way back.

"There's something else I've been wondering about—from what Captain Layna said about short compositions." She gave me a confused look. "She made it sound like some sort of epic feat that needed vast training. Even for Aunt Elena. But you do it. You always have."

I nodded. "I've actually been thinking about that all summer. From what I understand, in normal power compositions, the biggest issue is binding the power long enough to shape the working properly. As we know from the commonborns, once power is drawn on, it wants to explode out—violently. That's why mages always start with binding words. Mother doesn't have to use them because her compositions are so short there's no time for the power to get out of control, but she took a long time to train to that point."

"I guess I don't know much about that," Bryony said. "None of us energy mages have that issue given our access to power is naturally sealed before we're even born."

I nodded. "And as well as the control issue, power is also difficult because there's so much you can do with it. It's inherently shapeless and has to be molded to the mage's purpose. It takes a lot of skill to do that in few words."

"I always knew you were skilled." Bryony grinned at me.

I snorted. "That's not what I'm saying. I've been thinking about how it's different for you and other energy mages. You don't have to worry about binding words because you're drawing on your own energy directly to work your compositions—the energy you're using for your workings isn't unstable in the way that power is. And your range of potential compositions is so much more limited that length isn't really an issue either."

"Thanks," Bryony said dryly, but I just grinned, knowing she wasn't really offended.

"I've come to the conclusion that I'm using energy not power," I said.

Bryony raised an eyebrow. "Energy compositions can't lay building foundations."

"I mean for the first part," I said, "when I take control of a working. It's hard to describe, but it's like something in me senses the working and just...reaches for it."

Bryony narrowed her eyes, speaking slowly. "I suppose that makes sense. It does sound more like energy than power."

"But once I've taken control of the working, I'm using whatever the composition was originally crafted with—be that energy or power. So it was power I used on the foundation today. But I didn't need binding words or even lots of words at all because it wasn't shapeless power. It had already been contained and directed. I was just...twisting it. Which is one of the reasons I was so hesitant to take it over in the first place. The power has already been shaped enough that I can't just do whatever I want with it. I have to find a way to direct it that at least somewhat aligns with its original shape. Like when the assassin used a composition to empty my lungs. I was able to turn it around to fill my lungs instead, but I couldn't have used it to…I don't know, grow a flower or something."

Bryony frowned, clearly trying to follow my logic. "So you were scared that you wouldn't understand what the creator mage had directed the power to do and therefore wouldn't be able to control it. It sounds like that's not going to be a problem, though."

I nodded, letting out a breath. "It's a big relief actually." My face fell. "Not that I suddenly have any more options for practicing than I did before."

Bryony straightened in her chair. "That's one good thing about being back at the Academy soon. We'll have more opportunities there. I'm sure we'll be able to work something out."

"Hopefully you're right."

"I generally am," she told me with a twinkle. "And personally, if I were you, I would stick with the 'I'm a prodigy' explanation. You deserve it after thinking you had no powers at all for so long."

I laughed. "Why do I feel like you would absolutely claim to be a prodigy in my circumstances?"

"Because I'm shameless?" Bryony chuckled. "But now you'd better head back to your own rooms. We're going to have to go to the evening meal with work site dust all over us if we don't hurry up and get changed."

I looked down at my gown and then guiltily at my friend's bedspread. "I think I already got it all over half your room."

"Never mind that." Bryony waved away my concerns. "But this is our last meal with your family, and I don't want to be late."

She shooed me out the door, and I went willingly, her words having redirected my thoughts. As much as I found my mind turning more and more constantly to the Academy, I still didn't like the idea of this being my last meal with my family.

I had hated not being able to tell them the truth of my new abilities. It put up a barrier between us, even if they didn't know it was there. But I had still enjoyed having time with them again.

Especially now that my love for my brothers wasn't complicated by my constant need to suppress my resentment that they had both received abilities from our parents while I had not. I would miss them when I returned to the Academy.

We ate the meal in a private dining room reserved for my family. My aunt didn't join us, and I felt guiltily glad. Aunt Lucienne loved us, I knew that, but she was always queen first and aunt second. It was the reason I couldn't risk telling anyone in my family about my new ability. I couldn't risk the crown of either kingdom finding out my potential as a weapon—especially a weapon against my own mother.

The summer hadn't taken away my fear that as soon as either kingdom discovered the truth, I would be reduced to nothing more than a tool—and one too full of danger and potential to be allowed to travel freely between the kingdoms. My aunt's crown created a barrier that wasn't there when it was just my parents and brothers.

Her presence always affected Lucien as well. With us he could be himself, but when my aunt was around, he never forgot he was crown prince. It made sense she had taken him under her wing, molding him to be like herself. He was her heir, after all. But I had long suspected that it pained my parents to see their son so weighed down with responsibility.

They never tried to curb the time he spent with our aunt, though. They understood that being monarch was the kind of job you needed to be trained for from birth because it was a role that consumed all of you. Lucien would always have to put Ardann first, and it was better that he was raised to understand that from the beginning. But I still enjoyed the moments we got to spend just with our family, not thinking about what was to come.

I was the last to arrive, entering the room just in time to see Bryony present my mother with the sculpture, accompanied by an explanation of its history.

My mother embraced her in response. "Thank you, Bree. It's beautiful."

My father put his arm around my mother's shoulders. "The symbolism is perfect. It's a thoughtful gift, Bryony."

Mother turned slightly, and I suspected she was surreptitiously wiping her eyes against his jacket. But when she turned back to us all, she was all smiles.

"I'll put it here." She placed it in the center of the table, my father removing the vase of flowers that had been standing there before she asked, anticipating her want as he so often did. "Then we can all admire it while we eat."

We all sat down, my parents at the head and foot of the table and two of us on each side. The room would have taken a larger table, but my mother had always insisted this smaller one remain. She wanted us all to be able to talk comfortably.

Over the initial scraping of chair legs and clanking of cutlery, my younger brother, Stellan, leaned toward me. "I don't know that I'd want a flower growing out of my hand, to be honest," he said in an under voice.

I grinned at him. "Didn't you hear what Father said? It's *symbolism*, Stell."

He rolled his eyes. "I'm just saying. I'm all for grasping hands across the divide, and what have you, I'd just rather not have roots through my tendons."

"You're going to have to learn something about romance if you ever want to convince a girl to marry you."

"Ha!" He grinned back at me, showing all his teeth. "I think you're forgetting I'm a prince. And the lucky kind who doesn't ever have to be king. The girls will be falling all over themselves just as soon as I start at the Academy."

I snorted, although his words reminded me uncomfortably of Prince Jareth. Darius had always insisted his brother felt the same way as Stellan—that he saw the throne as something to be avoided rather than coveted. I wasn't so sure.

I took a mouthful of soup. "You're just lucky Lucien will graduate before you start."

We both turned to examine our older brother. If I looked like my grandmother, everyone had always said Lucien was the exact image of my father when young. And even I had to admit his bright green eyes were striking against his dark, almost black hair. Although we shared the hair color, I had sometimes envied him those eyes, although my mother always assured me the glints of gold in my own brown eyes were just as beautiful. But then, as my mother, she could hardly be viewed as having an objective opinion.

Lucien, sensing our scrutiny, looked up from his bowl and narrowed his eyes at us both. "What are you two plotting?" His voice held all the superiority of an older sibling.

"We're just marveling at what a fine specimen you are," I said in a tone of utmost innocence.

He choked on his mouthful of soup and had to pause to cough it back up. Once he'd recovered his breath, he gave me a baleful glare.

"Now I know you're up to something."

"Leave your sister alone," Father said. "It's her last meal with us, remember."

I gave Lucien the prim smile I knew always left him fuming and quickly finished my own bowl. Mother looked between us and shook her head, a smile on her face that was half-amused, half-indulgent. She was probably thinking of her own brother and sister.

"Maybe we can foist him off on Bree," Stellan said abruptly, continuing our quiet conversation at full volume. "Then the way will be clear for me."

Bryony, sitting across from him, looked up from her soup in alarm. "If you're talking about Lucien needing some extra energy compositions to keep on hand, then I'm more than happy to help out, but if it's anything else you have in mind..." She shook her head so vigorously she nearly lost a hair pin from the rather haphazard arrangement on her head.

Lucien grinned at her. "Thank you, Bree. It's always good to be reminded of how repulsive I am."

She rolled her eyes. "You are all too aware you're not in the least repulsive, Lucien." She paused to give Stellan a stern look. "But aside from the fact that I've been raised to consider you all family despite the lack of blood connection, not even the prettiest eyes in the world could tempt me anywhere near a crown." She shuddered dramatically.

"There you go, Lucien," I murmured. "Some consolation for you. At least you've got pretty eyes."

"The prettiest eyes in the world, apparently," Stellan said with a wide grin.

Bryony snorted. "I'm nothing if not fair. Although it's a sad waste. I'm sure some poor laborer somewhere could do with those eyes. You hardly have need of them, Lucien. Not when there are plenty of girls who do find a crown attractive."

"Let your poor brother be," Mother said, directing a quelling look at me in particular.

I instantly felt guilty. I had forgotten her words from a few days before about my aunt's desire for a marriage alliance with one of the imperial princesses. There was every likelihood poor Lucien wouldn't get the chance to choose his own bride.

"Stellan is just afraid of the competition," I told Lucien. "He's already thinking of when he'll be starting at the Academy next year."

"About that," said Stellan quickly, and the mood in the room instantly dropped.

My father's expressions could be hard to read, but I had long ago learned the tricks of interpreting them. Bryony might not have noticed anything at all, but to me he looked thunderous. I glanced at my mother who, even after more than twenty years as a princess, had never achieved my father's level of control. She was giving Stellan the look we all knew meant it was time to let something drop.

My brother pushed on.

"If you would let me join the sealing ceremony next week, then I could properly start at the Academy next autumn. Who knows when another opportunity will come up?"

"We've already discussed this," Father said flatly.

"And the answer is still no," Mother finished for him.

I looked back and forth between them before looking across the table at Lucien. He looked as confused as I felt. We both turned our gazes on Stellan.

"Sealing ceremony?" Lucien asked at the same moment as I spoke.

"You want to be sealed?"

Stellan, who had remained resolute in the face of our parents' disapproval, threw us both a guilty glance.

"Your brother has spent most of the year while you two were away trying to convince us to let him be sealed along with the next group of commonborns," Mother said. "I thought he had finally given up on the topic."

"I had," Stellan said. "Until I heard there was going to be a sealing ceremony next week. We don't have many of them anymore, so this is my best chance."

"But why would you want to be sealed?" I asked blankly. I glanced across at Bryony, expecting to see her sharing my confusion, but she looked merely thoughtful.

"It makes perfect sense if you think about it," Stellan said. "I know my royal status means they've bent the rules and allowed me to learn to read, but the Academy would be much easier if I could write as well. Mother knows that's true because she had to make it through all four years without writing herself."

"And I graduated just fine," Mother said. "As will you."

"We've already agreed to discuss it again after you finish first year, Stellan," Father said in a closed voice. "You're not yet sixteen. It's much too early to think of limiting yourself in any way."

"But that didn't work for Verene, did it?" Stellan asked before cutting himself off with a guilty look in my direction. Changing tack, he focused his attention across the table. "You understand, don't you, Bryony? An energy mage doesn't need access to power. All we can do with it is accidentally destroy ourselves. You're all born sealed, so I don't see why it's so strange I would want to be sealed myself."

Bryony opened her mouth but then looked at me and closed it again.

Stellan glanced at me as well and then at Lucien. "I know being a spoken energy mage makes me strange, but I'm still an energy mage. Everyone agrees on that. It's just another one of our oddities that I wasn't born with my access to power sealed like all the regular energy mages. But thankfully that's easy enough to remedy."

"But…" I struggled to find the words. At Stellan's age I had been desperately awaiting my sixteenth birthday, hoping against hope that some hitherto unsuspected power might emerge, and now my brother wanted to do the opposite and purposefully limit himself.

And yet, I also understood what it was like to dread starting at the Academy, knowing how different you were from everyone else. And in Stellan's case, he would be starting the year after Lucien graduated, not only different from his year mates but walking in our brother's impossibly large shadow. At the moment he was like a commonborn, unable to safely write without unleashing uncontrolled power, and so being sealed alongside commonborns actually did make sense. And unlike the power mage conducting the sealing ceremony, he would still be left with his ability intact since he appeared to have an energy ability which wouldn't be affected by sealing his power.

But looming over all of those thoughts was the knowledge

that had closed Bryony's mouth. The knowledge we had agreed not to tell my family—and by inevitable extension, my aunt. My brother thought my example proved his case, but he didn't know the truth. I was actually proof it was entirely possible he did have some power that hadn't yet emerged.

"I think Mother and Father are right," I said slowly, earning a betrayed look from my brother. "Sorry, Stellan, but I just don't think it's worth the risk. You can wait another couple of years."

A crease appeared between Mother's brows as she gave me a long look. I bit my lip, hoping I hadn't somehow given myself away. However she didn't challenge me, and immediately my concern was replaced with guilt. If I wasn't concealing the truth from my family, then my brother wouldn't be trying to get himself sealed.

I glanced at my father's implacable face. Sealing wasn't the sort of thing Stellan could do on his own in a fit of rebellion. He was safe for two more years. I resolved that if his opinion remained the same next summer, I would think of a way to warn him properly. I couldn't let him forever limit himself because of my lack of transparency.

Meanwhile, my mother had turned her attention from me to Stellan. Her face and voice softened as she looked at her younger son.

"I know it doesn't feel like it, but we're saying this because we love you. I'm truly sorry you children have had to inherit such a muddle of powers, but each of you is unique and special. Your Father and I couldn't live with ourselves if we let any one of you limit yourselves in an effort to be normal."

My father nodded. "Your mother didn't change our kingdom and end the war with Kallorway by being the same as everyone else. And I truly believe you children have the potential to do even greater things than we did. We brought the beginnings of change, but we were forced into taking small steps by the weight of the past and established opinions. You four are at the center of the next generation—the one growing up in the new world, with a new way of thinking. You're the ones who will truly live that change."

I grimaced, looking down at the plate of roast meat I had just served myself from the platters in the middle of the table. Aunt Lucienne had also talked about my being part of a new generation when she sent me off to Kallorway with the mission to uncover the minds of my year mates—and especially that of the Kallorwegian crown prince. But I couldn't say I'd seen a great deal of evidence of this new way of thinking that apparently gave my parents so much hope.

Most of the first years had given every appearance of following obediently in their parents' political allegiances, and none of them had appeared to give a thought to the common-borns at all. The thought sparked something in my mind, an elusive idea that slipped away before I could grasp hold of it fully, the chatter of my family distracting me from pinning it down.

Stellan made a quip about my father's speech, and my mother laughed, sending my father an affectionately mocking look and apparently taking Stellan's effort as a sign he was willing to let the charged topic of sealing drop. The conversation moved on, and I rejoined it, suddenly remembering that Bryony and I would be leaving in the morning. This was the last time I would hear my family laughing and joking together for nearly a year.

Although I tried to shake it off, the melancholy lingered with me for the rest of the evening. My mother must have noticed because she gave me an extra long embrace as we all parted for bed.

"It's so quiet here when you and your brother are gone," she said softly.

I forced myself to smile. "You're surrounded by an entire palace full of people. It can't be that quiet."

She smoothed back my hair, like she used to do when I was a

child. "But they're not the most important people. I hope you know that your father and I miss you."

I buried my face in her shoulder, my arms tightening around her. "I miss you too."

When I pulled back with a long sigh, she smiled at me, but it didn't light up her eyes the way it usually did. I gave her a final goodnight and left for my suite, wondering if she could sense what I had carefully refrained from voicing all summer. The palace at Corrin no longer felt like my only home, and something —or rather someone—called me back to Kallorway.

CHAPTER 4

*W*hen our carriage rolled past the stretch of road
that had once split the Wall, only the dead land
remained as a sign of what had once stood there. The work
removing the rocks had finally been completed, or so I had been
told.

I wasn't alone in the carriage this year, either, the journey
enlivened by Bryony's company. She had been extra bright all the
way from Corrin, and from her careful avoidance of any mention
of Darius's name, I could guess why. But she seemed to have
finally abandoned her efforts to lighten my mood, falling silent as
she watched the countryside pass by the window.

I stared out the opposite window myself but absorbed
nothing of the view. How strange it seemed that I hadn't seen the
Kallorwegian prince for so many weeks. And how much stranger
that a year ago I hadn't even met him. When I pictured his tall
form and the hidden spark in his dark eyes, my heart beat faster
despite myself, and I willed the horses to hurry.

But I feared our arrival in almost equal measure. How would
he react when he saw me? Would our absence over these summer

weeks bring back something of the closeness we had once shared? Or would the chill of our parting still linger?

My heart wanted to see the fire in his eyes again, but my mind remembered that nothing had changed in those weeks. I still had a strange new power that I couldn't share with a prince who had dedicated his life to seizing the throne at Kallmon. If I couldn't share the truth with my own family, I certainly couldn't share it with Darius who knew just as well as my aunt what it was to hold everything and everyone else secondary to your responsibility to your kingdom.

But it still felt wrong. He had been the one to rescue me when I had discovered the first part of my ability and had trained with me for weeks. He was a central part of that journey and the world I had lived in last year, and it wasn't my desire to cut him out now.

But he would be the first to tell me that royals had a responsibility to their kingdoms and people that came before their own desires. It was the only reason he was scheming for the throne. I just wished I knew which kingdom and which people I could safely entrust my new abilities to. I had hoped the summer and a return to my old home might bring some counsel on the subject, but I was no closer to peace on the matter than I had been when I finished first year. I could not let Darius use me against my mother and my family and the people of Ardann. But neither could I become a tool in the hands of my aunt against the people of either Kallorway or the Sekali Empire.

Not that I felt any great loyalty to either group of people as a whole. But their representatives burned brightly in my mind— Bryony and Darius. My best friend and the boy who haunted my dreams.

The carriage rolled on into Bronton and, like the previous year, we stopped for the night, although this time we stayed at the largest of the town's inns. When we crossed the bridge over the Abneris into Kallorway early the next morning, tension filled me. It wouldn't be long before I saw Darius again.

He had been closed off from me when we parted ways, shamed, perhaps, by his father's role in the attacks against me, and resentful of my continuing suspicion of his brother, Jareth. But he had still entrusted me with a secret message to my aunt, and if he hoped to avoid me completely this year, her reply would foil those plans.

She had called me in for a private audience as soon as I returned to Corrin for the summer and had listened to the carefully worded request I passed on from Darius. My father had learned to hide his true emotions through the same upbringing as Aunt Lucienne, but she was the greater expert. I could still sense her surprise, however.

I didn't know if it was surprise at Darius's plans, or surprise at the extent of my success. Either way, I could tell she was impressed with my efforts and with the trust I had won from the infamously closed Darius. Once her approbation would have filled me with joy, but now it only sparked feelings of guilt. I had set out a year ago, determined to prove myself to her, and now I was hiding something huge and momentous. I didn't deserve her approval.

"So the crown prince intends to seize the throne from his father," she had said, tapping her lips in thought. "An interesting problem."

"King Cassius is destroying Kallorway," I replied, refraining from mentioning he had also attempted to destroy me. I didn't want that story getting back to my parents. They might pull me from the Academy altogether. "Darius only wants to save his people."

She laughed at that, a short chuckle, although it seemed to hold genuine amusement. "I'm sure we all tell ourselves that. And for some of us perhaps it's true."

I wanted to leap to Darius's defense but restrained myself. It wouldn't help his case for my aunt to guess the extent of my partiality for the foreign prince. Instead I gave a more political answer.

"It seems to me the crucial element is that he has been promised the throne. And soon—not at some distant date upon the death of his father. King Cassius has assured not just Darius but his own supporters that he will step aside in his son's favor. From what I understand, it's the whole basis of his current hold on power. Darius merely intends to hold his father to the promises he has made to his kingdom."

I held silent for a moment, letting her ponder. As a reigning monarch herself, I could understand why the concept of over-throwing a ruler might make her uncomfortable.

"It is true that the prince's claims align with reports we have heard," she said at last. "Our intelligencers have long relayed rumors that Cassius promises to step aside for his son. And his efforts to delay the prince's commencement at the Academy would certainly support this idea. Cassius has held on to his throne by his torn fingernails for more than twenty long years. He is not the sort to cede power willingly."

"And he does not have reason to love Ardann." I chose my words carefully. "During my year in Kallorway, I was left in no doubt that King Cassius's hatred for us, and for my mother in particular, weighs too strongly with him to allow his forging closer ties with our kingdom. If Ardann wants to build stronger ties with Kallorway, then we would be well served to see Darius on the throne."

My aunt weighed me with a piercing gaze. "And you are confident that the son does not share his father's prejudices?"

"Entirely," I said with too much feeling, immediately regret-ting my eager response when I saw the speculative look that sprang into her eyes.

"King Cassius and Queen Endellion attended the Midwinter Ball that I hosted at the Academy on Ardann's behalf," I said quickly, hoping to cover my lapse. "I had the opportunity to observe the princes with both their parents. There is no love lost between Darius and his father."

"And what of Jareth and Cassius?" Aunt Lucienne asked, instantly latching on to another topic I preferred not to discuss.

I hesitated. "Jareth appeared...changed around his father. Less comfortable than I had seen him previously. But, on the surface at least, he appeared to be on reasonable terms with his father—and even better ones with his grandfather."

I didn't mention that I had spent a significant amount of time suspecting the prince of colluding with his grandfather to seize power from both Cassius and Darius. But it had turned out in the end to be the king, not old General Haddon, who was behind the attacks on me. Attacks that I still believed Jareth had a part in perpetrating.

"We have certainly always heard that he is the more sociable of the brothers," my aunt said.

I barely suppressed a snort. I doubted sociable was a word that anyone had ever thought to apply to Darius.

"Do you believe Prince Jareth is a contender for the throne?" Aunt Lucienne asked. "I have received no such reports, but then I had also received no reports that Darius was intending an imminent coup."

I shifted slightly. "I don't know that I'd use the word imminent." I hesitated again. "And I couldn't state Jareth's intentions with any certainty. But I know that his brother believes in him implicitly."

It was strangely painful to report this weakness in Darius—the blindness with regard to his brother. But if I wasn't going to tell my aunt the truth of the attacks on me, then I had to find a way to convince her that Jareth was not an option for the throne as far as Ardann was concerned.

"I do believe that if he ends up on the throne, it would only be through great duplicity," I continued. "In winning such a place, he would demonstrate he possessed the sort of character Ardann could never rely on. If we wish to see a strong and reliable ruler on the throne in Kallmon, a ruler who will hold his kingdom together and look to Ardann as an ally, then we must back Darius. I truly believe that."

I held my breath, waiting for her response. I wanted to believe that everything I had told Darius was true, and that Ardann did want to see a strong ruler in Kallorway. But there was always the possibility that my aunt's feelings on the matter were not so straightforward. Decades of war had left deeply entrenched mistrust of Kallorway in all layers of Ardannian society.

Once again, my aunt's eyes weighed me. I tried to look older and wiser than my actual years.

"You have impressed me, Verene," she said after a moment. "You achieved more than I thought probable in a single year. I am surprised that I find myself inclined to trust your judgment in this." She sighed. "But then perhaps I am merely believing what I wish to be true. It is certainly hard to see how—after more than twenty years—Ardann has any hope of moving forward with either Cassius or old Haddon."

"So it is truly a priority for you to see Ardann more closely allied with Kallorway?" I asked tentatively.

She sighed again. "Weakening Kallorway was a necessity when they were determined to use their strength against us. But in the long run it is in no one's interests to see the southern king-doms so divided. Kallorway's weakness weakens us all."

I frowned. It almost sounded as if my aunt had some specific threat in mind. She read my expression easily.

"You have proven you can be discreet, niece, so I will admit that there are unsettling rumors coming from the north."

"From the Sekali Empire?" My brow creased in sudden worry. "Don't tell me the Emperor has turned against us!" Was this the reason for my aunt's sudden talk of a marriage alliance for Lucien?

She shook her head. "Nothing so drastic. But it is my job as ruler to see beyond the immediate problems of today. I must see the dangers waiting to spring at us down the road. And you may call me fanciful, but my instincts tell me it is time for Ardann to mend the breaches with Kallorway."

I had never in my life considered my aunt fanciful. And I wasn't about to do so now. Unease sprouted inside me. The mission I had taken on the year before suddenly assumed new significance in my mind. Ardann had benefited greatly from the borders with the Empire opening, but there was danger to us there too. If unrest was coming to the great northern lands, who knew what might spill over into the south?

"So what answer shall I take to Darius?" I asked.

"You may tell him Ardann supports him," she said, her tone brisk now that her decision was made. "But we will not do so openly until he has earned legitimacy for himself. There will be nothing in writing. You will be my representative in this matter."

I drew in a breath. I hadn't expected her to trust me with so much responsibility.

There had been further conversations over the course of the summer as she instructed me on what help I might promise or provide Darius in different scenarios, but her basic decision remained unchanged. To aid me in my expanded role, she had even gifted me further communication compositions with a powerful enough range to reach from the Kallorwegian Academy back to the palace.

"It is a natural enough gift for me to give my niece," she said. "No one will think it remarkable to hear that her family misses her and wishes for more frequent communication."

I frowned down at them, knowing what a composition of such strength cost.

"It's true, you know." Her soft voice made me look up, startled. "Your family did miss you, and your father was more than willing to accede to my request. He considered the occasional day in bed to be a small price."

I sighed. I had been careful not to say anything that might push him into expending so much energy on my behalf, especially when I saw the crown already had him working so hard. Now I knew these had been what he was working on all along.

As a prince, my father wasn't part of any discipline and was never expected to assist with the sort of commonplace compositions other mages regularly produced. But royal strength was meant for more than just prestige or status. Some compositions required so much strength and control that they could be completed only by the strongest of mages—and even then, a day in bed might be required to regain the energy expended on such an effort. Keeping my parents on hand allowed my aunt to sacrifice fewer of her own days. No monarch wanted to spend even a day weak and vulnerable in bed, their energy entirely depleted.

"If you need to consult with me on a matter, use one of these," she said. "I have a trusted clerk standing ready at all times to receive your communication. And I will then reach out to you at the earliest opportunity. Or have your mother do so. Try to make sure you're alone until you hear back from us."

I nodded and carefully tucked the precious compositions away in my most secure pocket. These weren't ones that I needed access to at a moment's notice, and I wouldn't risk losing or damaging them.

Now, as we bumped across the Kallorwegian road, I touched the outside of my robe, over the place where they hid. I would be careful not to use them frivolously, but it still felt reassuring to have the option.

"We can't be far," Bryony said, sliding closer to the window and attempting to peer out at the road ahead. "I thought I just saw a glimpse of the Academy."

Sure enough, a lone house appeared outside the window, followed by another.

"This must be the nearby village." I moved to the other window. "We should be there within minutes in that case."

I caught a glimpse of a rider on a strong chestnut stallion. Captain Layna rode beside the carriage, escorting me back to the Academy as her final duty of the summer. But unlike the first time we had ridden this way together, she had brought only a single mage officer in support. I had spent the entire previous year at the Kallorwegian Academy without a single Ardannian guard, so the entourage that had accompanied me last year was deemed unnecessary.

I lowered the window and was about to call to her when her mount reared. Layna somehow stayed on his back while still keeping a hand free to thrust inside her robe. I didn't have a chance to see what composition she was retrieving, however.

"Attack!" yelled another voice as Bryony scrambled away from her window, almost falling into my lap in her haste.

"Someone is attacking the carriage," she gasped.

CHAPTER 5

$\mathcal{I}$ moved in the opposite direction, rushing toward the far window to try to catch a glimpse of what was happening. The carriage had come to a shuddering halt, but the view was too limited to tell why. I pushed open the door and jumped down. Bryony followed close behind, recovered from her initial shock.

I had expected to find us encircled by soldiers or perhaps brigands of some kind—although for either to attack a royal carriage was beyond shocking. I didn't expect to be greeted with nothing at all. I spun in a circle, trying to find what had so unnerved my companions.

We were still in the midst of the village, but the streets were deserted, and everything was quiet—strangely so. But an unnatural stillness wouldn't have made Layna's horse rear or sent Bryony leaping away from the window.

"What happ—"

I didn't get the chance to finish the question. A shadow moved between two of the houses followed immediately by a rush of power that surged in our direction. My hand dived for my most accessible pocket before I registered the feel of a bubble of power already around us. One of our two guards had long since shielded us.

I dropped my hand as the power that had been lobbed at us broke against the barrier of our shield. For a moment the shield held before dissolving, all sensation of power leaving the air around us.

Another shield sprang to life before I could even think about going for one of my own. It had most likely come from Layna, although my view of her was now blocked by the carriage.

Bryony grabbed at my arm. "What's going on?"

I swallowed. "That was a powerful attack. It took out our shield."

"What?" Bryony gasped.

"One of the guards released another one," I reassured her quickly.

"Still," she said uneasily. "Are we going to have enough?"

"I'm sure Layna is well supplied." I tried to inject more confidence into my words than I felt. If someone was fool enough to attack a royal carriage, they would presumably have come with significant attack power. Who knew how long they had been preparing for this?

"There!" Bryony pointed to another building further up the street.

A man darted out onto the street, narrowing his eyes as he looked back at us. He didn't wear a robe, or any other identifiable clothing, but he held a stack of parchment in his hands.

A clattering behind us made me whirl, but it was only our second guard, Lieutenant Beckett, climbing onto the roof of the carriage.

"In front," he called. "And behind."

My captain appeared, on foot now, her face grim.

"Who are they?" I asked. "What do they want?"

"You, I assume," she said in a harsh voice. "I should have asked for more guards."

I shook my head. "Who could guess something like this would happen? No one has dared attack a royal carriage in..." My voice trailed off as I tried to think if it had happened even once since the end of the war.

The man ahead of us ripped one of his compositions. A rolling bank of smoke appeared, racing down the street to engulf us.

Layna's hands flashed, and a wind sprang up, sending the smoke writhing and twirling into eddies and streams as it was pushed back. But somewhere behind the darkness, flickers of red flame had appeared.

Thunder cracked overhead and rain began to fall, instantly drenching us. I tried to peer through the rain and smoke but could no longer see our attacker or even the buildings lining the street.

"Verene." Bryony sounded nervous.

I glanced at her and saw her attention focused back down the road behind us. I remembered Beckett had said we had attackers on both sides and whirled to peer just as fruitlessly in that direction.

The sound of tearing parchment above our heads preceded a second wind which drove a funnel of clear air down the street. For a moment I got a hazy view of a second attacker, this one a woman.

"Can you feel her?" Bryony asked quietly.

For a moment I thought she was asking whether any power was rushing toward us. But as soon as I properly focused my senses, I understood her reference.

When my new abilities first appeared, the constant sensation of the energy of everyone around me had been overwhelming. But I had become so used to it now, that I barely noticed the energy of others. However, I had acquired enough subtlety for Bryony to teach me to recognize a particular marker—the slight difference in the energy of another energy mage.

"Are we shielded for energy?" she asked me.

I glanced back at Layna, still locked in battle with the man further up the street. "I don't know."

"Then do something," she hissed, as the woman, who was once again disappearing within the smoke, tore a composition.

"Take control," I whispered, nearly tripping over the words in my haste.

I could already feel the snaking energy coming for us. As soon as I finished the words, the full awareness of it washed over me, nearly making me reel at its strength. It latched on to first Bryony and then me, tugging at our inner reserves, trying to drain away our life force.

"Reverse," I muttered, fear making me act without thinking.

Immediately the thread of energy connecting us changed course, draining in the other direction and flooding into me instead of our attacker.

I gasped as the energy hit me. A feeling of momentary discomfort—familiar from my training with Bryony—turned quickly into a euphoric buoyancy.

The energy continued to flood toward me, my attacker draining shockingly fast. A moment later I realized my mistake. She had been draining both Bryony and me, which meant she was now losing energy to us both. My friend was actually bouncing up and down from the unexpected influx.

Another ripping sound from above released a wave of pure power that spread around us in every direction, dissipating the smoke wherever it came into contact. As the air finally cleared, the woman appeared, now lying collapsed on the ground, her face ashen.

"Cut," I whispered, and the flow of energy stopped. Her chest rose and fell in a shallow breath.

A warning shout from the front of the carriage made me glance backward as another wave of power slammed against our shield, bursting it with the strength of the attack.

Simultaneous ripping sounds from above and behind encased us in further layers of shielding, even as Lieutenant Beckett above us grunted and fell. He slid off the roof of the carriage, plummeting toward the ground.

Bryony reacted almost impossibly fast, racing past me to cushion his fall. The two of them collapsed to the ground in a tangled pile before Bryony sprang back up, reaching down to help the larger man to his feet.

"Something got through that time," he said unnecessarily. "Maybe you should get back in the carriage, Your Highness." But he sounded uncertain, as if he wasn't sure if I was safer out here where they could see me or tucked away behind walls of wood.

I nodded absently, not really following his words. It was hard to focus with the buzz of energy inside me.

At first it had seemed just like the familiar feeling of excess from Bryony's compositions to gift energy. But the more seconds ticked by, the stranger it felt. This energy fought against combining with my own. It twisted, pulling away from me before springing reluctantly back, making me rock every time.

Beckett frowned at me. "Are you all right, Princess?"

I nodded, panting slightly. "I'm fine."

I hoped my words were true. What was happening to me?

"We have to help Captain Layna," I said. "Are there more of them?"

As if in answer to my question, an even stronger wave of power hit us from the side, emerging from between two buildings. It broke through the first of our shields before fizzling out against the second.

Beckett already had a parchment in his hands, tearing it to once again give us a double layer of shielding.

"How many more of those do you have?" I asked, keeping my voice level with difficulty. The energy still fought inside me, the buzzed feeling of its presence at odds with my natural fear and the strange nausea produced by its attempts to escape from my skin.

"More," the lieutenant said. "But whether we have enough depends on their number and how well-equipped they are."

I appreciated that he didn't offer me platitudes or empty reassurances.

"We need to get moving," he said. "See if we can outrun them. Or at least get out into the open. If we could make it to the Academy…"

I glanced up at the carriage driver who was shaking in fright, even as he attempted to control his even more terrified horses. The thunder and rain had stopped, but the animals could sense something unnatural was going on.

"That's not going to be easy," Bryony said.

I led the way toward the front of the carriage, where Layna still stood with her back to us, the ground around her now littered with torn scraps of parchment.

"One of them is down," Beckett told her. "Although it must have been the princess who did it. It wasn't one of my compositions."

Layna nodded without taking her eyes off her opponent. "How many of them did you spot from up there?"

"At least three," he said. "But my visibility was limited by the buildings. There could be more."

Lightning arced through the sky, cracking against our shield and setting the carriage horses to rearing again. For the first time true fear shook me. With the energy mage disabled, we were safe enough behind our shields. But for how long?

I had still seen no sign of any locals, and the residents of the village were all commonborns anyway. They could do little to help us against such an attack—assuming they didn't side with our attackers.

A shout and the sound of running feet made us all flinch. My attempted control over my roiling insides faltered, and this time when our attacker's energy pulled away, it snapped free, disappearing instead of springing back toward me.

A heavy weight pressed me into the ground for a moment before my sense of self equalized. I wasn't exhausted, this was my normal level of energy. It had just felt like weakness for a few seconds after the loss of the unnatural strength.

Gold robes appeared in the street, accompanied by the red and gold uniforms of commonborn guards. I instinctively relaxed, but Layna remained taut, her attention sliding between her opponent and the new arrivals.

I recognized the man leading them, and my own wariness reasserted itself. Vincent, the captain of the Academy Guard, had been appointed directly by the king—a man I knew wanted me dead.

But Captain Vincent took one look at the situation and began barking orders to his team. The guards ran forward, swords outstretched toward the man standing openly in the street.

He cursed and tore several more parchments, fresh power springing to life around him. But the guards didn't hesitate, hammering away at his shield with their weapons, slowly draining it.

After a moment, I realized they were doing more than that. Working in coordination, they used their attacks to drive him back, herding him away from us and toward one of their two mage lieutenants.

"There's another between those buildings," Beckett called, pointing to the relevant gap.

The second Kallorwegian lieutenant took off running in that direction, a small stream of red and gold guards following.

"And one behind," Layna barked to Captain Vincent. "Incapacitated."

I glanced back behind the carriage. The street was empty.

I bit my lip. "She's gone. I'm sorry, I should have stopped to bind her."

Layna frowned at me. "That's not your job, Princess. And if we'd had more people, one of us would have done it. But we rightly had to keep our focus on current threats."

"Are there any more?" Captain Vincent asked.

Beckett shrugged. "Not that we know of. But they were hiding between the buildings, so it's possible."

The Kallorwegian captain frowned around at the empty streets. "This village is close enough to the Academy that I've interviewed every one of the inhabitants myself. I don't believe they would be part of any such attack."

"You're worried they're not just hiding in fear?" Layna asked. "You think the attackers might have dealt with them first?"

I gasped, the thought not having occurred to me.

"It's a possibility." Captain Vincent sounded genuinely concerned, and I warmed to him.

The lieutenant who had gone chasing off between the buildings reappeared, his breathing slightly labored. He stopped in front of us, saluting his captain.

"I'm afraid he got away, Sir. He was already running when we started the chase. We lost sight of him, and not even our compositions could pick up his track." He frowned. "It was like he disappeared. He must have had some highly effective cloaking compositions to hide his path."

"Did you see any of the people?" I asked. "The locals?"

"We're here." A grizzled, older man appeared, limping slightly as he exited a door of one of the larger buildings. "Sheltering out of sight."

He bowed in our direction. "We would have helped, but we have no mages of our own. And most of our able-bodied are lending Zora a hand up at the Academy. She often has a few days' extra work for locals like us, cleaning the place top to bottom in preparation for the return of the trainees." He nodded respectfully at the white robes worn by Bryony and me.

Layna glanced at Captain Vincent, and he nodded his agreement. "That's true enough. Although there would have been plenty still here—especially children and elderly."

His earlier concern now made even more sense, but the villager in front of us didn't look especially distressed.

"Those brigands sent an unnatural smoke straight up the center of the street shortly before you all arrived," he said. "We knew well enough to get out of the way at that point."

Layna regarded him with narrowed eyes. "Was it you who called the warning?"

He nodded. "Couldn't bear to see innocent folk ambushed like that. Even if you was better equipped to defend yourself than us. We don't want any trouble here. We've had trouble enough for several lifetimes being so close to the border."

"You did the right thing," Captain Vincent said. "You sent for me. I'm just sorry we couldn't get here sooner. But there isn't room at the Academy to be keeping horses for all of my guards. And when the request for help arrived, there was no mention of you, Your Highness." He bowed slightly in my direction.

"We sent young Eamon off before the carriage arrived," the village elder said. "We could tell they weren't ordinary brigands from the start—never minding we don't tend to get those out this way in the first place."

"No, they certainly weren't brigands," Captain Vincent said in a hard voice. He straightened suddenly, calling out a barked order.

We all turned to follow his gaze in time to see his second lieutenant kneeling over a body lying flat on the ground. The young man in the gold robe looked across at his captain.

"We had nearly worn down his shield when he just collapsed."

Bryony and I exchanged a glance. We had known there was an energy mage involved, one who could drain someone's energy. Maybe if I'd been paying more attention, I would have felt when she drained her companion's energy. But it hadn't occurred to me to worry about such a thing, and I'd been distracted by the conversation.

"We lost all three of them, then," Layna said, and I winced.

We were all alive, but if I hadn't made so many mistakes, maybe we would have one or two of the attackers to question.

"I don't suppose you recognized any of them?" Captain Vincent's tone didn't sound very hopeful.

Layna bristled. "Of course I didn't. I hope you don't mean to suggest you think those mages were Ardannian."

"I'm just considering every possibility," he said. "Which is my job. We're near enough to the border."

Layna relaxed slightly. "I suppose you're right. But no, I didn't recognize them. And we've had no hints of any threats against the princess the whole summer. I can't imagine an Ardannian adversary would have waited for us to cross the border before attacking."

The Kallorwegian captain nodded, accepting her words before asking his next question. "Do we even know they were mages?"

"That one isn't marked at throat or wrists." The lieutenant who had been examining the dead man joined us. "So he's no sealed commonborn."

"They were mighty familiar with their compositions," Beckett added.

"And that one visibly responded a couple of times before my composition hit him." Layna nodded at the body in the street. "I'd be willing to bet good gold he could feel power."

Captain Vincent nodded again. "I'll leave a couple of guards to interview the villagers, but I doubt we'll learn anything of interest at this stage. And if our tracking compositions aren't working, then I don't have the men to perform a foot search of the entire region. Which means, for now at least, our focus must be on getting the princess safely behind the Academy walls."

He turned to survey our carriage with a critical eye. "Is your vehicle still functional?"

Layna nodded. "They didn't attack it directly."

The carriage driver, having finally regained control of the horses, nodded his agreement. "She'll get us there, right enough."

I could see from the slight shake in his hands that he would be glad himself to be behind the Academy's high walls as fast as possible.

"Very well then." Captain Vincent turned to the village elder, but the man had already foreseen his request.

He waved forward a young girl and boy, each leading a saddled horse. They regarded us all with wide eyes, not speaking as they handed the reins to Captain Vincent.

The captain nodded his thanks and gestured for one of his lieutenants to join him. "We'll ride beside you. It's not far on horseback. The rest of my guards will follow on foot."

Within moments, Bryony and I had been ushered back into the carriage, and we were moving once again.

"What just happened?" Bryony asked in an undertone as soon as we were alone. "I thought Darius said his father wouldn't attack you again."

"So did I." I rubbed at the side of my head. "Maybe this attack wasn't the king?"

My friend regarded me with wide eyes. "How many people are trying to kill you?"

"Too many, apparently." I grimaced. "Did you feel how strange that energy was? It was like it was fighting me."

Bryony rubbed both her arms. "It was awful. I never thought I'd experience taking someone's energy like that, but I can see what Amalia was talking about."

As soon as she mentioned our instructor's name, I knew what had happened. I should have recognized it straight away, but there had been too much going on for me to think properly. Energy taken by force wasn't like energy willingly given, as in the case of Bryony or Tyron's compositions. The stolen energy strained to return to its rightful owner, eventually breaking free to do just that—unless its original owner was no longer alive.

All that energy churning inside me had returned to my attacker. No wonder she had recovered so quickly and escaped. What did she think had happened? Whatever she thought, it had unnerved her enough to flee instead of continuing to fight. My only consolation was that I didn't see how she could possibly guess the truth. I had been too far away for her to hear my words, and my ability was totally unique.

We rumbled through the entrance of the Academy, Captain Vincent calling out muffled instructions to unseen guards. The gates creaked shut behind us, closing with a thunderous clang.

Weary after the unexpected battle and the struggle with the stolen energy, I stumbled down the carriage steps and into the Academy courtyard. Layna swung down from her mount and gestured for me to head straight inside the building. I complied without protest, shivering slightly in my still wet clothes.

The wooden doors at the top of the gray stone stairs already stood open, so I hurried inside, Bryony on my heels. Inside the echoing entrance hall, I halted. Water dripped down to form a small puddle at my feet.

Several people had been walking through the large space, and all of them stopped to stare at us in surprise. But only one caught my attention. Darius.

CHAPTER 6

The prince had also paused, the slightest expression of surprise creasing his face at the picture we must create. But then he resumed walking, coming to stand a short distance in front of me. He gave a small, impersonal half-bow.

"Welcome back to Kallorway, Princess Verene. I hope you haven't met with some accident within our borders."

His cold tone made me shiver more than the moisture coating me.

"Only if you consider an outright attack in broad daylight to be an accident," Bryony said tartly.

For a moment, I could have sworn something sparked and flashed in Darius's eyes, but it might have been my imagination willing the emotion there.

"I heard Captain Vincent was called out with a squad of guards," he said, in the same detached voice. "I didn't realize you were involved. I trust he assisted your own guards in dealing with the brigands."

Bryony opened her mouth, no doubt to say they hadn't been robbers, but I jumped in before she could.

"I will leave the captain to give you the full report." I called on all my training as I tried to match my tone to his. "As you can see, we are unharmed."

"The crown has full trust in Captain Vincent to keep the Academy and the trainees safe," Darius said.

Bryony snorted quietly behind me, but my focus remained on the prince's face. What did he mean by that? Was there a warning in his words?

But his face gave nothing away, his impassive mask impenetrable.

Bryony shivered theatrically. "I, for one, would like to get to my room and get dry. If you'll excuse us, *Your Highness.*"

Darius didn't flinch at her contemptuous tone, merely standing aside and gesturing for us to pass. As we stepped onto the grand staircase, I couldn't stop myself from throwing a single glance over my shoulder. But Darius had already moved on out of sight, whether out the still-open doors or into one of the corridors, I didn't know. He had certainly not lingered for any last glances.

I shook myself and began to climb. Captain Layna had also entered the building and now shadowed us, several lengths behind. We reached the second landing, and I hesitated. Last year, I would have turned right here for one of the royal suites, and at the end of the year, Bryony had been staying with me. But I didn't actually know if I had been assigned the same rooms this year.

The head of the Academy's servants, Zora, appeared from down the corridor, bowing low at the sight of me and making no mention of my wet and bedraggled state. Her calm didn't surprise me—she had always seemed capable of taking any situation in stride.

"Princess Verene, welcome back. Your old suite has been prepared for your arrival."

"Thank you," I said, aware the words sounded wooden.

She turned to Bryony. "I'm afraid you still have four more

flights of stairs to climb, Bryony."

My friend hesitated, glancing at me, so I shooed her upward.

"Go! Get dry."

She took off, almost running up the stairs in her haste, and I turned toward my own suite. Zora kept pace beside me.

"If it pleases Your Highness, I have once again assigned Ida to your care."

I nodded. "Of course. I had no complaints with her efforts last year."

The head of the servants continued to walk with me, although I had no difficulty remembering where I was going. I had trod this path countless times before.

When I stopped at the right door, she handed me a key. I turned it in the lock, resisting the impulse to hold my breath. After an attack outside the Academy walls, the welcome left in my room the year before seemed inconsequential.

When I pushed the door open, however, no sign of any disturbance greeted me. Everything looked neat and clean, all the furniture in its correct places.

Zora, entering behind me, relaxed slightly, and I realized why she had led me all the way here. I wasn't the only one who remembered the year before.

I had never told my personal guard about the incidents of the year before, but Layna brushed past us both anyway, poking into every corner of the room and disappearing through the doorway on the right wall that led into my bedchamber.

She reappeared a few moments later.

"Everything is clear," she said. "I sense no power lingering anywhere."

I nodded my thanks.

"And these are for you." She handed me a tall stack of parchments. "As we discussed."

I thanked her more warmly as my hand curled around the precious gift. As soon as I had reached Corrin, I had expressed my appreciation of the compositions she had left me the year before to guard my door. And although I hadn't told her of the assassin who made it into my bedchamber, I did confess to being careless enough to let one of my year mates get their hands on one.

Guiltily, I had asked if it would be possible for her to make a modified version for this year—one whose secrets weren't compromised. She had agreed with enthusiasm, especially after I promised to let her superiors know how effective her work had been.

She watched with a slightly raised eyebrow as I immediately tore two, directing one toward the external door of my suite and another toward my bedchamber door. I carefully refrained from glancing at the tapestry on the left wall and the concealed door I knew lay behind it. Let Layna wonder why I felt the need for a double layer of protection. I wasn't going to tell her. Just as I wasn't going to shield the door that connected my sitting room with Darius's. Despite his cold greeting, a kernel of hope had lodged in my heart and refused to die.

Thankfully my captain's caution extended to all parts of her role, and she had supplied me with an ample number of compositions to guard two doors. No doubt she had been allowing for the protection to need frequent refreshing in case the power was drained from challenges. Thankfully my doors had been largely undisturbed the year before, just the presence of the guarding composition apparently enough to keep any unwanted guests away. With only the occasional refresh needed after the natural drain of power over the passage of time, I had managed to make last year's compositions last. This year should be even easier.

Zora's eyes lingered on Layna, but when my captain showed no sign of leaving, the head servant crossed to the door.

"I'll leave you to get cleaned up." She hesitated but then slipped out into the corridor without speaking further.

I watched her go with a creased brow. It was almost as if she had wanted to speak to me alone.

"Now that you're safely here, I should be going also," Layna said, pulling my focus back to her.

"You're not going to stay the night?" I asked in surprise.

"I would like to examine the village and its surrounds for myself before the scene is completely trampled," she said. "And then we will ride for Bronton before nightfall."

I twisted my lips. "I suppose you have to report the attack."

She raised an eyebrow. "Certainly I must do so."

I sighed. "Maybe you could downplay it just a bit?" I suggested. "Just to my parents?"

The sides of Layna's lips quirked up the slightest bit. "I'm afraid that wouldn't be possible, Your Highness," she said gravely.

I winced.

"However," she continued, "I expect I shall be called upon to make my report to the queen and my commanding officers rather than your parents."

I brightened slightly. "Yes, that's likely true." I could only trust that my aunt's vested interest in keeping me here would make her view the threat with less alarm than my parents no doubt would.

"You won't get in trouble for leaving me here?" I asked.

Layna shook her head. "The Academy is the safest place for you at present, Princess. As has clearly been demonstrated, I would need a much larger force to protect you on the open road."

I nodded. "And at least you can truthfully report that Captain Vincent and his guards proved more than capable of keeping me safe. And they would presumably be even more effective behind the walls of the Academy where they are also on their own turf."

"It has certainly relieved some of my concern to see the captain's squad in action," Layna said. "They are well trained."

I wanted to ask her if she thought my aunt and parents would call me back to Ardann once they got her report, but I restrained myself. Layna was an excellent personal guard, but she wasn't privy to the crown's policy concerns, and she certainly knew nothing of the factors that must be weighed in my aunt's decision.

I had hoped it wouldn't come to this, but I would have to trust that my newly assigned role would be enough to keep me here. Aunt Lucienne certainly had no other simple alternative for keeping a line of communication open with Darius.

I sighed softly. Not that Darius had looked interested in communicating with me. My eyes strayed to the tapestry before I pulled them away.

"I must be going," Layna said. "If we manage to discover the identity of your attackers, I'll send you word."

I forced a smile. "Thank you. You fought well, and I know you must have greatly depleted your supply of compositions."

Layna bowed. "There is satisfaction in using them for their created purpose. Not many opportunities present themselves in Ardann. Thankfully," she added quickly.

I smiled again to show I understood. "Well, you may be satisfied that your workings performed admirably."

"Thank you, Your Highness. And farewell." She bowed again and hurried out the door.

Leaving my sitting room, she almost collided with a figure in a white robe. The tall girl stopped in my open doorway, and Layna hesitated, meeting my eyes over her shoulder.

I waved my guard away. I might not like Dellion, but I no longer suspected her of wishing me harm.

Both of the elegant trainee's eyebrows were raised so high they almost disappeared into her elaborate arrangement of golden hair.

"I heard a rumor you had arrived looking like a drowned rat, but I must confess, I doubted it. It hasn't been raining lately."

"It was in the village," I said flatly, not in the mood for verbal fencing with her.

Her eyebrows, which had dropped down, rose again. "So the rumors of an attack are also true. How fascinating. Who wants to kill you, I wonder?"

"If you find out, let me know," I said.

"They're not bundling you straight back to Corrin, then?"

"Not for now." I wrung out a portion of my robe, hoping she'd get the message.

"A pity." She sighed and then smiled nonchalantly. "It's not personal, of course. Things would just be...simpler without you."

"If you'll leave me in peace to get into dry clothes, I'll promise not to take offense," I said lightly.

She laughed and wandered away from my doorway, not bothering to close the door behind her. I sighed and crossed the room to do it myself.

As I cleaned myself up, making use of the selection of clothes I'd left here the year before, I found I believed her. I didn't think it was personal. But Dellion was the granddaughter of General Haddon and niece of the queen. And while it didn't seem they had been the ones trying to kill me last year after all, they still weren't happy about the interest the king's supporters had shown in me—or rather in the alliance with Ardann I represented. If King Cassius and my aunt managed a proper treaty, it might tip the delicate balance of power too far away from the general.

I considered her words and attitude as I twisted my hair inside a towel. She had sounded almost weary of the pressure she had alluded to being under from her family. As if she would have preferred to be free to view me as just another year mate. Possibly even a potential friend.

I chuckled at that thought. Dellion might be less wedded to her family's opinions than I had thought, but the predatory air to her movements and the competitive glint in her green eyes were all her own. Even without their involvement, I had no doubt she would have seen me as someone to prove herself against.

But maybe it could have been a friendly sort of rivalry. Maybe it still could be.

A knock sounded on an outer door, and I hurried out of my bedchamber. My heart sank, despite myself, when I realized it had come from the corridor door and not the one behind the tapestry. Opening it, I found Ida waiting outside.

She bobbed a curtsy. "Welcome back, Your Highness." Tension radiated from her as she brought my bags inside, and several times she opened her mouth only to close it again.

Once she had finished putting away my gowns, collecting those that needed pressing, I had her place her hand on my door and spoke her name.

"Now you'll be safely able to come and go," I told her. "Just like last year."

She dropped into a second curtsy, made awkward by the pile of garments in her arms.

"Thank you, Your Highness. And thank you for under-standing about the attack." The second sentence seemed to burst out of her. "We were all ever so shocked to hear of it! A dangerous attack in our own village! Of course none of us would have anything to do with such a thing. We've all been in a tremble to think what might have happened to our families if they hadn't hid themselves away."

She glanced up at me as if checking to see whether I carried any resentment toward the villagers for not rushing to my defense.

"It is a good thing they did so," I said. "Or things might have turned out ugly indeed. But from what I understand, no one was harmed in the end."

She nodded vigorously. "Thanks to the good captain."

"I didn't know you were from the local village." I could hear the hint of guilt in my voice. Ida had cared for my rooms all last year, and I knew almost nothing about her.

The realization sparked something inside my brain. The

elusive thought that had tried to grab hold of me during my last meal with my family finally formed properly. I knew nothing about the Kallorwegian commonborns.

In all the briefings I had received from my aunt and her intelligencers on the state of the Kallorwegian court, the two different factions, and my potential year mates, I had never heard anything about the commonborns—sealed or unsealed. What did they think of their king, their queen, and their prince? Who did they support to hold the throne?

It should have occurred to me to ask when I was receiving the briefings. Commonborns might not sit on the Mage Council or have a direct say in the forming of laws, but I had seen that they wielded power of their own. After two decades of sealing, their merchant families had amassed enough wealth to ensure their voices mattered.

"Oh yes, Your Highness," Ida said. "Born and raised. Zora prefers to work with locals when she can, and if there's extra work to be done, she'll take on anyone who can carry a pail and rag."

I nodded, remembering the village elder's words. It made sense that Ida would have grown up working at the Academy whenever there was extra help needed.

"And when the sealing first started," she continued, "she hand-picked those of us youngsters who were the hardest workers and put our names forward to the duke for one of the ceremonies. She said she needed a dependable workforce who could be trusted in the mages' rooms."

"I'm glad your village and the Academy were not forgotten, despite your distance from the capital," I said.

"Oh no, Your Highness. The duke wouldn't allow that." A slightly flustered look came over her face, and she dropped into another curtsy.

I regarded her curiously. I was forcibly struck with the impression that Ida knew a great deal more about how things worked at the Academy than I did. But I could tell that openly questioning her would only cause distress. Instead, I tucked the matter away for further consideration. If my aunt didn't know the opinions of the commonborns, then maybe it was up to me to find some answers for myself.

CHAPTER 7

*D*espite the temptation to request a tray in my room, I trudged down to the dining hall for the evening meal. Bryony waved enthusiastically to me from the long table second from the right. Apparently now we were second years we'd moved up in the dining hall. I walked toward her while letting my eyes roam over our previous table.

A number of trainees already sat there. Some chatted enthusiastically, clearly already familiar with each other, while others sat in near silence, looking everything from morose to terrified. But many of their eyes were focused on our table and two sandy heads in particular. I kept my face in a flat mask, but my interest in the first years instantly disappeared.

I had to pass the two princes to reach Bryony, and Jareth leaped to his feet at the sight of me, forcing me to a reluctant stop in front of them.

"Princess Verene!" He gave me an elegant half-bow. "It is an honor as always. I heard about the, ahem, excitement of your arrival, and I'm delighted to see you looking so well."

I gave me the slightest curtsy I could manage, trying to decide what was more agonizing—talking to Jareth about my attack when I suspected him of having played a hand in it or talking to Jareth in front of a silent, icy Darius who was no doubt aware and disapproving of every suspicion in my mind.

"I'm glad to have safely arrived," I said in a carefully neutral tone. "I greatly appreciated the assistance of Captain Vincent."

"Ah yes." Jareth smiled. "Vincent has always been an excellent guard, both vigilant and skilled. My grandfather wouldn't have selected him for the role otherwise."

"Your grandfather?" I gave him a sharper look, distracted from my discomfort. "General Haddon chose Captain Vincent? I had understood he was assigned here by the king."

"Well, yes, he was in a way, I suppose," Jareth said. "My father was the one to insist that if both his sons were attending the Academy, then a new captain was needed to ensure our safety. But my grandfather is the Head of the Royal Guard. He was the one best placed to make the actual selection."

"That makes sense," I said slowly.

"Grandfather chose Vincent?" Darius asked, showing interest in the conversation for the first time. "Why didn't I know that?"

"Didn't you?" Jareth looked at his brother in surprise. "I assumed you knew. I suppose I must have overheard Grandfather talking about it at some point."

"So Father requested and later approved him, but Grandfather actually chose him...That changes things," Darius said in an under voice.

For a brief moment, our eyes met, and I felt the same burning connection that had drawn me to him before the summer. I easily understood his unspoken message. Both sides of the Kallorwegian court had played a part in selecting the captain, which greatly increased the chances of his neutrality—and subsequent trustworthiness. But then Darius's shutters slammed closed, his indifference returning as he turned his attention to his food without any direct acknowledgment of my presence.

I swallowed, ice chasing the rush of heat out of my body as I scrambled to recover my own mask. Jareth looked from me to Darius, frowning, but said nothing. I forced myself to give him a nod and then urged my feet to move, carrying me further down the table to my waiting friend.

With each step I took away from the brothers, my mind cleared a little. So Jareth had known more about Vincent and his assignment to the Academy than he had ever told Darius. My first instinctive desire was to discuss the significance of that with Darius. But even in the days when we had been open with each other and worked together, I had never been free to discuss my suspicions of Jareth. Darius would no doubt take Jareth's assurance that he had thought Darius knew at face value and refuse to consider any other possibility.

"What did Jareth want?" Bryony asked quietly when I sank into a chair beside her. She glared down the table at the younger prince, as always far more open with her thoughts and opinions than I was ever free to be.

"To congratulate me on my escape, of course. Ugh." I began filling my plate with food, not wanting to think about the prince and how he continued to fill me with such unease.

"So you still think he's involved somehow?" Bryony asked. "And that attack was connected to all the ones last year."

I shrugged. "It seems the most logical assumption. And there's just something I don't trust about Jareth." I groaned. "Not that I could ever convince Darius of that."

"It's hard to be objective when it comes to family," Bryony said.

"Don't defend Darius." I took a large bite. "I'm currently determined to be irritated by him." Maybe if I could hold on to my irritation, my heart would stop hurting so much every time he looked at me with that distant, disinterested expression.

"My apologies," Bryony said instantly, although her eyes laughed at me. "Naturally, in that case, his lack of suspicion toward his brother is a sign of gross stupidity and negligence. If he had any sense at all, he'd place all his faith in your superior judgment."

I chuckled reluctantly. "When you put it like that..."

Bryony grinned and picked up her fork. "If it makes you feel better, I believe you. I think I know what you mean, too. There's something about Jareth that just doesn't quite feel right."

She took several bites of her food before speaking again. "What happened to Captain Layna, by the way?"

I explained my guard's intentions, and Bryony grimaced when I got to the end. "Your family had better not send word for you to start packing. I've committed to three more years here, and I don't want to have to do them on my own."

"What? You don't think Dellion would make a good substitute best friend?"

Bryony rolled her eyes. "You must be feeling recovered from our ordeal if you can make jokes like that."

"In truth, I'm ready for my bed," I admitted. "It's hard to believe classes start tomorrow morning. I feel far too distracted to focus on anything so mundane."

"A couple of hours of beating someone with a sword will make you feel better," Bryony said cheerfully, and I groaned.

"Please don't remind me of your unnatural obsession with your blade. The rest of us don't find constant sword fighting nearly so invigorating, you know."

She shrugged. "Your loss."

The mention of combat class set us to speculating about what we might face in the arena during the year, and the meal quickly passed. By the time I let myself back into my suite, I no longer felt so eager to head straight to sleep.

Instead, I paced up and down my sitting room, playing out every aspect of the attack in my mind. I had binding compositions in one of my pockets. If only I'd used them on the energy mage. If I had, the two captains might even now be interrogating two prisoners. Or I could have requested my guard to bind them.

I sighed and massaged my head. I could do nothing to change the past, but if I ever found myself in another such situation, I would know better.

A knock interrupted my pacing, and my eyes flew straight to the tapestry. I hesitated, wondering if my mind was playing tricks on me. But it sounded again, definitely coming from the hidden door.

I hurried over and pushed the heavy material aside, pulling the door open. Darius stood on the other side, alone, thankfully.

It was such a familiar scene, and yet, at the same time, everything about it felt wrong. His face remained closed off, and he offered no greeting. After a moment, I stepped back, gesturing for him to enter my sitting room. He did so silently.

For several unending seconds, we stood and stared at each other. Something flashed in his eyes as he looked me over, but I couldn't read it.

"Captain Vincent tells me your guards' shields held until he arrived."

I held myself rigidly. "I am unharmed—as I told you in the entrance hall. I'm sure Captain Layna will report to my aunt that your guards provided timely and sufficient assistance."

"Queen Lucienne will still wish to know who would perpetrate such an outrageous attack." His level tone conveyed nothing of the emotion that might be expected to go with such words.

"I imagine she will. As do I."

"I have informed Captain Vincent that I wish to be directly involved in the investigation. We will discover the person or persons behind the attack."

I raised an eyebrow. "So it's not your father, then?"

He moved slightly in what could have been a flinch. "It's too early to speculate."

"Excellent," I said in a caustic voice. "It's good to know there are so many people in your kingdom who wish me dead."

This time it was definitely a flinch.

"I offer you my official apologies, Princess Verene."

I sighed, deflating. It wasn't official apologies I wanted from him.

I had spent so many hours imagining seeing him again, but now it felt like I was trapped in some sort of nightmare. Where was the Darius I knew? The Darius beneath the careful ice.

A heavy silence fell between us, but I didn't have the heart to break it. He was tense, I could read that much, holding himself carefully, as if all his muscles were coiled and taut, ready for action. But when he spoke it was in a carefully controlled voice.

"Do you have a message for me from Queen Lucienne?"

I fought down a flush, instantly feeling foolish. I had been so distracted by first the attack and then my own emotions, I had forgotten the issue of greatest interest to him. This must be what had brought him to my room on my first night.

"Ardann will support you and your claim. But my aunt will not commit publicly until you have won legitimacy. She wants nothing in writing and has assigned me as her delegate in this matter. All communication will go through me."

Some of his tension dissipated, although he didn't truly relax. "You'll be staying then?"

My brow creased as I tried to decipher his unreadable gaze. It wasn't the response I had been expecting. Did it mean that somewhere buried deep beneath that ice, he still cared on some level? Did it mean he wanted me here?

Or was that wishful thinking on my part?

I shrugged. "She hasn't heard about the attack yet. But as long as I'm safely inside the Academy, I think there's a good chance."

"You *are* safe here in the Academy." His expression remained carefully controlled, but his voice sounded almost violent.

"I have confidence in Captain Vincent," I said, curiosity compelling me to add, "Especially after what your brother said today."

"Yes." Darius nodded his agreement, although for some reason he didn't seem pleased with my statement of belief in the captain. "That was reassuring to hear."

I raised an eyebrow slightly. Reassuring about Captain Vincent, perhaps—less so about Jareth. But I didn't say anything aloud. The last thing I needed was more of a barrier between us.

"I would send my personal reassurances to your aunt regarding how carefully you will be guarded," he said, "except you tell me she has forbidden direct communication between me and Ardann."

"Let's wait and see what happens," I said. "Such reassurances might not be necessary."

"Very well." He fell silent again.

Sudden weariness descended over me. "At some point we should speak further about exactly what support Ardann might be able to offer you from the shadows. But there is no hurry, and I'm tired after the events of the day."

"Of course." He bowed, the deepest one he had ever given me. "I will leave you to rest."

He turned and started toward the door, but irrational panic flooded me. I couldn't let him go like that. After everything that had passed between us, surely we hadn't been reduced to such formality and distance.

I rushed after him, catching him just as he passed through the door. He spun at the lightest touch of my hand on his arm, one foot already through into his own room.

I instantly let my hand drop, my fingers tingling.

"What's going on, Darius?" I asked, my voice coming out as a whisper. "Why are you like this?"

I had known at the end of last year that he was angry at my mistrust of Jareth, but this seemed like more than that. This felt like something big and heavy and suffocating.

For the briefest moment, I thought he meant to sprint through the door without answering. But then he looked down at me and let his mask drop.

I gasped and staggered back a step. The fire I remembered was all still there, but his expression was twisted and tortured, as if he was now the one being burned.

"I'm scared, Verene." His voice was a ragged whisper. "I've never been scared like this before."

My hand flew to my throat. "Darius, I..." I reached out to him, but he pulled back, something like horror crossing his face—as if he couldn't believe what he had just admitted.

"Please forget I said that," he said roughly, and propelled himself through the doorway, pushing the door closed behind him.

I stayed immobile, frozen with shock as I tried to process his reaction. I had seen Darius angry. I had seen him determined and threatening and cold. And I might be one of the few people in the kingdom to have seen him open and vulnerable. But I had never seen him scared.

If Darius was scared, what did that mean? And, more importantly, what had made him so afraid?

CHAPTER 8

he morning bell pulled me out of sleep, groggy and disoriented. It had taken me far too long to fall asleep the night before.

I stumbled blearily down to breakfast, amazed at how easily I fell back into the old familiar routine. The dining hall was already full when I arrived, and Bree sat with Tyron, chatting brightly.

I slid in beside them and greeted the Sekali boy. "I didn't see you here last night. Have you only just arrived? Did you have a good summer?"

He grimaced. "I got in far too late and collapsed straight into bed, I'm afraid. And I'm consequently starving."

As if to prove his point, he loaded his plate with what looked like it must be a second serving of everything on the table.

"I was just telling him about our summer in Corrin," Bryony said.

"It sounds much more interesting than mine." Tyron pulled a face. "And not as hot, either." He scanned the table. "It looks like everyone made it back. I have to admit, I wondered if we would see you again, Verene."

"Really?" I frowned at him. "Why?"

He shrugged and then grinned. "I suppose I thought your family might decide you'd done enough penance."

Bryony laughed. "As if spending time with us could ever be penance! Plus, you're forgetting I was there with her. I would have dragged her back here one way or another."

"That's true," he admitted. "Your determination isn't something I would ever doubt."

He polished off his plate and started serving himself thirds. "I heard some interesting comments about your arrival at the Academy yesterday. It sounds like I missed something exciting."

"I don't know about exciting, but it was certainly wet," I said wryly.

"Verene looked as elegant as ever," Bryony added, "but I'm afraid I most closely resembled a drowned rat."

"Actually, I have it on the best authority that I also presented the appearance of that particular animal."

Bryony looked shocked for a moment at my declaration, her eyes flying to Darius as if she suspected the prince of having raced after me to my room so he could lob insults at my appearance. But a moment later her gaze moved further down the table, and she rolled her eyes.

"Let me guess. Dellion. The worst part is that girl gives the strong impression she has never in her life resembled any kind of rodent."

"No, it's a little hard to imagine such a comparison being applied to her, isn't it?" I eyed the other girl dispassionately. "But I've heard rumors that large predator cats live in the high mountains, although I've never actually seen one. I imagine them being something like Dellion."

A startled laugh burst out of Tyron before he immediately looked guilty.

"Don't worry," Bryony said kindly. "We won't tell her you laughed."

Another bell drove us all away from the table, and we streamed out of the dining hall together. Royce, looking no less unpleasant but a great deal more surly than when I met him the year before, rushed past me without speaking. His father was not only Cassius's cousin but had always been his closest friend. Did Royce's family know anything of what had happened here last year?

When Wardell and Armand passed me, they both nodded in a way that seemed friendly enough. Given their uncle was Head of the Creators and aligned with the general, I considered the attitude of the cousins to be a positive sign.

Frida and Ashlyn actually called proper greetings, though.

"I heard you were attacked by brigands on the way back to the Academy," Ashlyn said breathlessly. "Was it thrilling?"

"Not as much as you might think," Bryony said.

Both girls looked disappointed, but someone behind us snorted. I glanced back to see Isabelle close behind us.

"As if being attacked by robbers would be *exciting*." She directed an unimpressed look at the two grower trainees. "It's obvious the two of you live near enough to the capital not to have to worry about them yourselves." She transferred her attention to Bryony and me. "Welcome back. I'm glad you're both unharmed."

I smiled at her. "Me too. And welcome back to you, as well. I hope you didn't have any such trouble on your travels."

She shook her head. "The commonborns on our lands sometimes do, but brigands aren't usually foolish enough to attack a party of mages." She frowned. "It's surprising they attacked you, and so close to the Academy."

I shrugged. "Perhaps they thought I was wealthy enough to make the risk worthwhile." I kept my voice light. "We've been busy discussing what Mitchell might have us doing in the arena this year. Do any of you three know?"

My distraction tactic proved effective, Frida immediately launching into a far-fetched idea about how we would be battling monsters created by the compositions of our instructors. When we all gave her incredulous looks, she claimed her older brother had sworn it was standard training for second years.

Ashlyn wrinkled her nose. "You should know better than to believe anything *he* says. I bet it's just more of the same group bouts."

"I hope so," Isabelle said unexpectedly.

When I gave her a questioning look, she grinned. "I've been practicing over the summer and have come back with a whole collection of compositions."

Both of the other girls nodded.

"My mother had all sorts of visitors all summer long," Ashlyn said, "including a number of growers. We got some excellent tips." She and Frida exchanged conspiratorial smiles.

We had arrived at the training yard at this point, and Wardell looked over with a satisfied grin. "My uncle had an enormous family gathering at his estate, and he was full of congratulations for Armand and my excellent selection of discipline. And practical suggestions as well, of course."

Ashlyn rolled her eyes and turned her back on him. Her mother might be Head of the Wind Workers, but they were closely enough aligned with the growers that Ashlyn would have plenty of access to senior mages in her chosen discipline.

Isabelle beside me began stretching, apparently unperturbed that Wardell and Armand had an uncle who led the creators, and Ashlyn's mother was Head of the Wind Workers. Once upon a time my attempts to look equally relaxed about the conversation would have been a struggle.

Everything was different now. The others in the group might still think of me as the only one without power, but I knew I was a true mage at last. Instead of internally bemoaning my situation, I found myself wondering what it would be like to take control of one of the compositions they were all boasting about. My year mates were only second years and wouldn't have as much knowledge as the creator mage who had botched the foundation, but it would likely be an interesting exercise all the same.

Mitchell appeared and led us through warm ups and a series of general exercises before instructing us to pair up and engage in free practice bouts. I barely kept the disgust off my face. We were second years now, but he showed no more interest in actually teaching us than he had last year.

My parents had always insisted that if you wanted to be truly competent at something, then you couldn't skip putting effort into the basics. It was a lesson they claimed to have learned from their own combat instructor back in their Academy days. Mitchell, however, had no such interest in his students' well-rounded learning. In the arena he seemed like a true instructor, but in the less interesting sessions in the training yards, he barely seemed present.

I suspected we only saw so much of him outside of our arena days because of the presence of the princes in our year. They warranted the attendance of the senior combat instructor, but I imagined his usual process involved leaving lessons like this to junior instructors while he himself focused on whichever year level was assigned to the arena.

Sparring with Bryony always took up my full concentration, but when I swapped to fighting Tyron, I had the chance to continue my earlier thoughts about my ability. Now I was back at the Academy and surrounded by compositions that had no purpose outside of training, surely I could find a way to practice. There must be some scenario that would allow me to do so unnoticed.

I was so distracted by the question that Tyron actually won one of the bouts. His look of surprise and hurried apologies were almost comical, and I had to assure him that while I might be royalty, I was also friends with Bryony and therefore inured to losing sword fights.

"What has you so distracted?" Bryony asked as we returned to the Academy for lunch.

"I'm trying to work out how I can practice," I whispered back. "Properly practice, with more than just you."

"Have you thought of anything?" she asked.

I frowned. "Nothing ideal. There should be more opportunities here, but at the same time, it also feels more dangerous. In the middle of an emergency, no one's paying close attention, but in class…"

Bryony wrinkled her nose. "I see what you mean. If I think of anything, I'll let you know."

Neither of us came up with any flashes of brilliance through lunch or composition class—where Alvin seemed to take the opposite approach to Mitchell and assume that over the summer break we must have forgotten everything we'd learned in first year. With nothing at all to stimulate my mind, it was torturously hard to resist stealing constant glances across the small aisle that was all that stood between Darius and me.

I kept wondering if I had imagined our final intense interaction the night before. There was certainly no sign of anything remotely like fear in his face or bearing as we listened to our composition instructor drone on.

We all separated after that for discipline classes where Amalia greeted us with her customary bad humor. Her manner was so reassuringly familiar, that I beamed back, which only earned me an even darker glower.

"See," Bryony whispered beside me. "She looks exactly like that senior creator. No wonder that poor boy muddled up his composition."

I kicked her under the table, as Amalia narrowed her eyes at us.

"I trust you have spent your summers uselessly and frivolously and have returned to me worse than when you left."

It wasn't a question, and none of us dared respond.

"Bryony and Tyron, you will now craft an energy composition so I can assess the extent of the damage."

Part of the problem, I thought, as I watched them, was that I didn't want to interfere with any of my year mates' training. If I started hijacking their compositions, both they and our instructors would think the error lay with them.

Unless...I sat straighter in my chair at the sudden thought. Unless I took over their compositions only to instruct them to do something so close to their original directions that no one would notice. There would be no point to such a thing in the real world, but as a training exercise it had merit.

It would give me the chance to experience taking over a range of different types of compositions. And the subtlety required for such an effort would probably help hone my skills better than anything else. If I repeated the exercise enough times, maybe some of the knowledge I momentarily gained while connected to the composition would even stick.

I grinned at the thought, earning another sour look from Amalia. But the smile was already falling off my face on its own. Thinking about all the different sorts of compositions I might sample at the Academy led my thoughts to those I would not have the opportunity to try...Like the unexpected experience of taking energy which had so thrown me off during the attack.

"Excuse me, Senior Instructor." I dutifully used the title she had demanded, not wanting to annoy her until I had a chance to ask my question.

"Yes, Your Highness." She also used my correct title, although her voice held no respect.

"Do you keep in contact with your old student? The one you told us about who can take energy?"

She narrowed her eyes. "What business is it of yours?"

I considered my words carefully. "I was just wondering if his duties ever bring him within reach of the Academy. I'm sure we would all appreciate the chance to talk to him and observe his work. It's rare to have the chance to meet an energy mage who takes energy, and it sounds like he honed his skills to the highest level under your tutelage." I stopped myself, afraid I'd been too obvious by laying the praise on so thick.

But after a moment she grudgingly answered.

"If he is in the area, he always stops by. I do not expect him this year, but if he does appear, I may consider asking him to attend one of our classes."

I smiled and thanked her. I wasn't sure what I had been hoping to hear. The energy mage who had attacked us had been a woman—although it was possible she was a more ordinary type of energy mage and had been using compositions supplied by someone else. But even if he had been involved with the attack, he would hardly have stopped in to see his old teacher on the way to the ambush.

"It must be a strange feeling," Bryony said. I sent her a warning look, but she continued. "To take someone else's energy by force and feel it fighting inside you to return. Did he struggle with it?"

"We all have our struggles," Amalia said. "And one of yours seems to be focus. Since neither you nor I will ever have the chance to experience such a sensation, I recommend you drop the matter from your mind. Your composition is still waiting."

"It was a strange feeling, though," Bryony said later in my suite. "And a fairly horrible one, to be honest. I feel sorry for that other trainee. Imagine having to feel that every day."

"I'll feel sorry for him as soon as I'm confident he wasn't involved in that attack," I said.

Bryony looked thoughtful. "Do you think it's likely? Doesn't he work with the healers now?"

"He works with the Armed Forces." I gave her a significant look. "Who as far as I know are still aligned with the throne...and King Cassius."

She wrinkled her nose. "I'd forgotten that. But that woman

was definitely an energy mage, and I can't believe the king would have two of them working for him. We're rare enough as it is—and even harder to find in Kallorway."

"I hope you're right." I sighed. "The thought that he has even one working for him is disconcerting enough."

"Darius may be acting awful to you right now," Bryony said, "but I do believe he'll find out who was behind that attack. Especially now he's working with Captain Vincent and not trying to do it on his own."

I groaned. "I hope you're right. Because I thought I'd finished with suspecting everyone around me at the end of last year."

"If we're lucky," Bryony added, "he'll find some evidence to convince him of Jareth's duplicity. And then you can have your prince back."

I snorted and smiled, but her words haunted me in bed that night. Because I no longer believed that getting Darius back would be nearly that simple—if I could claim I ever had him in the first place.

CHAPTER 9

I could barely contain my impatience through combat the next morning, eager to get to composition class. I just hoped Alvin would actually let my year mates compose today instead of lecturing the whole time.

I got my wish, and for once I listened closely to the instructions he gave them. Now that it came to it, a small flutter of nerves had started in my chest, and I preferred to start by knowing what the compositions were supposed to be achieving. I still believed I would be able to understand the purpose for myself when I connected with the composition, but I didn't want to take any risks with my first experiment.

In composition class, trainees learned a variety of basic compositions, regardless of their chosen discipline. Alvin had announced at the start of class that as second years, we were going to begin learning about compositions that interacted with living things.

He laughed merrily at Frida's horrified expression. "Do not fear. I'm not going to start you out experimenting on each other. You're not yet ready for such advanced workings. Today we will be composing a flower."

He produced a small pot of dirt with a flourish, beckoning Isabelle forward to help him hand out the rest of the pots lined up against the wall behind his desk. Neither Bryony, Tyron, nor I received one, but that didn't matter. I would be using the pot of one of my year mates for my own private experiment.

I had already chosen my first victim—Royce. Not only was he the least likely to say anything if he thought his composition had gone awry—his pride wouldn't allow such an admission—but I was also the least pained at the thought of accidentally causing him an unearned reprimand. Part of me would have loved to take Jareth's composition and twist it out of recognition, but that instinct was exactly why it wasn't safe to meddle with any working of his. I had already decided I wouldn't touch any composition of either of the princes.

"Each pot already contains a seed buried in the dirt," Alvin explained. "If you were working on crops, or even just on a permanent garden bed, we would also need to consider aspects such as providing water and nutrients to the growing plant. But for today, we are not going to worry about such things. Imagine, if you will, that you have spied the object of your affections and wish to present him or her with a token of your esteem."

He grinned at what he clearly thought a clever sally while Dellion openly rolled her eyes. I certainly couldn't imagine her ever composing such a lover's token.

"What sort of flower is it?" asked Wardell.

"Compose it into being, and you'll find out," Alvin said with a twinkle in his eye.

Dellion rolled her eyes again, but she turned to the empty parchment in front of her with a determined expression. My other year mates did the same, with varying levels of enthusiasm. My impatience mounted as they scratched out the binding words and began their actual compositions.

Surreptitiously I tried to watch Royce, although both Bryony and Tyron sat between us. I had no hope of reading the exact words he wrote, but he did seem to be writing at a fast pace. He was signed up to study the armed forces discipline, but perhaps he had been practicing in his gardens at home over the summer.

I almost smirked at the thought of Royce producing showy flowers to present to girls in the capital. It would take a lot more than a flower to make Royce an appealing romantic proposition.

"Once you've completed your composition, please work it so we can all admire the results!" Alvin called over the quiet sounds of multiple pens moving at once.

I bit my lip, now openly staring toward Royce. I had no idea how long a composition like this would take to work, and I might need to be ready to move fast. When he put down his pen, I tensed, reminding myself not to hold my breath.

As soon as he finished tearing the parchment through, I whispered, "Take control."

As the rush of power released by his working moved toward the pot, I was already connected with it. I could feel it reaching for the seed and feel its intention to spur new and sudden growth. Relief flooded me. Even if I'd missed every word Alvin said, I would have understood the purpose of the composition.

The power poured into the seed, causing it to split and sprout, unseen beneath the dirt. Within moments, greenery poked up into view. I didn't have long.

"Grow tall and large," I whispered, under my breath.

The power burst upward in a stronger, faster rush than before, the stalk growing from the soil at an unnerving rate. A bright purple blossom appeared, at first tightly sheathed and then, within less than a breath, bursting open. The petals unfurled, and the power died away.

I leaned forward so I could get an even better look. It was beautiful.

Every part of me buzzed. I had directed that power. I had

created that flower. I had done it with borrowed power, and with the help of the seed, of course, but the sense of euphoria still swept me up. Doing something so purposeful felt surprisingly different from reacting in a moment of danger and urgency.

I took a deep breath and looked around the rest of the room. Everyone except Armand now had a pot in front of them with a purple flower. And I could already see a green sprout rising from his.

I bit my lip. Everyone had the same flower, so they must have all been given the same type of seed. But Royce's was noticeably the tallest and largest of the blossoms. I might have overdone it a little in my rush. Working out how to channel the power was going to be the most difficult of my tasks. It was hard to make a decision ahead of time, before I felt the shape of the composition, but once I had connected with it, I usually only had seconds to respond.

Alvin walked up and down the desks, stopping in front of Tyron and Royce. He chuckled as he looked over Royce's flower.

"It's a fine specimen, Royce, I won't deny it."

Royce puffed up slightly, but Alvin continued to talk.

"But beware when it comes to living things such as this. As you know, power cannot create matter. If it is created from nothing, then it will remain only as long as power continues to sustain it. What we have done here is not create a flower but encourage one to grow unnaturally fast. But as I mentioned earlier, we have done it at an unsustainable pace, not giving it the proper tools it needs to grow healthy and strong. There's a reason our growers don't produce harvests in such a manner."

"But you said that doesn't matter here," Royce said.

"It's true that I set you all the task to create a flower meant for a short-term purpose only. But this flower has grown to such a size that I suspect it will not last long enough for your intentions to be fulfilled. Look." He pointed at one of the petals. "It's starting to wilt already."

I tried to see what he meant, but it was hard to do from this angle. Glancing around the room, I again compared the other flowers to the one I had created, frowning to myself. I had told it to grow large, but I hadn't expected it to so outstrip the intention of the composition.

"Whoops," Bryony muttered quietly, grinning at me.

She didn't seem to have any compunction at my having brought a lecture down on Royce's head. But even though he was consistently unpleasant to almost everyone, I felt a few small pangs of guilt.

I tried to relive those few moments of controlling his composition, even as the full understanding of its scope was already slipping out of my mind. The problem, I concluded, was that I had overestimated Royce. The creator back in Corrin had made a terrible mistake in his composition, but he had still understood the fundamentals of what he was crafting. His accidental overlay of the competing instruction had destroyed an otherwise sound composition.

For those few moments I had controlled his foundation, I had only needed to redirect it in the manner he had originally intended. His own knowledge and expertise had ensured that it operated correctly from there. But this composition had been different.

Royce had no expertise in the matter of creating flowers, and the composition had already been flawed on creation. I had thought he was writing quickly, and it looked like I had been right. He would have done better to take a little more time and care over his choice of words. He wasn't the only one either. Several of the flowers were already wilting by the time the class neared its end.

A little of my guilt lifted. I had only exacerbated a problem Royce had already created. But it was a good lesson for me as well. If I was going to be taking control of the compositions of other beginners like me, then I needed to be more prepared.

In fact, I needed to study just as hard as they did—as if I was the one crafting the composition from the beginning. The wave of understanding that came when I connected with a composition would be essential for situations where the knowledge of the mage in question far outstripped my own. But it wouldn't do me nearly as much good at the Academy.

In one way the experiment had been a complete success, however. No one was looking at me—no one even seemed to have any undue interest in Royce. I had successfully practiced with my ability—and had learned a lot in the process—with no one any the wiser.

Even as I thought it, the weight of a pair of eyes drew my gaze sideways. One person in the class was looking at me, his inscrutable gaze making it impossible for me to guess if his interest had anything to do with what had just happened. There was no reason to think Darius—or our instructor—could possibly have felt my involvement. Not if I was right and I was using energy to make my initial connection with the composition.

But still Darius's eyes burned into me. He had said I could assure my aunt I was being watched over at the Academy. Apparently I would have to be wary of that in the future.

That night, when I returned to my suite well after the evening meal, my mind still whirled with my experiment. I itched to try it again. Distracted, I walked straight through my sitting room, headed for my bedchamber door and my bed.

But a flash of purple caught my eye, making me slow. When I got a good look at the spot of color, I stopped completely. My first instinct was to glance wide-eyed around my sitting room, but I was alone, just as I had thought myself.

Walking slowly over to the small side table beside one of the sofas, I picked up the brilliant purple flower that lay there. My eyes flashed to the tapestry, but it lay just as still as usual, giving no sign that anyone had used the door it hid.

And yet, how else had this flower gotten here? Ida could have brought it, perhaps. Another trainee—or even instructor—might have requested her to leave it for me, and she likely wouldn't have seen any harm in doing so. It was just a flower.

Or a token of love, a dangerous voice in the back of my head whispered. *One created by someone with enough power that it still hadn't wilted.*

I told myself I had no reason to suspect such a thing, but I still slept with the flower under my pillow all night. The next morning, my heart beat extra fast when I saw Darius at breakfast, but he paid me no more attention than usual.

So I threw myself into the distraction of my new experiments. I paid far more attention to Alvin's previously tedious lectures than I had ever done in the past. I was even grateful for his constant need to go over the most basic material again and again. In my spare time, I returned to my old haunt of the library, studying the art of composing.

I often encountered Isabelle there, usually lost in the section on wind working. At first I thought she might be hiding in the library since she was somewhat at odds in our year without any particular friends. But every time I saw her, she seemed cheerful and genuinely interested in her reading.

The first time I passed her perched in a puffy armchair with her gaze focused out a narrow window instead of reading, I paused awkwardly. But she turned to me with a broad smile.

"Isn't it cozy to be hidden away in here, looking out at the world? I can tell you like it as much as I do."

I blinked, taken aback. "It is pleasant," I said after a moment. "And warm. Bryony would be out in the training yards all year round if she could, but it's much nicer in here."

Isabelle grinned. "It is starting to get a bit cold out there, isn't it? When you're studying wind working, you don't get much of an escape from the outdoors. I think that's why I like to spend time in here."

"You've mentioned your family live on the coast and your estate includes a lot of farmland. I've always pictured you striding up and down wind-swept beaches or through wet and muddy fields. Don't tell me you actually have a hatred of the outdoors!"

She laughed, the merry sound startling in the quiet library. "Oh no, I don't hate the outdoors. Wind working would have been a terrible choice if that was the case. I just enjoy the contrast —the library seems even more warm and cozy after time spent outside, and after long enough ensconced in here, I start to itch for fresh air again." She looked around. "Plus it reminds me of home."

I looked around at the enormous library blankly.

"Home is a great deal smaller, of course," Isabelle added, the laugh still in her tone. "And with infinitely fewer books." Her voice took on a wistful quality. "But it's cozy like this."

I felt a swell of fellow feeling. The library had always reminded me of home as well, although for different reasons. It was strangely reassuring to know that some trainees in Kallorway missed their families, just as I did. Not everyone had parents like King Cassius and Queen Endellion.

"I hope I can visit the north coast one day," I said. "I haven't had the chance to see much of Kallorway yet."

A fleeting look of discomfort crossed Isabelle's face before she spoke in a more stilted voice than she'd used before. "My family would be happy to host you if you ever want to visit, of course."

I thanked her, wishing I could take back my words. I had meant them in a friendly way, but it sounded like Isabelle—or perhaps her family—had no interest in royal visitors from the world of courts and politics. And could I really blame them?

I steered the conversation to wind working, and her previous ease soon returned. After that, we often stopped for a short chat when we crossed paths in the library, and I sometimes asked her questions about power compositions that occurred to me during my study.

But as helpful as I found the research, it was still secondary to actual experience. Each time Alvin had the trainees complete a practical exercise, I chose one of my year mates to practice on. I tried to rotate around equally between them, although given I couldn't use Bryony, Tyron, Jareth, or Darius, that only left seven options.

Now I was learning how to craft a composition for myself, I got better at noticing flaws in their workings. Where possible, I tried to leave the flaws there—or even exaggerate them, if it was safe to do so. I couldn't bear the idea that even Royce might leave the Academy having failed to learn some basic and essential lesson because of my interference.

I caught Jareth watching me with a questioning, almost calculating look at times, and when he finally cornered me after the evening meal one day, I discovered why. I would have liked to be curt in response, but Darius lingered behind him, and his presence made me consider my words more carefully. It was clear that while Darius hadn't asked directly, both princes were interested in the progress of my secret ability.

It might have been easier to lie outright, but with Darius standing there, I couldn't bring myself to do it. Instead I drew on all of my court training to return an answer vague enough to be true but which left them with the impression that I no longer trained with Bryony not because I had outgrown her, but because there was no further way to develop such a limited ability. As far as they knew, my ability was restricted to redirecting energy being given or taken through an energy composition toward myself.

To my relief, Jareth seemed to accept my answer. And after he left, it occurred to me that his understanding of my ability would be enough to explain my effective defense against the energy mage during the attack in the village. Maybe I hadn't tipped my hand as much as I thought.

I spent the first week of classes with a constant minor tension at the back of my mind as I waited to hear my family's response to the attack. And when Captain Layna reappeared at the Academy, my heart sank all the way into my boots.

But when she announced she'd come alone, my horror turned to confusion. I couldn't imagine my family sending anything less than a platoon to guard me through two days on the open road, given the circumstances.

"Don't worry," she said, with a knowing grin. "I haven't been sent to haul you away. From what I hear, Queen Lucienne managed to talk your parents down on that topic. Instead I've been sent to assist Captain Vincent in his investigations."

I raised an eyebrow. "And how do Captain Vincent and Duke Francis feel about that?"

The Academy Head was famously neutral, and I wasn't sure how either the king or General Haddon would feel about an Ardannian captain nosing around in Kallorway.

"Well, since it was Captain Vincent himself who suggested the attackers might have come from Ardann, he can hardly complain now about my being sent to assist," she said triumphantly.

I chuckled. "That does sound like my aunt. So you'll be here at the Academy, then?" I brightened at the idea of having another familiar, trusted face around.

"I'll be stationed here," she said. "But I'll be bunking in the guards' barracks, and I expect I won't actually be here that often. Given how tight a ship Captain Vincent runs, this is the least likely location to find any hint of your attackers."

I held back a wince, wishing I could believe that as easily as she did. But then I doubted Captain Vincent would be investigating his two primary charges.

"I'm glad to have you here, anyway," I said. "You'll report anything you find to me as well as back to my aunt?"

Captain Layna nodded. "Those were the queen's instructions."

I smiled, touched again by the faith my aunt continued to place in me. The smile fell away when Layna left my suite, however. Every day that I developed my ability in secret, telling no one but Bryony about my efforts, was a betrayal of that trust. And every time Darius looked at me with closed, cold eyes, it got harder and harder to believe the flower had come from him, or to remember why I was keeping my ability secret from my own family.

Only two things stopped me from doubting my decision. One was Bryony, the friend whose loyalty never wavered. I had been so worried about my aunt sending me to use my ability against Kallorway, but over the summer she had said it was the Sekali Empire where trouble was brewing. Bryony was Sekali, as was her family, and it didn't matter what my aunt commanded, I would never be able to see her as the enemy.

The other person who stopped me was Darius himself. Not because of the lingering feelings for him that still bubbled beneath the surface, no matter how I tried to suppress them, but precisely because of the closed expression on his face. I had seen behind that illusion and seen something that burned him so badly he could barely contain it. Darius had grown up as the tool of a king, and I had seen what he had been shaped into. He had no freedom to be himself or even to reveal a hint of his true emotions, and he trusted almost no one, living his life without friends and almost without family. I couldn't bear to risk the same thing happening to me. Not for any king, queen, or emperor.

That night was the first night I glanced at the tapestry on my wall and remembered that the previous year, Darius had shielded it with a composition crafted to allow me access.

But I had changed the compositions guarding my doors over the summer, and he might easily have done the same. My courage failed me, and I didn't test it either then, or on the many nights afterward when I stared at the woven feature and wondered what exactly was driving Darius to hide the person I knew existed under all those layers.

CHAPTER 10

*T*he weeks wore on, and the weather grew colder. I gave up waiting in daily expectation to hear of progress in Layna's investigations. But though she hadn't discovered my attacker, neither did she return to Ardann. I began to suspect that my parents had only capitulated and agreed to leave me in Kallorway if my aunt found a way to send my personal guard to watch over me.

I welcomed the daily combat lessons as an escape from both the churning emotions I couldn't quite overcome and the intense mental stimulation of my new studies and secret experiments. But the rest of the class were less satisfied that our lessons continued to be limited to sword fighting in our training yard. I even heard Armand complaining almost loudly enough for Mitchell to hear him. The third and fourth years had been training in the arena since the second week of the year, and none of my year mates could understand why we weren't doing the same.

"I'll admit, I'm looking forward to getting back to arena battles," Bryony said one morning as she gazed toward the bubble of power that encircled the open-air structure.

"Don't tell me you of all people are getting sick of poking people with that sword of yours." Tyron raised an eyebrow. "I might die of shock."

She laughed. "I'm not sick of the bouts. I just enjoy the arena battles as well."

"I can attest to the fact she's not lost her enthusiasm for unnecessary amounts of swordplay," I said. "She still makes me come out here to practice on rest day mornings."

Tyron shivered. "Yes, she tried to convince me to join you once."

Bryony turned her nose up at both of us. "I'm just being a good friend and trying to stop you wasting your days away in bed."

"There are bells to prevent that kind of thing," I muttered, but I didn't protest too loudly. Darius had just passed us in the training yard, and my heart flipped over, stuttering for a moment and then beating far too hard. He walked with a deadly grace, his drawn sword in his hand and one of his most commanding expressions on his face. No doubt he had just demolished whatever unfortunate year mate had been partnered with him for the last bout.

For some reason seeing him in the training yard always reminded me of the time he had carried me to safety after I first discovered my ability. Even after all these months, I could far too easily conjure up the memory of his strong arms around me and my cheek warm against his chest. For all I complained about Bryony's extra practice sessions, I wished myself in the middle of one now with no distractions but our training. I had discovered the year before that physical activity was the only thing that could clear my mind, and I needed those moments of tranquility that Bryony forced on me even more now than I had done then.

"Tomorrow morning," Mitchell announced, cutting across our conversations, "we will be training in the arena. You may gather directly there at the bell."

"There you go," I told Bryony. "He heard you."

"As if Mitchell would ever listen to a word I had to say," she scoffed. "But never mind that. The arena at last."

The sense of palpable excitement at breakfast the next morning suggested that most of our year shared her feelings on the matter. Even Frida had abandoned her grim predictions about the terrors we would face and was excitedly talking about the compositions she meant to test. Compositions meant for combat could only be safely worked within the arena shield, and all the trainees lived in fear of releasing one anywhere else. According to the rumor, a number of years ago a trainee had not abided by these restrictions, and the duke had expelled him from the Academy for accidentally demolishing several walls.

"And you know what happened to him then," Frida said in a foreboding voice when she told me the story. "Sealed."

Armand had been in earshot at the time and walked away with a disgusted expression on his face. Frida watched him go, unrepentant.

"He's just sensitive because his father is sealed," she told me. "Of course his father went whimpering straight to the general afterward, but it's not something that can be reversed."

I watched his retreating back with interest. So Armand's father had been sealed and had then switched allegiances. Did that explain something of why Armand himself was so reserved and withdrawn compared to his cousin? Despite his connection with the Head of the Creators, I couldn't imagine his family had much sway within their faction.

But whether or not it was true that a past trainee had been expelled for such crimes, the story was effective at discouraging the current group from risking experimenting outside the arena. So effective, in fact, that I suspected Duke Francis of having invented the tale himself. If so, I congratulated him on a masterful strategy.

Despite my own preoccupation, I found the excitement

contagious as we filed into the arena after breakfast. I hoped Mitchell intended to let us all take part in the first day's battle, whatever it might be.

Not that I intended to use my ability. Now that I better understood the dangers of taking over the composition of an inexperienced mage—let alone in a rushed, high pressure situation—I didn't want to risk making a dangerous mistake. But I had managed to participate well enough in first year despite my lack of ability, so I had every expectation of being able to do so now as well.

None of Frida's stories of us facing off against monsters composed into being by our instructor eventuated. Instead Mitchell called for those trainees studying to join the growers, the Royal Guard, and the Armed Forces to stand to his left. Frida, Ashlyn, Dellion, Jareth, and Royce stood and made their way down from the seats. When he called for Tyron to join them, I felt a small swelling of hope that Bryony and I would end up on the same team—an unusual occurrence.

He then called for the creator, wind worker, and law enforcement trainees to come down. Wardell, Armand, Isabelle, and Darius stood, followed by Bryony when he tacked her name on at the end. Only five of them were making their way down to stand at his right, compared to the six at his left, but he still hesitated as his eyes rested on me. From some of his groupings in first year, I guessed he was hesitant to assign equal teams when Darius's skills so far outstripped the rest of us—an inevitable consequence of both his natural strength and his two years of private training.

I challenged Mitchell with my gaze, and he finally called my name, gesturing toward his right. I almost bounded down the stairs to join Bryony, carefully not allowing myself to brush too close to Darius.

"Yes!" Bryony cried. "We're going to be unbeatable."

But when Mitchell announced the rules of the battle, he had a surprise in store for us.

"You may use any compositions *except* those relating to your chosen discipline," he said.

"What?" Howls of protest rose from both sides.

"But that's not fair," Royce said. "We haven't been preparing other compositions."

"Well you should have been," Mitchell said coldly. "It is never a wise idea to become predictable. An enemy will take advantage of it, no matter your strength. I am sure you all have shields, at least, and they are not discipline specific, so I expect every trainee to contribute." He paused, his eyes resting on Bryony and me. "Well, every trainee capable of doing so."

Bryony sighed. "That's me out then," she said apologetically to our team. "I only have the one composition, and it's very much within my 'discipline'. If you can call being an energy mage a discipline."

"You'll still be valuable for your skills with a sword," Darius said calmly, assuming leadership as he did for every team he fought with. "Wardell, Armand, and Isabelle, what do you have beside shields?"

Wardell grimaced. "Nothing, I'm afraid. Although I have a fair few shields. I loaded my pockets with creator compositions when I knew we were in the arena today."

"I have a number of binding compositions," Armand surprised us all by saying. When his cousin gave him a questioning look, he shrugged. "They seem like a generally useful sort of thing to have on hand."

I examined him more closely, remembering Frida's revelations. Maybe there were some advantages to not being completely secure in your position.

"I've been experimenting with fast growing vines," Isabelle said. She also received a number of surprised looks, but she continued calmly. "Ever since I worked with the growers to make use of them in one of our early battles last year. It didn't seem a truly effective strategy unless I could do it on my own."

"A wise thought," Darius said. "It's always better not to rely on others."

I kept my face still. I hated that he felt that way but, contradictorily, I also wished he would apply the belief to his brother. I glanced across at Jareth who appeared to be in animated conversation with Dellion. Tyron stood beside them, looking slightly bemused. I grinned at him, and he waved back.

Darius was also examining our opponents, but there was no friendly glint in his eye.

"They've lost the advantage they would have had from having two guards and a soldier," he said. "None of those three will be able to use their combat compositions, and I don't imagine the grower girls will have many workings of that sort to hand. So we should hit them hard and fast with combat-focused compositions of our own. Wardell, you can provide shields for Bryony and the princess. They'll be leading the way with their swords, so they'll need effective ones. Isabelle, see if you can take out some of their opponents with your vines. Just remember that you can't provide any water for them, or you'll be disqualified, and possibly our team with you."

She nodded, although from what Alvin had taught us, it could be argued that water fell just as much within the purview of a grower as a wind worker.

"Armand, you stand ready with your binding compositions to take out anyone who loses a shield."

"And what of you, Darius?" I asked, intentionally using his name after he had relegated me to my title only.

"I'll be the one breaking down those shields," he said coldly. "Unless you have a better suggestion."

I held his eyes for a moment, but he didn't back down, and I was the one to look away. Apparently I could consider myself punished for using his name so freely in public.

There was no time for more discussion anyway. Mitchell called the start of the battle, and most of the trainees scattered, scrambling apart to give themselves time to retrieve their chosen compositions. Bryony and I charged our closest opponents, however, trusting in Wardell to get us shielded before we actually reached them. He didn't let us down.

I encountered Dellion first, but she had already managed to work her own shield, so my first blow bounced away. She retreated anyway, trying to preserve her shield by staying out of my range. I pushed my attack forward, but my focus wasn't on the haphazard blows I tried to land on the invisible bubble around her.

I was too busy fighting an internal battle of my own. A number of times now, when faced with danger, I had reached out with my ability despite having only a limited understanding of it. But now I had been training, and it turned out my ability was like a physical muscle.

The more I practiced with it, the more it responded instinctively without needing conscious direction. What I hadn't anticipated was how much the energy and chaos of these mock battles reflected the intensity of an actual threat. My energy wanted to reach out and latch hold of Dellion's shield, and it required conscious effort on my part to prevent it.

With her shield in place, Dellion had time to draw her own sword, so when her power fizzled and disappeared under my blows, my next thrust was met with the ring of steel against steel. She was looking at me oddly, though, so I knew she could tell something was off with my fighting.

Without the distraction of her shield, I renewed my efforts with my sword, but the reprieve didn't last long. With her free hand, she pulled out another parchment, ripping it with her teeth to release a fresh barrier. This one only blocked my more deadly blows, letting the others through, but I couldn't capitalize on the opportunity when I was struggling to bite back the words that would give me her shield.

I didn't even notice my own shield was gone until the tip of her blade danced up my arm, ripping the sleeve of my robe and leaving a long, shallow cut in my skin. Energized by the small victory, she pressed forward while simultaneously withdrawing yet another composition.

This one, when she ripped it, clearly wasn't a shield. Dancing orbs of fire sprang into life and circled above her head. They cast an almost fiendish glow over her, making her wide grin look reckless and dangerous.

I could feel the heat of them from where I stood, the length of two sword blades away, and before I knew what I was doing, I had whispered, "Take control."

I instantly realized my mistake, but it was too late. The orbs streaked away from her toward me. To an observer, it must look like she had sent them to attack me, which meant I had only the briefest moment to fix my mistake before they began to circle above my head instead of hers. How would I ever explain that?

They wanted to attack someone—it was their crafted purpose —so, in panic, I gasped, "Attack!"

The balls of flame went flying in all directions. I whirled, trying to see who might be in their path. I had sent them out without guidance, and they raced toward everyone in my vicinity.

The first person my eyes latched on was Bryony. She was fighting Jareth, dancing in and out of his reach, laughing. But the prince had already succeeded in destroying her shield, and she was helpless before the incoming fireball, not even seeing it coming.

"Get down!" I screamed, sprinting toward her, my sword lying forgotten behind me.

She started, turning toward me as I launched myself across the remaining distance. I reached her at the same time as the fireball, knocking her to the ground in a sprawling tangle of limbs.

"Verene!" she had time to gasp, and then the tip of a sword appeared at each of our throats.

We froze.

"Yield," I said, my voice shaking, and Bryony echoed me.

The swords, and the two wielding them—Jareth and Dellion, our two strongest opponents—instantly disappeared. Slowly, I pushed myself up onto my feet and held out a hand to help Bryony.

"I'm not sure if I'm supposed to be thanking you or blaming you," she said, her cheerfulness a little forced. She was obviously disappointed to be removed from the battle so quickly.

"Definitely blaming me." I fought back the moisture that wanted to spring into my eyes. "I made a big mistake, Bree."

She stared at me, dropping her voice so low I almost couldn't hear her words. "You mean that was you? With those fireballs?"

I nodded miserably. "I wasn't planning to do it, but I took over Dellion's composition. And then I had to do *something* with them. Goodness knows what she thinks just happened."

"Hopefully she thinks there was a flaw in her composition, and she just lost control of it," Bryony said. "I don't see how she could guess the truth."

I groaned. "And meanwhile, I managed to take both of us out of the fight. And who knows who else? I can't even bring myself to look."

Bryony cast a glance back over her shoulder and grimaced. "Maybe better not to."

I groaned again. "I didn't expect it to be so hard. My mind knew it was a training exercise, but my body felt like it was in danger, and it wanted to act."

A gasping moan interrupted me, and Bryony and I both spun around. Someone else had been "killed" and was slowly departing the field of battle. But unlike us, Isabelle moved slowly, carefully holding one arm still across her chest.

Bryony rushed forward to support her under her good shoulder, but I stayed frozen in place, my eyes glued on the raw burn that marred the full length of her forearm. Isabelle saw me looking and managed a weak smile.

"I don't know what Dellion was thinking with such an uncontrolled working, but it was certainly effective in the end."

I knew I should step forward and help her, like Bryony was doing, but I couldn't make myself move.

"Raelynn?" I managed to ask, finally thinking to look around the arena for the healer.

"Those fireballs took out Frida as well," Isabelle said, "but she only lost a little bit of hair. Mitchell put out the flames before they could do any damage and then sent her to fetch Raelynn. Unfortunately she was sitting all the way over there." She tried to point to the far side of the arena but winced at the movement.

"Here, sit down." Bryony guided her onto the lowest tier of seating. "I'm sure she'll be here any moment."

"Oh, poor dear!" called a familiar voice, puffing a little. "Just sit tight for a minute." Raelynn appeared, her healing case slung over one shoulder.

As soon as she reached us, she put it down on the seating and began rummaging inside. Before long, Isabelle had been treated with a pain relief composition followed by a burn treatment.

She gave a long sigh of relief as she examined the healthy skin of her arm. "Thank you," she said with feeling.

"My pleasure." Raelynn beamed at her. "I was disappointed no one in your year chose healing. It's such a satisfying thing to see the pain leave someone's face. And no one is ever sorry to see you arrive." She chuckled before turning to Bryony and me. "And what about the two of you? Any injuries?"

I shook my head. "Only to my pride. I managed to take us both out of the battle without sustaining a single scratch."

She chuckled again. "An achievement indeed. You can count yourself fortunate if you ask me."

Frida approached, having circumnavigated the arena floor at a slower pace than the healer.

"It's too bad you can't heal my hair." She plucked at the burned strands disconsolately.

"Never mind, dear." Raelynn patted her arm. "We can chop it shorter, and no one will even notice."

"But I don't want it shorter." Frida's heart wasn't in the complaint, though. She already knew she would have to get it cut.

I climbed higher up the seats, choosing one positioned some distance from my year mates and the healer. Bryony slowly joined me.

"It was an accident, Verene," she whispered. "And Raelynn is always on hand for arena battles. They know trainees have accidents."

"I can't compete in the arena," I said, feeling the weight of the words, but knowing they were true. "I just proved exactly why my ability isn't safe to use in a situation like this. And I also proved that I can't stop myself from using it. It's too dangerous."

Bryony chewed on her lip, looking worried. "But you can't just choose not to participate in combat class. You don't mean you're going to go home?"

I shook my head. "I'm not going home. But I'll find a way. I just need to think on it."

Bryony still looked doubtful, but she didn't say anything. I finally forced myself to look toward the remaining battle, just in time for Mitchell to declare Jareth and Dellion's team the victors. I groaned again.

The rest of my team were already straggling back toward the seats. Darius came from the rear, stalking through their midst to take the lead. I swallowed. He looked thunderous.

When he reached the seating, however, he stopped to talk to both Isabelle and Raelynn in a quiet voice. As soon as he was satisfied that his team member had been successfully healed, however, he strode up the steps toward Bryony and me.

I stared at him in confusion, my overloaded brain trying to

understand what was happening. Darius never approached me and never spoke to me unless forced to do so.

"What was that?" he snapped.

I stared at him, scrambling to think of an answer. How did he know what had happened? How could he possibly know?

"I—"

"There are many ways to avoid a fireball," he said in a freezing tone. "All of them are preferable to tripping over your own feet and taking down one of your best teammates with you. With both of you plus Isabelle gone, and Jareth and Dellion freed to come against the rest of us, we didn't stand a chance."

I gaped up at him. Normally I would have responded sharply to such an attack, but I was too conscious of my own overwhelming guilt to do anything but stare at him.

"What? Nothing to say, Princess?" His voice taunted me, more hurtful than a slap.

I saw the rest of our year, along with our instructor, staring up at us in shock and steeled myself. I might not have it in me to defend myself, but I wouldn't let them see my pain either.

When I continued to say nothing, Darius turned and strode back down the stairs.

"Verene," Bryony whispered, horrified.

I shook my head, not meeting her eyes. "No, don't say anything. I deserved that, even if it wasn't for the reasons he thought. I injured Isabelle, and it could have been far worse."

"That doesn't make what he did all right," Bryony muttered, always the rebel.

But as if to underscore my words, Mitchell had begun a public reprimand of a mortified-looking Dellion. Apparently none of us were to be using anything as dangerous as fireballs until we were sure we could control our own compositions.

Every word he said hit home, further convincing me I couldn't risk returning to the arena. I just had to find a way to convince Mitchell to allow me to withdraw without failing second year.

CHAPTER 11

*J*stumbled through classes for the rest of the day, not meeting anyone's eyes and keeping my ability locked tightly inside. I had let myself grow overconfident, and Isabelle had paid the price. Along with poor Frida's hair and Dellion's pride.

But by the time I had paced up and down my sitting room fifty times, my emotions had subsided somewhat. I was still determined to find a way out of arena combat, but I could also see the truth of Bryony's words. Trainees spent four years at the Academy precisely because they were not expected to be instant masters of their skills. And we fought in a shielded arena with a skilled healer on hand because we were expected to make mistakes.

Just because no one else knew of my training, didn't mean I wasn't training just like the rest of them. And I had to let myself make mistakes.

As my initial feelings of guilt eased, I found my pacing taking me closer and closer to the tapestry on my wall. What had happened to my team in the arena might have been my fault, but Darius didn't know that.

His criticisms had been unjust. But, more importantly, they had been completely unlike him. The crown prince didn't lose control in public, and I had never heard him speak to anyone in such a way over an error in training.

This wasn't even the first time my new abilities had caused me to fail my team in the arena. He hadn't known the true cause when it happened last year, either, and yet when we spoke in private, his only concern had been for me. Any lingering doubts that something strange was going on with Darius hardened into certainty.

Without stopping to think it through for once, I pushed the tapestry aside and opened the door. Only once the door was already in motion did it occur to me that I should have knocked.

I rapped awkwardly on the open panels. Now that I was here, I didn't want to take that final step into his sitting room. I didn't want to know if he had reset his shields to exclude me.

The room stood empty. It looked just like it had on my one previous visit, almost a mirror image of my own except for the deep burgundy furnishings. We had been interrogating an assassin on that occasion, and my eyes moved to the place where he had sat before flitting quickly away, the memory an unpleasant one.

It hadn't occurred to me that Darius might not be here, and I was about to withdraw again when the closed door to his bedchamber opened. He stared across the length of the sitting room at me, both of us frozen in doorways.

"Verene?"

"I need to talk to you." I swallowed, trying to regain some of the certainty that had sent me through his door. "Right now."

Something flitted across his face that I couldn't read, and he gestured for me to enter. We met in the middle of the room.

"What you did today," I said. "After the attack—"

"I'm sorry." He cut me off before I could continue. Reaching out a hand, he took a single step toward me before stopping and rocking back on his heels. "Verene, I'm so sorry."

Any lingering anger faded away at the torment on his face.

"I'm worried about you," I said in a soft voice. "And I want to know what's going on. Because I know *something* is going on."

He ran a hand through his hair and barked a harsh laugh as he turned partially away from me. "You're worried about *me*. Of course you are. I've been nothing but horrible to you since you returned, and yet you're concerned about me."

I took two steps toward him, causing him to step back. I stopped.

"Yes, of course I'm worried. I know you, Darius. Even if you're determined to pretend I don't. You promised me at the end of last year that I would be safe in Kallorway now, and yet I was attacked just outside the Academy. And no one seems to be able to work out who was responsible."

He sucked in a breath, pain flaring on his face, so I hurried on.

"Maybe it's foolish, but despite everything, I still believe you're a person who can be trusted to keep your promises. I trust you, Darius, so I know something deeper is going on here than you're letting me see." I willed him to meet my eyes again. "Won't you trust me back? Please?"

"Trust you?" The words seemed wrung from him. "You're one of the few people I've ever trusted. It's everyone else I don't trust."

I took another step forward, and this time he didn't step away, although the pained look on his face deepened.

"Then, please, tell me what's going on," I begged.

A shudder rippled through him before he straightened, his posture stiff. "You're wrong to place so much trust in my promises. I believe it *was* my father behind the attack, although neither Captain Vincent nor Captain Layna has managed to secure any definitive proof."

The news wasn't a surprise, but it hit me harder than expected, and I swayed slightly. Darius responded instantly, closing the distance between us to place a supportive hand on my elbow. He guided me to the sofa a short distance behind me, and when I sat on it, he dropped to one knee, grasping one of my hands in his.

"Please know that I would never willingly break my word to you, Verene." His ragged voice tore at my heart, his eyes burning into me. How many sleepless nights had those eyes seen?

"I believe you," I said, and for a brief moment he closed them, calming his breathing.

My heart raced, intoxicated by his closeness and the raw vulnerability I had so missed. Something had happened to tear him apart, but this was still the Darius who haunted my dreams. I would have barged in here weeks ago if I had known this was all it would take to see his true self again.

But when he opened his eyes, he had regained his control. He stood swiftly, letting my hand drop.

"Something has changed in my father." Darius's tone was harsh but no longer ragged. "He is…out of control. Something— or someone—has managed to tip him beyond reason. He has always been cruel and power-hungry, but he has also been care- ful. Now he has lost that caution." He frowned. "Perhaps my starting at the Academy had something to do with it."

"So what does that mean?" I asked. "Am I not safe here?"

"No," Darius said swiftly. "You are safe within the Academy walls. My father still dares not act openly, and Captain Vincent is trustworthy. I am convinced of that now. He guards this place like a fortress. Nothing has changed for you. I'm the one who has changed."

I rubbed at the side of my head, feeling a headache developing.

"Don't do that," Darius said, a new soft note in his voice that caught me off guard. My eyes flew to his. "You always rub your temples when you're stressed. But this is my stress to carry."

I looked away, trying to hide my flush. He was right. I did

massage my temples whenever I was stressed. I didn't realize he knew that about me.

"You may be the crown prince," I said. "But you're also a trainee at the Academy. What can you do about your father, even if he is out of control?"

"I have never had the luxury of being merely a trainee," he said, the harsh note back in his voice. "Now more than ever. I've done the only thing I can do—I've moved forward my time-line. I can no longer wait for graduation to force my father's hand. I must do it now. He can no longer be trusted on the throne."

I gasped, jumping back to my feet. "You're going to seize power now?"

"This year, at least. If I can."

I stared at him wide-eyed.

"Oh, I don't think the Mage Council will actually crown me before I'm a fully qualified mage," he said. "But I can still claim the throne and tie my father's hands."

I tried to pull my racing thoughts together. "Is that why you were so harsh to me today? It was a…a performance?"

He nodded, a brief look of pain crossing his face before he clamped back down hard.

"This has happened too soon," he said. "I don't have every-thing in place yet. Which means my only hope is to take my father by surprise—to take both sides by surprise. It has never been more important that I appear to be neutral. And you…" He sighed. "You are not neutral, Verene. You know the chaos you caused last year just by accepting a Midwinter invitation."

"I understand," I said slowly. "I told you I knew something was going on. But what I can't understand is why you didn't just tell me all this as soon as I arrived. And not just because we're friends—or at least I thought we were. I'm also a representative of the Ardannian crown, remember. And Ardann has promised to help you."

"Friends?" He sounded almost startled. "Is that what we were?"

I flushed, not sure how to respond.

"You're right, though," he said heavily after a moment. "I should have sought your assistance immediately as your aunt's representative. I was..." He trailed off, and although I waited hopefully, he didn't finish the sentence.

My eyes narrowed. Clearly I had not gotten to the bottom of Darius's complicated tangle of motivations and emotions. And equally clearly he didn't mean to share them.

"As Ardann's representative," I said after a moment of heavy silence, "I will help you in any way I can without compromising my crown."

"Of course," he said quickly. "I won't ask for your official support. Not until my plan has succeeded."

I nodded, and the moment hung between us. I had offered myself as Ardann's representative, not as Verene, and I could read in his eyes that he understood the difference.

Darius might not mean his public actions toward me, but neither had he chosen to be open with me—not when I first arrived back, and not completely even now. Which meant I needed to guard my heart.

I still believed he was the best future for Kallorway, and I would stand his friend in the political games he played. But I certainly couldn't risk telling him the truth of my abilities. A brief flash of guilt filled me at that thought. I had claimed I trusted him and asked for his trust in return, but I was no more being completely open with him than he was with me. But I could not give in to that feeling. I could not afford to let my emotions rule me.

Only when I was safely back in my own room did I acknowledge, even to myself, that I had already been trying to guard my heart since the end of last year. But neither absence nor daily exposure had proven enough to drive the prince from the corners of my heart. I only had to see his tall form for my heart to leap out of control.

Well, I concluded grimly, *I would just have to try harder.*

~

I attempted the effort in the only way I knew how. Distraction.

I threw myself into my secret training with even more focus. I had learned to use my abilities instinctively, like a muscle, but now I needed to learn complete mastery over them. It was the only way I would ever be able to safely train in an environment like the arena. But until I achieved that goal, I needed to find a way to remove myself from danger.

Every time my thoughts tried to turn to Darius in the days following our conversation, I forced them instead onto the issue of how to avoid arena training. It meant I spent a lot of time contemplating the issue.

In the end, I decided my answer lay in the strange and unexplained delay in the start of arena battles for the second years. When we had finally come to battle, Mitchell had paused when he looked at me. I had thought in the moment that he was trying to decide where to assign me, but what if it was more than that? I had been attacked multiple times last year, but few people knew of it. The open attack against me in the village had been different, though. What if the furor it had caused had made Duke Francis hesitant to allow the other trainees to attack me in battle—even in training? I could imagine the incensed messages he might have received from my aunt and parents after they heard Captain Layna's report.

My strategy decided, I waited for the next time Mitchell announced the second years would spend the following morning in the arena. And as soon as class finished, I approached him. I assumed my most regal air, hoping he would believe I spoke with more than the authority of a single second year trainee.

"I'm afraid I can no longer participate in arena battles," I said. "Please let me know how you would like me to complete replacement work so that I don't fall behind in your class. Perhaps I could complete written assignments analyzing the strategy I observe in my year mates' battles?"

I had been working hard to hide my tension, but apparently I needn't have been concerned. Mitchell actually looked relieved. The out of control fireballs in our first battle must have confirmed all the instructors' fears about the risks of having me in the arena. If I had been the one hurt instead of Isabelle, my family might have tried to claim it wasn't an accident at all.

"I can see no need for written assignments," he said. "You may observe the battles from the shielded arena seating and take part verbally in the strategy discussions after the fighting is concluded. I have no concerns about your physical sword skills, and you can continue to bout in the training yard."

I thanked him and hurried back to the Academy, not wanting to miss lunch. Bryony had waited for me, just out of range of our conversation, and I responded to her raised eyebrow with a broad smile.

She shook her head. "It must be nice to be a princess," she muttered.

"Sometimes." My smile dropped away as my mind filled with thoughts of Darius and the complicated politics that both bound us and tore us apart. Now that I had succeeded in freeing myself of arena battles, I would need something else to focus on whenever his dark eyes intruded on my peace.

CHAPTER 12

$\mathcal{T}$he answer came in expanding my training. I was familiar at this point with the compositions of each of my year mates and could connect with them with ease. I wanted a greater challenge.

The next time Alvin began composition class with a composition of his own, I was ready. As soon as he tore the parchment, I whispered, "Take control."

Only Bryony sat close enough to hear me, and she gave me a startled look. I ignored her, focused on those crucial few seconds while the working ran its course.

After so much practice controlling the compositions of my fellow trainees, connecting with one done by an expert was heady. The power he had gathered was tight and controlled, and layers of understanding blossomed in my mind. I could see not only the words he'd used to shape the power but the depth of intention behind them.

We were back working on plants again, and he hadn't just told this seedling vine to grow thicker and stronger, he had directed the level of its growth with a fine-tuned understanding. The power leached all available nutrients from the soil, pushing them into the plant to allow an explosion of unnatural growth that would remain strong enough for the vine not to wither and die within hours.

I knew immediately that most of my year mates would not be capable of a composition like this. Not for years, at least, and for some, maybe never.

It should have made my task easy, but I realized in a split second that it actually made it far more difficult. There was no chaos of battle to hide my actions here, and Alvin clearly knew exactly how he had directed the power to behave.

Panicked, I instructed the power to do exactly what it was already attempting to do. When the vine grew—not with quite the dramatic display of the purple flowers, but still with impressive speed—Alvin smiled. He continued with his instructions as if nothing unexpected had occurred, and I breathed a small sigh of relief.

Bryony gave me a quizzical look. "What did you do?" she whispered.

"Nothing," I admitted.

She frowned, no doubt confused, but didn't attempt to question me further in the middle of class. I didn't interrupt any of my year mates' compositions that lesson, my mind distracted with what I had discovered inside Alvin's working.

Already the exact knowledge on plant growth I had so easily grasped in the moment was fading away. If I had been able to access power normally, I couldn't have replicated his efforts. But something of the feel of his composition lingered.

I had stumbled onto something valuable. While I would have to think carefully about small ways I could adjust instructor compositions that wouldn't be detectable, I could also learn without diverting them at all.

Two days later, Amalia announced in our discipline class that the time had finally arrived for us to start visiting other classes. I had always known that was the eventual intention, but the timing couldn't have been more perfect for my purposes.

No one was interested in me, of course. As far as they were concerned, I was trailing along just to observe. But I felt almost euphoric at the access our visits would give me to expert mages across a range of disciplines.

When Amalia led us into the first class, a number of unfamiliar faces greeted me. I hadn't expected the class to be so big until I remembered that discipline classes were mixed across the year levels. It was easy to forget when Bryony and Tyron were the only energy mages currently at the Academy.

Amalia had chosen to start with the wind working class, and an undercurrent of excitement threaded through the room. Not every group of trainees who studied at the Academy got the chance to train with energy mages.

The wind worker instructing their class deferred to Amalia, and she explained that we would be working with this class for two weeks. To start, the class would watch Bryony and Tyron compose and then work an energy composition. Isabelle had already had the chance to experience receiving some of their energy in our arena battles, but the trainees from other year levels would each be given such an opportunity.

In return, Bryony and Tyron would observe some of the specialist compositions the class had been learning. The two energy mage trainees would then work together with the class to develop ways the ability of the energy mages could benefit the compositions of the class.

"Surely that's obvious," one of the fourth years drawled. "We'll be able to complete much more powerful compositions."

Amalia gave him such a withering look that he sank back into his chair. I had to stifle a smile. Clearly this class had yet to be exposed to Amalia and her teaching style.

"Certainly that is one benefit—the most obvious one. The true rewards will come if you are capable of looking beyond the obvious." It was clear from her tone that she didn't expect such a feat from him.

When she looked at the rest of the class, no one else said a word.

My role in the lessons was to sit in the back and observe, which perfectly suited my purposes—as would all the demonstrations apparently planned for the next few days. But since they started with Bryony and Tyron, I didn't immediately interfere.

Even Amalia understood they couldn't compose endlessly, however, so it would take a number of days to produce enough energy compositions for all the wind worker trainees. Thankfully for me, that meant by our second combined class, the wind worker demonstrations had begun.

To give the class full rein to work, we met out in the grounds. I caught a glimpse of the grower class working in the extensive Academy garden beds, but Amalia led us past both the training yards and the gardens to a large stretch of open ground on the far side of the Academy.

Several outbuildings sheltered on the edge of the wall, but a substantial patch of clear space stood between them and the Academy itself. I had never noticed this part of the Academy before, perhaps because there was nothing here of any particular visual interest.

"It's best if we have the Academy building between us and the stables," Isabelle said to me quietly when she saw me looking around. "Captain Vincent doesn't like it when we terrify his horses."

No doubt wanting to impress us, the wind worker instructor began by composing an enormous whirlwind, which roared around the confined space without so much as ruffling our hair. After that she had a couple of her fourth years produce first lightning and then rain.

By the time they had completed the workings, I was almost bouncing with excitement, eager to connect with one of them and see what it felt like on the inside. I chose to start with the instructor, not confident to fiddle with such a powerful working if it might not be entirely stable to begin with.

When she explained that she would next show us the whirlwind again, but in a smaller form, I was initially disappointed. But as soon as I whispered the words to take control of the working, all such feelings flew away.

A smaller whirlwind might look less impressive, but it was actually harder to compose because it required more control. Once the air started spinning, it wanted to draw more air into it and grow in size. I didn't try to change anything about it, merely releasing it to do its pre-shaped job and marveling at the expertise required to safely complete such a working. My mind filled with an instinctive understanding of not only the wind dynamics of the funnel itself but all the flow on impacts on temperature, weather, even cloud formation. A responsible wind worker didn't interfere with the weather until they understood the full consequences of their actions.

When the whirlwind died out, the power dissipating, disappointment filled me. I had admired the intricacies of our composition instructor's workings, but they were nothing to the feeling of pure power from holding the weather itself in your grasp.

In the classroom, Bryony had been ushered to the front, but now that we were standing in a clump outside, she had stubbornly stuck to my side. When I finally regained proper awareness of my surroundings, I found her frowning at me.

"Are you sure that was a good idea?" she asked.

I waved her words away. "Nothing went wrong, did it? I wish you could feel it, Bree. It's incredible."

She didn't look convinced, but I was already concentrating on the instructor's words, wondering what compositions she might have the class demonstrate next.

The fourth years were given the most access to Bryony and Tyron, presumably because the younger trainees had two more years after this one to work with the energy mages. It was fascinating to feel the difference in the compositions of the fourth years compared to the second years. Their workings had noticeably more power and control, but they still couldn't match those of the instructors.

After our two weeks with the wind workers, Amalia moved us on to the creators, and then the growers, which involved spending most classes out in the gardens, despite the increasing cold. This new access to compositions proved almost absorbing enough to overshadow thoughts of Darius in my mind, and I could feel my understanding of not only my own ability but compositions in general growing by the day.

Bryony never sat with me in these classes—she was always the center of attention, while I lingered unobtrusively in the back. When she did glance back my way, an unhappy expression on her face, I always waved her off. This was her moment to shine, and I was too distracted to feel lonely or overlooked anyway.

When she said we needed to talk and shadowed me back to my suite after breakfast one rest day, I had a pretty speech prepared in my mind to reassure her. But her first words took me by surprise.

"I'm worried about you, Verene. I'm worried you're losing yourself."

I stared at her, all my prepared sentences slipping away.

"Losing myself? What do you mean? I've never enjoyed classes so much. It's amazing, Bree!"

Her face didn't lighten. "Yes, that's what I'm worried about. You know I was excited for you to discover you have an ability after all, but this…"

I frowned, instantly defensive, as she continued.

"You don't just have an ability, you have a powerful one. And you haven't told anyone about it—not even your own family."

"But you were the one who said I shouldn't tell them!" I protested. "And I think you were right."

Bryony grimaced. "So do I. I stand by that advice. It's necessary for your own protection. But the unfortunate side effect is that you're doing your training in secret. You sit there, with none the wiser, tapping into powerful compositions—more and more of them. Nothing seems to make you pause anymore. If you had openly acknowledged your ability and were receiving guided training like the rest of us, do you really think they'd let you do so much? That they'd let you take over any composition you wanted without permission or regard for its power or destructive potential?"

I opened my mouth to retort before slowly closing it again, an unwelcome flush heating my cheeks.

"No, I'm sure they wouldn't," I said.

Bryony drew a long, shaky breath, and I realized for the first time how nervous she'd been about this conversation. I hadn't even noticed—already preparing to brush her off.

"I understand that there's no other way for you to practice, and I can see that you're careful not to interfere too much. I'm not saying I think what you're doing is *wrong...*" She drew a deep breath. "I just think power is dangerous. And I think it's especially dangerous for someone who never had any and spent so long wishing for it."

"You're worried I'll get lost in it," I said slowly, repeating her initial comment.

"I'm sorry." She sounded nothing like her normal, bubbly self. "I've been worried about saying anything in case I was just being selfish."

"Selfish?" I frowned at her.

She wouldn't meet my eyes. "Have you even noticed that we don't spar on rest day mornings anymore?"

"I..." I paused and looked around my suite, as if surprised to find myself here instead of out in the training yards with my sword in my hand. "It's gotten so cold," I finally said, without conviction.

"I don't get the impression you've been spending time at the library like you used to anymore either. Isabelle mentioned something the other day about hardly ever seeing you there."

A heavy silence sat between us that I couldn't remember ever experiencing with Bryony before. I thought back to all those unhappy glances she'd thrown me from the front of various classrooms. Embarrassment flooded me at how condescendingly I'd responded, even if it had only been within my own mind.

I hadn't noticed my own obsession or the distance it was driving between us. I had been drunk on the power of the compositions I was stealing, on the access it gave me to so many minds. Not that I could read anyone's thoughts, of course, but just dipping into their hard-won knowledge and expertise had been heady enough. How addictive it had become to feel that rush of understanding without first having to do the work to earn it.

Another thought intruded. Darius.

Bryony wasn't the only one I had abandoned when my quest for distraction had proven so effective. I had told myself to guard my heart, but instead I had tried to drive him from my mind. And in the process, I had forgotten my responsibilities. I had promised I would help him as the representative of Ardann. But what had I done to contribute?

I looked back at Bryony's strained face. In my quest to escape my own emotions, I had hurt one of my closest friends— someone who had stood by me like family and always watched my back. Now that I saw the damage, I was horrified. How had I not recognized what was happening?

Nothing had ever mattered more to me than helping those I loved. It was the only reason I had desired to have power in the first place. Bryony was right. I had been losing myself.

"I'm so sorry." I threw my arms around her with a sob. "You're utterly and completely right. I've been a complete fool. And a horrible friend. I don't know why you put up with me."

She disentangled herself with a watery smile. "We're basically cousins, aren't we? Which means I'm obligated to put up with you." Her smile grew. "And besides, even at your most abstracted, you were still better company than Dellion would be."

I chuckled weakly. "I'm not sure how much reassurance I can really draw from that comparison."

"In all seriousness, though, you're a good friend, Verene. I wouldn't want you to doubt that. I'll admit, when we were children, I was just desperate to have a friend to play with—any friend I didn't have to keep secrets from. You can imagine how delighted I was the first time we visited your family when I discovered we were the same age." She smiled in fond reminiscence. "And then when we got older, I liked how determined you were despite not having any ability at all. Sometimes my own ability felt like an impossible burden, but you were never willing to let anything drag you down."

I knew from her tone of voice that she wasn't referring to her openly acknowledged ability to give energy, but the other, secret, one.

"Sometimes I've thought about how different our lives are," she said. "I don't mean with our abilities. I mean with your rank. You're a princess, and you could have turned out very differently from how you did."

"That sounds a little ominous."

She shook her head. "No, it's a compliment." She gave a rueful smile. "Or it's meant to be. I don't mean that you're a bad princess. I just mean that somehow despite everything, you're willing to acknowledge when you've made a mistake. You're willing to listen to *me* of all people and try to change. I've always thought that was the most important quality of all."

"What? To be willing to listen to you?" I asked with a chuckle.

She laughed. "No, although it's a quality I'm highly in favor of, naturally. I mean to be able and willing to acknowledge weakness and attempt change." She looked thoughtful for a moment. "I think I get that from my mother. She doesn't often talk about her life back when the energy mages were known as the Tarxi and lived in hiding in the mountains. But she's sometimes said that their problem was they couldn't change. Or some of them couldn't, anyway. Generations had passed, but they were still holding on to the injustices of the past and nursing their resentment. They couldn't see that we needed a fresh start."

"Until they did," I said. "And I'm so glad you all came down from the mountains."

Bryony gave an exaggerated shudder. "Me too! Can you imagine me spending my life foraging for food on some icy rock?"

"Not at all. But then you're far too fierce for that. No doubt you'd have been fighting mountain lions, or some such."

"Well, I prefer being here and fighting the human versions." She winked at me, reminding me of my description of Dellion on our first day.

"You would certainly have been wasted on the mountain lions," I said. "And they are no doubt happy to be left in peace again without humans invading their territory."

"Talking about fighting..." Bryony said in her most wheedling voice.

I winced. "I'm truly sorry about abandoning you on rest days, Bree, but even you have to admit it's freezing outside in the mornings."

"We could still run inside, though. Like we did last year." Her hopeful look almost made me laugh.

"That's true," I said. "We could. In fact, why don't we do it right now?"

"Yes!" She leaped up and down, her face wreathed in smiles. There wasn't much that could keep Bryony suppressed for long.

I smiled back. The mindless exercise would do me good. Maybe I could regain some of the perspective I'd allowed myself to abandon in the last weeks.

CHAPTER 13

*P*ounding up and down the stairs and along the hidden servants' corridors proved even more cathartic than I'd hoped. It had been nearly a year since Bryony and I ran this route last, but everyone we encountered flattened themselves against the wall at our approach as they had learned to do in winter of our first year. And they smiled at us as we passed.

Seeing them only reminded me how much I had let myself be consumed by my focus on my ability. At the start of the year, I had resolved to discover more about the position of the Kallorwegian commonborns—for the sake of both Ardann and Darius —and yet here we were approaching Midwinter, and I had done nothing toward that goal.

As we ran, I kept an eye out for both Ida and Zora, but we encountered neither of them. When we finished our exercise, I dragged Bryony back to my suite. I wasn't going to make the mistake of shutting her out again.

"You just spent the whole summer break in Corrin," I said, after telling her what I wanted to discover. "Have you noticed a difference between our commonborns and the ones here?"

"Definitely," she said, without needing to pause and consider.

"The issue of the commonborns always made me a little uncomfortable when we visited Ardann in the past from the Empire. I didn't grow up with the same sort of barriers you're used to. Of course there's still a distinction between mages and everyone else, but it's different when everyone can access words, it's..."

"Better," I supplied, in case she was too polite to say it. "Mother has always wished it could be like that in the south. But we just don't have enough mages."

"I know," Bryony rushed to say. "And I noticed a difference this summer."

I gave her a surprised look. I couldn't think what might have changed since her previous visit.

"I don't think anything had changed in Corrin," she clarified. "I think it was just that I was seeing a different comparison. I was used to seeing Ardann compared to the Empire, where everyone is sealed. But seeing it compared to Kallorway...well, your commonborns seem much better off."

I nodded. "I always expected it to be more formal here, but it seems like it's more than that."

"So what's our plan?" Bryony asked.

"That's what I still need to work out. But I think my best hope is starting with Ida."

Unfortunately, the servant woman always came to clean my rooms while I was in class. And while I reduced the amount I was practicing my own compositions, I still needed to attend classes. Ida kept my rooms supplied with a pile of bell compositions, but I didn't want to use one to summon her just for an interrogation. I suspected I was unlikely to get the answers I wanted with such a direct approach.

When I woke up several mornings later with a sore throat and runny nose, I knew my opportunity had arrived. Hurrying straight to Raelynn's healing rooms, I found no sign of the healer. My next stop was the library, where the library head, Hugh, greeted me with enthusiasm. If I had needed it, his attitude provided further proof that Bryony had been right. She wasn't the only aspect of my life I had been neglecting. Even the sight of the books gave me a pang of guilt. Their pages held many lifetimes of accumulated knowledge, won through hard effort, not stolen with a shortcut, as I had attempted.

Hugh himself gave me no recriminations on my recent absence, however, merely directing me straight back to the corner where his office door hid. Inside I found Raelynn. I should have known she would be with her husband as usual. I could have saved myself time and come straight here.

Thankfully she had her healing case with her. I suspected she even slept with it tucked beside her bed.

Healing my cold took only moments, although she spent several extra minutes chatting sociably, asking me about my classes and commenting on the recent cold turn of the weather. I tried not to show my impatience.

But since I didn't know what time of day Ida usually appeared in my rooms, I didn't want to waste any time out of them. Finally Raelynn turned back to the topic of my healing, reminding me that I should spend the day resting despite now feeling as healthy as usual.

"But you know that, Your Highness," she said. "This healing won't have taken as much out of you as healing that awful break last year, but it still needs a day of rest at least. I'll let your instructors know and tell the servants to send up your meals on a tray."

I thanked her effusively and almost ran from the library. Would Ida bring the trays of food herself? She must have done so in the past on the occasions when a tray had been left in my sitting room. None of the kitchen servants would have attempted crossing the guards on my door.

I almost collided with Bryony at the door of my suite, her hands full of rolls to replace my missed breakfast.

"There you are!" she said. "I was coming to drag you out of bed. Where have you been?"

"With Raelynn. I had a cold."

Bryony gave me a bewildered look. "You sound strangely triumphant about that."

"This is my chance." I pulled her into my sitting room. "I've been instructed to spend the day resting, of course, so I'll have the chance to catch Ida."

Enlightenment broke across Bryony's face. "Brilliant!"

A bell sounded, and she thrust the food into my hands and rushed for the door. "Let me know what you find out," she called over her shoulder as she disappeared.

The pain and discomfort were gone, thanks to Raelynn, but I did feel unnaturally weary. I dragged the cover off my bed and propped myself up on one of my two sofas, wrapping the warm material around me. I had initially worried the day might be unbearably boring, but I now realized my true concern should be the danger of falling asleep. If Ida came in and found me sleeping on the sofa, she would no doubt creep straight back out again.

But the thought of everything and everyone I had been neglecting lately had reminded me how long it had been since I wrote my family. So I set myself up with a makeshift writing desk on my lap and spent the morning hours writing several letters.

The healing fatigue must have had a sentimental effect because the exercise made me so homesick I nearly used one of my father's precious communication compositions so I could speak to them in person. Only the thought of the toll it had taken on him to produce them stopped me, along with the memory that the message would be sent straight to my aunt. She had entrusted them to me for official use only, and the secret I was keeping from her only made me determined not to betray any other part of her trust—a resolution I had nearly lost sight of in the pursuit of my ability. Thank goodness for Bryony's intervention.

Ida didn't appear until lunchtime, when she delivered my tray of food. I brightened instantly at the sight of her, but she looked startled.

"Oh, I'm sorry, Your Highness! I thought you'd be in bed. I was only going to leave this on the table there."

"Please don't apologize." I gave her my most winning smile. "It's pleasant to see another face after so many hours alone." I drew in a deep breath through my nose. "And that smells delicious."

"I'm sure it is, Your Highness. The duke's cooks are excellent."

I jumped on the tiny opening. "Don't the servants eat the same food? I would have thought it was simpler for the kitchen to prepare one meal for everyone in the Academy."

She paused from arranging the tray on a small table within my reach to give me a shocked look.

"The same food as the trainees? No, of course not, Your Highness. We have our own kitchen and our own cooks in one of the outbuildings."

I frowned. "That doesn't sound efficient. And Zora strikes me as efficient above all else."

Ida grinned. "She's certainly that. But some things aren't up to her. It's always been done this way at the Academy."

"But practices can change." I nodded toward where her long hair partially hid the intricate markings that ringed her neck. "Like sealing for instance."

"Some things have certainly changed for the better under Zora's rule," she said cautiously. "Some of the stories my gran used to tell would strike fear into your heart." She dropped her voice ominously low. "Ice cold washes in the middle of winter."

"Goodness! I'm glad to hear Zora provides you with warm water, at least. Just the thought makes me want to get an extra blanket."

Ida grinned. "You wouldn't find me here if anyone was trying to dump freezing water over my head, I can tell you." An alarmed look crossed her face as if she'd only just remembered who she was talking to. "But we eat well enough, Your Highness, you don't need to be worrying about us. And we keep warm enough in our tunnels."

"Your tunnels?"

"Oh, aye. I suppose you wouldn't know about those. All the main outbuildings are connected to the Academy with a series of old tunnels. There are storage rooms down there and everything. That way we don't have to go back and forth outside in the dead of winter."

I couldn't help but consider that perspective on the tunnels' existence to be overly generous toward the original creators of the Academy. Now that I had seen how many lessons actually took place outside, I rather suspected they hadn't wanted the servants to be traipsing about in their view. But it sounded like it was a mutually beneficial arrangement, at least. Even in milder weather, the servants wouldn't want to find themselves walking through the middle of a whirlwind or accidentally struck by lightning.

"I'm glad to hear you're so well provided for," I said.

"I'll come back later to tidy up then, shall I?"

"If you don't mind." I transferred a bowl from the tray to my lap. "That would be lovely."

She dropped a curtsy and hurried from the room, leaving me to my meal. While I hadn't discovered anything of particular import to my purpose, I still felt the connection had been worthwhile. She had talked more openly than I had expected, which boded well for the future.

When she returned later that afternoon, I used her earlier reference to her grandmother to ask about her family. It turned out they had been locals to the area for generations, and although most hadn't been full time servants at the Academy like Ida, many of them had picked up extra work from time to time.

I could tell from the way she talked about her family that she loved them, and it sounded as if they were the reason she stayed.

Zora had been canny in choosing those commonborns she had put forward for sealing. It would have been easy for someone like Ida to be tempted to use her sealed status to seek a better position elsewhere.

"So you get plenty of chances to see them, then?" I asked.

"Oh, yes, Your Highness," she said as she fluffed the cushions on the other sofa. "Zora is generous with all of us with days off and the like. Plus she often has work for the villagers up here."

"She seems like an excellent head servant."

"Oh, there's never been one like her, that's for sure." Ida chuckled, as if at some joke, but despite my hopeful silence, she didn't expand on what she found so amusing.

When she departed, I was left with the strong impression that whatever political leanings the servants might or might not have, their loyalty was first and foremost to Zora herself. If I could find out who she supported, I would likely have my answer.

When I felt the ball of energy that I knew must be Darius return to his suite in the evening, I was tempted to knock on the door between us. But what did I really have to report? Nothing of especial relevance. And the days when we could openly discuss theories and conjectures were gone. I owed it to my heart not to give in to such inclinations. If I was honest with myself, I just wanted to see him after a day spent mostly alone. And that was exactly why I couldn't cross over to his door.

The next morning I was recovered enough to return to class, so I didn't see Ida again for some days. But when Bryony visited my suite the next rest day afternoon, she spilled a bottle of juice she had somehow managed to purloin from the kitchen all over my rug.

I surprised her by responding with enthusiasm, and when she realized I saw it as a prime opportunity to summon Ida, her exclamations of apologetic dismay changed to veiled hints that it had all been part of her superior strategy. When Ida actually appeared, however, Bryony was full of humble apologies, and the servant was soon laughing and smiling while she cleaned up the mess. Few could resist Bryony's bright and irreverent manner when she chose to turn on the charm.

"So, what did you think?" I asked Bryony, when the spill was at last cleaned to Ida's satisfaction and the servant had departed.

She grinned. "I think we've had it wrong all along, and it's not Duke Francis who runs the Academy at all. Clearly it's Zora."

"I suppose you haven't met her." I tried to remember the times I had spoken with her the year before while arranging my Midwinter Ball. I couldn't remember Bryony being present at any of them. "She really is a wonder, though. The most efficient woman you ever met."

"No wonder the duke hired her then." Bryony returned to the cake she had been eating before the juice accident. "He seems the type to admire efficiency."

"He certainly appears to have enough wisdom to let her run the servants as she sees fit."

"Well, if you need me to spill something else, it's a task I'm willing to undertake for the good of the cause." Bryony polished off the final bite. "As you can see, no sacrifice is too great to assist your noble quest, Princess."

I laughed and assured her I'd let her know if I needed her services, but I was the one to knock over a vase less than a week later. I wasn't usually so clumsy and even wondered if my subconscious was creating an accident on purpose. Whatever the cause, I once again summoned Ida.

But when I finally dared to ask the mildest of questions about the politics of the capital, using my most nonchalant voice, she instantly went quiet. We had no more conversation that day. Which left me with a burning question. Was Ida scared or was she hiding something?

CHAPTER 14

The next evening, a knock on the outer door of my suite startled me. I rarely had visitors at that entrance who needed to knock. When I opened the door to find Zora waiting in the corridor, my surprise grew. For a moment we assessed each other in silence, and then I gestured for her to enter my sitting room.

I could think of no reason for the head servant to be visiting me, which only confirmed that the timing was far from coincidental. Apparently I had rattled Ida enough to send her to Zora. Although that knowledge still didn't provide an answer to my question.

"Your Highness, I hope you'll forgive the intrusion," Zora said smoothly, once she was inside with the door closed behind her.

"Your presence could never be an intrusion, Zora. Please sit down."

"I would prefer to stay standing if you don't mind." She paused. "Although I thank you for the invitation."

"Certainly." I remained standing as well.

"I am merely here to inquire if Ida's service has been to your satisfaction of late."

"I have no complaints, I assure you. She has always performed her duties admirably."

"I'm glad to hear it. She has always been a diligent worker, or I would not have assigned her to you."

"As I said, I have no complaints. Why? Has someone else complained about her work?"

"No indeed. I merely consider it incumbent on me to check on those within my care from time to time. We live close together here at the Academy and are more than a team. I would consider us more like a family."

"A family that I'm sure you run with excellence and precision," I said. "It's clear that Ida would not consider seeking a position elsewhere, although her sealed status must put her in higher demand than many other servants."

"There are few in this region who have reason to employ servants."

"But this is not the only region in Kallorway." I kept my voice light. "As I said, I congratulate you." I met her eyes boldly. "I'm surprised you haven't ever considered a position elsewhere yourself. I imagine someone with your skills and vision might rise high at the capital."

"I will never leave the Academy," she said, her voice flat.

"Then the Academy is fortunate indeed. I cannot regret your choice, although I fear you are somewhat wasted in your current position. If you'll allow me to say so."

"You're a princess, Your Highness," she said, a note of humor in her voice. "You can say what you please."

I chuckled. "If only that were true. I think there are few of us indeed who can truly say what we please. Especially in Kallorway." I paused. "Or has that not been your experience?"

"I like you, Princess Verene," Zora said, her manner changing suddenly. "I have ever since you arrived. So I would caution you not to make the mistake of thinking the Academy is Kallorway."

"We are remote here, of course," I said cautiously. "And out of touch with the ways of court, I suppose."

She gave a bitter laugh. "No one in Kallorway is free from the poisoned influence of the court. But it is true that we are somewhat shielded here."

I raised my brows at her open comment. Something in her manner reminded me of my conversation with Hugh and Raelynn the year before. They had seemed to have the same barely disguised contempt toward the court. Perhaps such an attitude was necessary to accept long term residence in such a remote location.

"I bow to your greater experience." I carefully kept my voice neutral.

She weighed me again with her eyes. "You may have an opportunity to judge for yourself soon enough."

"To judge the court?" My mind flew immediately to the upcoming Midwinter celebrations. But I had heard no rumors of the duke repeating his invitation for guests to join us at the Academy.

"I have heard the king, in his gracious wisdom, has issued an invitation to the duke." Her tone turned *gracious wisdom* into a biting insult.

"An invitation for me?" I frowned. Why would he send an invitation for me to the duke?

"An invitation for the entire Academy. Apparently he wishes to return the hospitality we extended to him last Midwinter. And so he is to hold a ball for you all at his castle in Kallmon. For the trainees and instructors and their families." She gave me a wry smile. "Or so I hear."

"I suppose," I said lightly, "if the rumor is true, then I'll hear an official announcement from the duke soon enough."

"Yes, I suppose you will," she agreed. "If the rumors are true." She eyed me calculatingly. "If anyone wanted to see the true state of Kallorway for themselves, the court at Kallmon would be a fine place to start. Although I could understand if the duke had some hesitations about allowing his trainees to travel outside the safety of the Academy walls."

Understanding finally dawned. I hadn't heard anything about it because the duke had received the invitation but was undecided on how to answer. And I was likely his primary concern.

"No doubt you are right," I said. "And I'm sure we can trust the duke to arrive at the wisest conclusion."

A sardonic light entered her eye. "As you say, Your Highness." She gave me a perfunctory curtsy, and I thanked her again for her visit and for assigning Ida to me. I kept my face and voice light and open, but as soon as the door closed behind her, I began to pace the room.

I couldn't trust Cassius's sudden desire to invite me to Kallmon. But I was also unlikely to get a safer opportunity to visit than in the midst of the entire Academy. Zora said the capital was the place to go to see the real Kallorway, and I believed her. But if I had understood her message correctly, she thought the duke would need some encouragement.

Drawing a deep breath, I retrieved one of my communication compositions.

My arms felt strangely reticent as I instructed them to tear the parchment, as if they had a mind of their own and hated to use the valuable working. But timing might be critical here. I ripped the paper cleanly in half.

A ball of power unfurled and hovered in front of me. I leaned forward to speak directly into it.

"I need to speak to Queen Lucienne about an opportunity that has presented itself."

The power folded itself around my words as if they were physical things that could be held in your hand. I could almost feel them hovering still in the air. But for several beats nothing else happened. Was I meant to do something? But as the silence stretched out, the power finally moved, picking up speed as it dove straight through the wall of my room. I could feel it for some distance, speeding away toward Corrin.

I knew such compositions only worked if someone stood waiting to receive them, but my aunt had assured me she had assigned someone to the task. Which meant there was nothing now to do but wait—alone, as she had instructed me.

It felt like a great many minutes but was probably only half an hour before a rush of power swooped into my room, making me leap to my feet. It hovered in front of me as a ball, my aunt's voice emerging from inside.

"Verene? Are you alone?"

"Yes, Aunt," I replied, once again leaning toward the hovering mass of power, although I felt a little foolish doing so. I wasn't actually sure it was necessary.

"We don't have long," she said. "What is this opportunity, and why do you need my guidance?"

"I have reason to believe King Cassius has invited the Academy to the capital for the Midwinter celebrations, but Duke Francis is hesitant to accept. His hesitation is due, I suspect, to whatever promises he has made to you and my parents about my safety."

"And you wish to go to the capital."

"I believe it is too good an opportunity to miss. I have been able to learn much here at the Academy, but my picture will always be incomplete unless I see the court itself." I hesitated. "And there are strategic reasons for wishing the Academy and the court to be in the same place at the same time. You committed Ardann to helping Prince Darius, where we could do so without overt involvement, and I believe this is such an occasion."

"How so?"

"The prince has confided to me that he has moved up his timeline. King Cassius grows increasingly unstable, so Darius intends to force his father's hand this year."

"Interesting." She was silent for a moment while I held my

breath. "After the attack on you, I am inclined to agree with the young prince's assessment. And if this is a chance to resolve the matter once and for all, then we cannot have you be the barrier standing in his way. I will inform the duke that since so much time has passed since the attack without sign of further danger, he is free to allow you outside the Academy. As long as Captain Layna and a sufficient number of guards accompany you, of course."

"Do you really believe it safe?" I asked.

"Not in the least," she said briskly and without sentiment. "But I trust in Captain Layna's judgment as well as the duke's natural caution. If the Academy is to travel to the capital, you will no doubt do so under the protection of Captain Vincent and his guards. And, of course, the instructors of the Academy are a significant force in their own right. I cannot imagine anyone attempting an attack on such a party. Is there anything else you need while we have this opportunity?"

A sudden thought flashed through my mind.

"I am interested to meet some of the sealed merchant families of Kallorway during my visit to the capital. I don't suppose you might have any reason to suggest that if Faylee Robart has any business to complete in Kallmon, Midwinter would be an ideal time to travel there?"

"The head of the Robart merchant family? Hmmm. She would certainly serve your purpose, given both her many connections and her old friendship with your family. If I can arrange it, I will. And I'll ask her to keep an eye out for you."

"Thank you, Aunt."

"It is I who thank you for taking risks in the service of Ardann, Niece. And now I must return to the reception your message called me away from. The power of this composition will fade soon anyway."

"Farewell, then." I bit my lip and added in a rush, "Tell my family I love them."

A softer note sounded in her voice. "I will do so, Verene. Although I fear they will not soon forgive me for this decision. Take care of yourself."

The power cut out before I could reply, and I was left leaning forward over an empty piece of air. I quickly straightened.

I had succeeded then. And I would have the chance to see Kallmon at last.

This time I didn't hesitate to cross to the tapestry and knock on the door behind it. I had an unassailable reason to talk to Darius now, and if the vision of a purple flower insisted on intruding on my mind, I could only attempt to tamp it down.

He pulled the door open himself, as if he had been standing close this time, and the sight of him left me breathless. He looked tired and rumpled, but somehow no less strong. It took all my willpower not to reach forward and straighten his wayward hair. I even swayed slightly toward him, making something spark in his otherwise dark eyes. But I kept my hands at my sides, and he squashed it a moment later.

"I heard voices," he said. "Are you all right?"

I nodded. "I was talking to my aunt."

Both his eyebrows rose, and he glanced around my sitting room as if expecting to see the queen of Ardann stashed in a corner somewhere.

"Your aunt? What has happened? I hope there's no bad news from home?"

"No, indeed. I contacted her." I stepped back, gesturing for him to come properly into the room.

"I haven't heard anything of your plans recently," I continued. "Do you have a strategy for how to take your father by surprise?"

He ran a frustrated hand through his hair, giving me an indication of how it had ended up in such a state. "I'm still working on that. It is not an easy task when isolated so far from the court."

"I may have a solution for you on that matter."

"You?" He frowned down at me. "I don't want you playing in this, Verene. My father is too dangerous."

I drew myself up. "You're forgetting that I act as the representative of my kingdom. I have offered you Ardann's help, and I intend to deliver. Are you aware that your father has issued the duke with an invitation for the entire Academy to attend a Midwinter Ball in Kallmon?"

"I have heard rumors he had plans for Midwinter, but I have yet to receive exact confirmation. Surely the duke himself did not confide such a thing to you when he has not spoken to me?"

"No, but I had it from an excellent authority," I said. "And it struck me that this might be your chance. But I currently stand as an impediment to the duke's accepting the invitation since I am bound inside the Academy walls. So I have requested that my aunt remove that particular block to the plan. I believe once he has her permission for me to travel, the duke will accede to the king's wishes. And not even your father could suspect you of plotting your way to the capital when he issued the invitation himself without your knowledge."

"Verene, you can't travel to Kallmon." Darius sounded dark and angry, but I stood my ground.

"I think you missed the important point," I said. "Here is your access to your father and the Mage Council and the court itself."

He took several steps toward me. "No, I missed nothing. You cannot leave the safety of these walls."

Inside I melted a little at his concern for me, but I forced myself to sound confident and strong.

"Captain Layna is to travel with me as my personal guard again. And I have no doubt the duke will also bring Captain Vincent and most of his guards. Surely you cannot think any assassins would dare assail such a group as we will make. The entire Academy, Darius."

"And once we arrive at the capital?" he asked.

I hesitated. "I am not defenseless. And I am sure Captain Layna will not leave my side. Bryony as well, I imagine."

For a moment he read my face in silence, his expression harsh, and his eyes burning. But he must have seen the certainty there.

"If you are determined to be so foolhardy, then Captain Vincent will not leave your side either. I will ensure it."

"Thank you," I said softly.

He groaned. "I wish I could promise that I wouldn't leave your side either, Verene. But—"

"But you will have other duties and priorities," I finished for him. "I understand, truly I do."

The vision of a purple flower danced behind my eyes. *Just tell me everything,* I pleaded with him silently. *Tell me the full truth of what is going on and let me help you properly.*

"I wish…" His voice trailed away while I held my breath hopefully.

"What do you wish?" I whispered at last.

"Too many things that can never be." His harsh voice broke the moment. "But I will see you return safe to the Academy, Verene."

"I certainly intend to do so," I replied. "I only hope you return with a crown."

"Hope is something I have long left behind," he said with blazing eyes. "But I will win the crown without it."

CHAPTER 15

*S*everal days later, Duke Francis announced the king's invitation to the entire Academy. If he thought the timing of my aunt's communication about the ending of my travel restrictions to be strangely coincidental, he never mentioned it to me.

He did, however, call me to his office to gravely explain the measures that would be taken to ensure my safety. They included the reinstatement of Captain Layna as my personal guard for the time we were outside the Academy walls. I thanked him and gave no indication I was already aware of the arrangements.

At every meal the dining hall buzzed with chatter about the upcoming holiday, and I didn't hear of a single trainee who had refused the invitation. Most of them reported their families would be traveling to Kallmon to join the festivities and seemed excited about a visit to the capital. A few seemed less pleased with the arrangement, but apparently personal preferences didn't weigh into the matter—not when it came to a joint invitation from both monarchs.

"This is outrageous," Dellion exclaimed on the way to combat class one morning, several days before our planned departure.

We all turned to look at her, and Royce sniggered openly when he saw she had put her boot in the waste left behind by some unknown horse.

Ashlyn made a sympathetic face. "I'll admit I'll be glad when it's time to actually leave. I'm not sure how many more horses and carriages the Academy can hold."

"Has the entire Academy ever traveled anywhere in convoy before?" Tyron looked around at the bustling courtyard where yet another carriage was being backed into a large storage shed. "I hadn't quite considered the logistics of such an undertaking."

"I doubt it," Jareth said. "Everything has been strange since we started here. The Academy had never hosted the monarchs for a Midwinter Ball before last year either."

Everyone carefully avoided looking at me, although personally I suspected Jareth himself had a little something to do with the unusual happenings of the last year and a half.

When the third new carriage of the morning arrived halfway through our combat class, causing Frida to lose concentration and drop her defense, Mitchell called a halt to our bouts. He sent Frida back to the Academy in search of Raelynn, Ashlyn in attendance and a trail of blood drops behind them.

"There is clearly no point in attempting a lesson when you are all so distracted," he said with a disapproving expression. "I shall register my complaint with Duke Francis, but in the meantime, I am canceling combat classes until after Midwinter."

Wardell whooped loudly, despite Mitchell's forbidding expression, and Isabelle hid a chuckle.

"Sorry, Bryony," Tyron said with a grin. "Don't be too disappointed. I'm sure it will feel like no time at all until we're back in regular classes again."

She just laughed and shook out her hair. "Even I can appreciate the occasional holiday. I'm dying to see Kallmon. I wonder what it's like?"

"Cold and gray," Armand said from her other side.

We all turned to him in surprise. He didn't usually volunteer any information.

"Does your family live there?" Tyron asked.

"For some of the year," he said. "I much prefer the months we spend at our small estate in the south."

If I remembered correctly, General Haddon had an estate on the south coast. Maybe Armand's parents had changed allegiances due to being neighbors with the general.

"Well anyone would rather live on the coast than in a city," Isabelle said. "That's just natural."

"Speak for yourself." Dellion tossed her hair. "I love the capital. Being out on the estate is so boring. Unless someone is holding a party or something. We all had a fabulous time at Grandfather's estate on the coast last summer." She glanced at Jareth who grinned back easily at her. As cousins, they had been at the large family gathering together.

"But being at the capital at Midwinter will be amazing," Dellion continued. "Absolutely everyone will be there, and there'll be all sorts of festivities. And the shopping."

"Oooh yes, I'm looking forward to that," Bryony agreed.

"Are you not looking forward to it, Isabelle?" I asked the quieter girl.

She looked thoughtful. "I'll miss having my normal holiday at home. Especially since my family can't make it all the way to the capital just for a ball. But I'll admit, I'm curious. I might not love cities, but I've always wondered what Midwinter in Kallmon is like."

"I grew up in Corrin," I said. "So I don't know anything other than a city Midwinter, but I'm curious as well. I've never been to Kallmon."

"At least the trip has been good for one thing," Wardell interjected. "I'll take an extra break from lessons any day."

Most people seemed to feel the same as Wardell. One by one, the other instructors followed Mitchell's lead, and I didn't hear any of the trainees complaining. In the library, I overheard Hugh telling Raelynn that the instructors were all worried about distracted trainees making some sort of fatal error in their compositions.

"We don't want another one bringing half the Academy down," he had said with a chuckle in his voice, making me wonder if the story about the expelled trainee was true after all.

Finally only Amalia was left teaching, and much to her displeasure we had to return to our usual room to focus on energy studies only. She grumbled a number of times about trainees needing to learn to work through distractions, and I must have been infected by the holiday spirit more than I realized because I actually answered back.

"But don't forget we're all unstable youth," I told her with a grin. "I imagine the theory is that we'll all have steadied somewhat by the time we actually graduate."

Tyron looked terrified on my behalf, but Amalia actually snorted a laugh.

"Unstable is the right of it. Although it sounds overly hopeful to think the mere passage of time will fix many of you."

She actually let us out early after that, a miracle that made Bryony exclaim all the way to the evening meal.

"I never would have expected Amalia of all people to be prone to such indulgences," she said. "She seems the type to hate holidays."

"I suspect it's the prospect of an empty Academy that's put her in a good mood," Tyron said.

"What, isn't she coming to the capital then?" I asked.

He shook his head. "I heard she managed to weasel out of the invite by convincing Duke Francis to leave her in charge of the Academy in his absence."

"Ha! That sounds like her," said Bryony, "and explains her good mood."

As we had visited more discipline classes, I had discovered it wasn't only the wind worker instructor who deferred to Amalia. Eventually someone had told me she was the head of all discipline studies at the Academy. So as a senior instructor, she was as logical a choice as any to be left in charge. I suspected Duke Francis would have liked to use the same excuse himself if duty hadn't required he accompany us.

Three days before Midwinter, we gathered in the front courtyard at dawn. The duke had decided we were to do the trip in one long day's travel, so the instructors had to corral a group of sleepy, complaining trainees. But the cold morning air soon woke up even the most determined sleeper among us, and excited chatter drowned out the moans.

I had expected us all to pile haphazardly into the mass of waiting carriages that had accumulated at the Academy over the last week. But the duke—or perhaps Zora—had everything arranged with far more precision than that.

By the time we arrived, the carriages had already been harnessed and prepared, and stood in a long line stretching out of the gates of the Academy. Instructors moved among the trainees, dividing us into groups and sending the fourth years out of the gates to carriages at the front of the line.

As always, I was acutely aware of Darius's presence. Nothing in his demeanor gave any indication of either fatigue or emotion at returning home for the holiday, and he climbed fluidly into the carriage the duke indicated. I noticed it had no decoration or crest of any kind on its panels, and when Jareth tried to follow his brother, he was directed instead to a different carriage.

When Bryony, Tyron, and I were ushered into a third unadorned carriage, two down from Jareth's but not at the end of the line, I realized the royal trainees were being purposefully spread apart, hidden in the mass of trainees, instructors, and servants who made up the enormous party.

For several minutes we sat waiting inside the still carriage, and then the door opened again, and Alvin joined us. He gave us all a hearty smile and began to talk with enthusiasm about both the journey and the capital.

Bryony, who had previously been a bundle of bouncy excitement, looked a little horrified at the discovery we were to have an instructor riding with us.

"It could be worse," Tyron leaned over to whisper to her. "We could have Mitchell with us. Can you imagine enduring his dour face for that many hours in a row?"

She laughed. "Poor Darius is probably saddled with him."

Tyron rolled his eyes. "They'll be well-suited then and will probably spend the whole journey in silence."

My heart contracted, and I quickly looked out the window. I knew how Darius must seem to those watching him from afar, but I hated the thought of what the long day would be like for him with only Mitchell and all the pressure of his upcoming coup to keep him company. What kind of conversations would we have if the two of us had been assigned to travel in the same carriage alone? It was far too tantalizing a thought, so I thrust it aside.

Eventually the carriage began to move, and we rumbled through the Academy gates. Our long procession joined the main road on the other side of the village, traveling west for a short time before beginning to curve directly south toward the capital.

At first the journey was merry enough, Alvin and Bryony supplying most of the conversation with the occasional whispered aside from Tyron to make us laugh. I suspected Alvin of hearing at least some of them, but his good humor never abated. Apparently at least one of our instructors was pleased to receive a Midwinter invitation to the capital.

Having seen the expertise and strength of his compositions from the inside, I had no doubt he had been placed in our carriage for my protection, if it came to that. But there was no sign of any disturbances as the hours rolled by. I had seen Captain Layna from afar in the courtyard, but as soon as the carriage rolled out of the Academy walls, she and her mount appeared at my window, and they hadn't moved in the hours since.

We stopped at a large inn for lunch, all of us more than ready to get out and stretch our legs. Layna stuck close to my side during the chaos of the meal, as did Alvin and both my energy mage friends, so that I felt as if I were hedged around by a wall of people. I didn't complain, though, despite my longing for a measure of space. Every one of these people was willing to place themselves between potential danger and me, and my gratitude overrode every other emotion.

When I nearly bumped into Jareth, however, I gave an exasperated sigh. But I quickly turned it into an empty smile in response to his excessive apologies. With so many people around me, it was hard to believe our collision could be an accident, but I didn't want to cause a scene.

I looked up from accepting his apologies, only to unexpectedly meet Darius's eyes across the expanse of the room. They seemed to be pure black from this distance, and there was no doubt they were fastened on me. What did he think of his brother hovering so close around me?

As always, in public I could read little of his expression.

When we piled back into the carriages, it was almost a relief, but that emotion soon wore away. Eventually even Bryony fell silent, and we all began to wince every time we hit a small bump. No one was ever prepared for so many hours in a carriage.

To my disappointment, darkness fell before we arrived in Kallmon, limiting my view of the city. One moment we seemed to be on the open road, and the next ominous stone walls loomed before us. I crowded against one window, while Bryony and Tyron took the other, Alvin watching us all with an indulgent expression.

Despite the darkness, we were clearly expected, and the gates still stood open for our arrival. Enough light blazed from multiple hands to light the gloom, a mix of mage lights and regular lanterns. The front carriage must have been waved through because we barely paused, moving into the city in the same procession that had brought us through the countryside.

My overwhelming initial impression aligned with Armand's summary. Everywhere I looked, I saw gray, although the darkness no doubt exacerbated the effect. In Corrin, the city was arranged in concentric semi-circles, leading up to the palace and its grounds at the northern height of the city. You passed first through the sections that housed the commonborns, and then through the mages' shopping district before reaching the mage estates and finally the Academy, University and palace.

I had expected something similar here, my eyes searching for narrow houses crowded against each other and the occasional market square. But from the moment we passed through the gates, I saw only large, elegant homes surrounded by either small but carefully manicured formal gardens or else vast fenced grounds.

As the carriage jostled on over the cobblestones, my frown deepened.

"Where are the houses of the commonborns?" I asked. "Where are the public buildings? Surely Kallmon cannot house only mages."

"No, of course not. But the commonborns do not have houses along the main streets." Alvin gave me a curious look. "Is Corrin arranged differently? Four main streets enter Kallmon—one each from the north and west, and two from the south. The homes of the capital's mage population line all four of them. The common-born districts can be found deeper into the city, between the streets."

"Wouldn't want any of the mages to have to sully themselves by passing through those areas," Tyron muttered, earning a reproving look from Alvin.

"Surely it is natural for a city to wish to present itself well," our instructor said.

I frowned, watching the houses of the mages pass by the window. I would have considered practicality a more important factor, and it didn't seem convenient for the commonborns to have their parts of the city so distant from the main thoroughfares.

"Doesn't it make the public buildings difficult to access?" I asked, thinking of the new building whose creation we had nearly seen go awry in Corrin. "Don't your sealed complain?"

Alvin frowned. "I'm not entirely sure what public buildings you refer to. Do you mean the recruiting offices for the Armed Forces? I believe there is one large barracks at one of the southern gates."

"She means the healing clinics and the law enforcement centers, and the offices of the sealed. That kind of thing," Bryony chimed in. "In Corrin many of them are located on the main roads since both commonborns and the mages who work there need easy access to them."

Tyron, who had been watching Alvin's face closely, shook his head. "I don't think they have those sorts of public buildings in Kallmon."

"What? No healing clinics? Or law enforcement centers? Surely they must." I stared at our instructor.

"Law enforcement have a barracks of their own, of course," Alvin said, wary and uncomfortable now. "I believe it is located at the western gate, so we didn't pass it. And the healing discipline has their headquarters in one of the wings of the castle."

"So you have no healing clinics the commonborns can access," I said slowly. "Not even the sealed?"

Alvin cleared his throat. "I believe there are some healers who will work for anyone able to pay their fee. But they travel to the homes of the afflicted. And of course the commonborns have healing assistants of their own, other commonborns like themselves. I suppose they must be located in the markets and such places. I've never given the matter much thought."

"Clearly," I said, unable to keep the coldness from my voice.

I had wanted to understand the state of the commonborns in Kallorway, but I hadn't expected it to be so bad. Even before sealing, Ardann had healing clinics and other such services available to all. Admittedly, the use of mage healers required a fee—we just didn't have the numbers to provide their services to all. But in the years since my parents' marriage, they had increased the number of commonborn healing assistants located at the clinics, ensuring they, at least, were freely available to all. Their capabilities were limited compared to the mage healers, of course, but they trained alongside them and benefited from the increases in knowledge gained by the healing discipline's mage researchers.

A sense of foreboding rose inside me. I hadn't expected to fall in love with Kallmon, but I suddenly suspected I wasn't going to like a thing about this city.

CHAPTER 16

*T*he carriages continued traveling south through the northern half of the city. The great castle loomed ahead of us now, its outline visible against the moonlit sky. Again it looked nothing like the elegant white marble spires of my home in Corrin.

Instead the castle mirrored the gray of the city, its square shape only softened by the round towers topped with decorative battlements. But despite myself, I had to admit it had a certain presence in the dark night, not elegant exactly, but strong and commanding. Rather like its prince, in fact.

The gates of the castle also stood open for us, and the enormous courtyard was large enough to fit all of our carriages. Despite the lateness of the hour, King Cassius and Queen Endellion stood waiting at the castle's grand entrance to receive us, General Haddon lurking behind his daughter.

I watched Darius greet all three of his relatives without any change in expression, although Jareth had an embrace for his mother and an easy smile for both his father and his grandfather. My mind wanted to read something ominous in his expression, but it was too dark, and I was too far away to see such subtleties.

Duke Francis appeared, ushering me forward to take my turn greeting the monarchs, and I was suddenly conscious of my travel-worn state. But the feel of someone at my back made me glance over my shoulder to discover both Captain Layna and Captain Vincent shadowing me closely, one on each side. The presence of the twin gold robes bolstered my confidence, adding greatly to the impression I must make.

When I swept my curtsy in front of the king and queen, Cassius gave me a mere cursory glance, his eyes lingering on the two guards behind me. Something like irritation flashed through his eyes, much to my satisfaction. If he had thought I would present an easy target in the capital, he was already discovering his mistake.

The queen murmured standard words of welcome, which I answered in equally formal tones, but over her shoulder, my eyes caught on Darius about to enter the castle. A smile of thanks slipped across my face. We had only just arrived, and he had already come through on his promise that Captain Vincent would guard me in the capital.

But his eyes darkened at my expression, his face growing colder rather than more friendly in response, as his eyes moved straight past me to his parents. I carefully schooled my own features, turning my smile on the queen instead, although inside I was fighting tears. It had been a long day, and I wanted my bed.

The suite I was shown to by a stiff, formal servant contained two bedchambers and a vast sitting room that dwarfed my one at the Academy. I discovered, to my relief, that Bryony was to have the second chamber. I had half-expected Layna to insist on sleeping in the sitting room as well, but instead discovered a cot made up for her in my actual bedchamber.

"Really?" I asked her with a raised eyebrow.

Her expression didn't change. "My instructions from Her Majesty were explicit. I do not mean to let you out of my sight."

I sighed. "Very well." I forced myself to smile. "Thank you, Layna. I do appreciate it."

She allowed herself a small smile. "You're forgetting this is my job, Your Highness. I didn't select the Royal Guard so I could do shifts protecting the walls of a palace. I'm right where I want to be."

I regarded her doubtfully but didn't argue, too tired to consider whether anyone could truly wish to be on constant high alert in the homeland of an enemy.

~

When I woke the next morning, Layna was already up. She had stationed herself in the sitting room, leaving the door to my bedchamber propped open. I closed it just long enough to wash and dress before joining her.

Layna had used the time to throw open all the curtains of the sitting room, and I moved over to one of the large windows to examine the view. The window looked south, over the back of the castle and the city beyond. Everything still looked gray, but in the bright winter sun it had a life to it that it had lacked the night before.

Turning, I gave my room a more thorough look. Deep purple had been used for the curtains and upholstery and peeked through in decorative elements on the rug. I thought immediately of Darius, turning back to the window before Layna could see my rising flush. Would the color purple ever stop having such an effect on me? For my own sake, I hoped so.

Bryony shuffled out of her room with an enormous yawn, giving the room a sour look.

"Where's your usual morning cheer?" I asked.

"I left it back in those endless hours in that awful carriage," she said.

"I thought you lived in the Sekali Empire," Layna said. "You must be used to long journeys."

Bryony dropped onto a sofa. "We don't attempt to make the trip all in one day. I don't know what possessed the duke to stuff such a journey into a single day."

I flashed her a look, my eyes traveling significantly to Layna, and Bryony grimaced.

"I'm sorry. You're right, I do know, of course, and thoroughly approve and all of that. Or at least, I will once I have the chance to actually stretch my legs."

I smiled sympathetically. Bryony wasn't someone who coped well with being cooped up.

"The official ball isn't until Midwinter night itself," I reminded her. "So I was thinking of exploring the city today. That should help." I hesitated and glanced at Layna. "If you don't mind."

"I'm here to protect you, Your Highness, not control your movements. You don't have to ask my permission. Although I do approve of anything that keeps our location and movements as spontaneous as possible. That's a defensive strategy in itself."

"Excellent, then it's a plan." I rubbed my hands together. "Now what about breakfast?"

Layna pointed to a side table where a number of trays had been laid out. "Three servants dropped those off some time ago."

Bryony leaped to her feet. "Why didn't you say so immediately? I told you all I needed was some food in my belly."

I exchanged a grin with Layna as the Sekali girl fell on the trays ravenously as if she had been starved as well as stuffed in a carriage all the previous day. I joined her at a more sedate pace, although my stomach gave me away by rumbling loudly.

By the time we had finished the food—Layna assuring us she had eaten before we awoke—I was ready to send my compliments to the king's chefs.

"Whatever else Cassius does," I said, "he certainly eats well."

Bryony nodded her approval before stretching and finally giving her usual bright grin.

"I vote we get moving right away. If we stick around here too long, someone might show up to drag us to some mind-numbing official function."

A sharp rap on the door made her face crumple. "See, I told you," she muttered, but not loudly enough for the sound to travel into the corridor.

I started to move toward the door, but Layna gestured for me to stay back. Opening the door herself, she kept her second hand out of sight, a composition gripped at the ready.

As soon as I saw who was on the other side, however, I gave a glad cry and hurried forward.

"Faylee! You came!"

Layna frowned but stepped back to allow me to greet the older merchant woman in my doorway. I pulled her inside and immediately turned to Bryony.

"Bree, this is Faylee. She's the head of the mighty Robart merchant family, and an old friend of my family, especially Aunt Saffron. Faylee, this is Bryony, an energy mage and my fellow trainee."

"A pleasure to meet you." Faylee smiled warmly at my friend. "And don't be too surprised, I'm older than I look."

I chuckled. It was a familiar refrain from the merchant woman, who didn't look like she could possibly be in her early forties. She had confided in me once that it was the reason she had risen to be head of her family at such a young age. She claimed it gave her an advantage in business negotiations since people tended to underestimate her. Personally, I suspected her position also had a little something to do with her determination and intelligence—not to mention her close connection to so many royals.

Bryony smiled back. "As long as you haven't come to drag us off to spend hours bowing and scraping and smiling through our teeth, then it's a pleasure to meet you too." She looked at me. "Although I didn't know you had any Kallorwegian merchant connections."

"I don't. Faylee lives in Corrin, and the Robarts are Ardannian."

"Primarily Ardannian," Faylee corrected in a satisfied voice. "We have recently expanded our network to Kallorway, and I have therefore stationed a junior cousin in Kallmon." She grinned evilly. "This is a surprise visit. I do so love taking the younger members of the family by surprise."

I laughed. "I can imagine. And was he caught carousing and ignoring his responsibilities?"

Faylee sighed. "Nothing so exciting, unfortunately. He's rather staid and married to a lovely girl we coaxed over from a competing merchant family. She's just had their first baby, so he was dancing attendance on her at home in a most dutiful manner."

"Ha! Caught out! There's a new baby. That's the real reason you were so eager to visit him, admit it."

Faylee had limited herself to a single son and daughter of her own, satisfying her love of babies with the constant offspring of her vast extended family.

She grinned, unrepentant. "I am nothing if not a dutiful subject of my monarch. If there were squidgy baby cheeks to be squeezed, it was nothing but coincidence."

Both Layna and Bryony looked confused, but I grasped the merchant woman's hand. "Thank you for coming. I really do appreciate it."

She smiled and patted my cheek. "Anything for you and Ardann, Verene. You know that."

"Do you have some people for me to meet?" I asked.

She nodded. "If you can be spared from the castle. I only have today, I'm afraid, because I promised my family I would head home tomorrow."

"We're currently plotting to sneak out of the castle before anyone can announce any alternative plans," Bryony said. "So I suggest we all move fast."

"I like her," Faylee said to me with a grin.

I grinned back. "Most people do. And as far as we know, we are free to spend the day how we like. Most of the trainees have family here for the festivities, so no doubt they'll be spending the time with them."

"In that case," Faylee said, "my carriage awaits."

We started down the gray stone corridor, Captain Vincent emerging from the shadows to join Layna at our backs. Faylee regarded him with a raised eyebrow, but when none of the rest of us commented, she stayed silent also.

It didn't take us long to reach the main staircase and then the entranceway below. No one challenged us, and I saw no sign of any of the Academy instructors as we escaped into the crisp air outside.

I didn't know what means Layna had used to communicate with the stables, but mounts were waiting for both her and Vincent. They swung up into their saddles as the rest of us climbed into the waiting carriage, and we were soon outside the castle walls.

Faylee's coachman kept to the main road for a short time only, passing some fancy shopfronts that I hadn't seen in the dark the night before. Positioned near the castle, they were clearly for mage customers. Did Faylee's family have wares in any of their windows?

We didn't stop at any of them, however, turning instead onto a narrower way that led us into the depths of the city. Here the houses stood much closer together, in some places built in long connected lines. But vines grew up many of them, giving life to the uniform gray. The traffic on the street drove the two captains away from the windows. Layna signaled with her hand that they would ride ahead of and behind the carriage.

"I'm glad to see you have such vigilant caretakers," Faylee said approvingly. "Your family will be glad to hear of it."

"I can't move without tripping over someone," I told her in a wry voice. "I defy any assassin to get anywhere near me."

"Assassins don't necessarily need proximity, don't forget," Faylee said in a more serious tone.

"Yes, of course, but I'm shielded. Neither of you can feel it, but Layna has had me in a bubble of power ever since we left the Academy."

I exchanged a glance with Bryony. And I had defenses of my own, although I couldn't tell either my bodyguard or my old family friend about them.

"So where are we going?" I asked, wanting to change the subject. "I hadn't initially realized I would have to stray so far to meet the influential commonborn merchants of the city, but I'm rapidly gaining the impression that the situation for commonborns in Kallorway is different indeed from in Ardann."

Faylee glanced at Bryony.

"You can talk freely in front of Bree," I said. "I trust her completely."

Faylee nodded once and then grimaced. "There's a reason it's taken us twenty years to expand into Kallmon. You don't realize just how useful all those compositions are until you don't have access to them anymore."

"Can't you supply them from Ardann?" I could imagine that Kallorwegian mages might be reluctant to sell compositions to Ardannian merchants over their own local families, but the Robarts had always been well supplied.

"It's not the supply that's the issue." A grim note entered Faylee's voice. "It's the law. Commonborns, even sealed commonborns, are not permitted to work compositions."

My mouth fell open. "Not permitted? As in…never? But—"

My words faltered as my mind spun over the many limitations such a ruling would create. So there were no mage and commonborn pairs working in tandem in Kallorway then. I had assumed there was just no need for them at an Academy over-flowing with mages.

The reason for the law became apparent after a moment's thought, although it left a sour taste in my mouth. King Cassius himself was sealed. If the sealed commonborns could work compositions from unsealed mages, then what made them different from him? The proud Kallorwegian king could never stomach such a situation. But to cripple his entire kingdom for the sake of his pride...

No wonder Darius was determined to seize power. Kallorway needed new leadership.

"How did I not know about this?" I asked at last.

"You're too young to remember what it was like during the war," Faylee said. "But most of us still remember. Kallorwe-gian commonborns are hardly a high priority for Ardannian mage society at the best of times, and after the war most people rejoiced to see Kallorway growing weaker while we grew stronger." She shrugged. "And now the antics of the king and his father-in-law take up the attention in Ardann, leaving few to care about the state of the Kallorwegian commonborns."

I shook my head. This information only confirmed my thoughts from the beginning of the year. The position of the commonborns had been an oversight in my briefings. Perhaps they had been left out precisely because they held so little power at court compared to their Ardannian counterparts. But I still believed they could have a part to play.

Loud music pulled my attention back to the window in time to see a market square go flashing past. I had the impression of many stalls and of laughing crowds and green garlands before the carriage moved on. I recognized the decorations from the year before, although they lacked the splash of red from the Ardannian berries.

"That looked jolly," Bryony said. "Are you sure we can't stop there?"

Faylee smiled. "Midwinter markets are scattered throughout the city and are well-frequented. They do make an appealing picture, don't they? Everyone is busy buying supplies for the upcoming holiday, and everyone seems to be in a better mood than normal. Some things aren't so different between Kallmon and home." She rubbed her hands together. "It's an excellent time of year for merchants."

"So will we stop at one?" Bryony asked hopefully.

Faylee glanced out the window. "I don't want to give your poor guard a heart attack by taking you to a crowded public market. We're going to a private residence instead. But don't worry, Bryony, it's almost Midwinter, so there will still be festivities."

Minutes later, we stopped at an unobtrusive pair of gates in a gray wall. The wall sat flush with the front of a tall, slim home which on the other side joined with the beginning of a whole row of such houses. I could see from Bryony's face that she didn't think whatever was behind this wall was likely to compare to the Midwinter market, but she didn't say anything.

I, on the other hand, sat forward eagerly. Who did Faylee consider important enough to bring me to meet? And what would they think of me?

Although the news about Cassius's law angered me, it was also an opportunity for Darius. The oppressive environment toward commonborns couldn't endear any of them to their current king. And the arrival of families like the Robarts—able to describe to them a different style of mage-commonborn relations —would only stoke the flames of discontent.

The gates opened, allowing us through, and we alighted from the carriage. Bryony straightened and gave a squeak of surprise.

"But it's enormous." She stared round-eyed around the huge

courtyard. "I would never have guessed there was so much back here."

Faylee hid a smile. "The merchants of Kallorway might not have the advantages we enjoy in Ardann, but they are not all paupers, you know. There is still gold to be made in trade, especially in the years since the borders opened. And as much as King Cassius might dislike it, his kingdom still has need of its commonborns. He can't drive them out completely."

Behind the quiet facade, an enormous mansion stretched out with stables and a vast garden. Intricate lanterns had been hung from many of the bushes and trees, although they weren't lit in the bright sunlight. Green garlands adorned surfaces in every direction, and bright golden streamers had been twisted and strung up beside them.

A small child, wearing an enormous golden dress, trotted around the edge of the building, stopping at the sight of us. She stared for a moment, mouth hanging open, and then turned and fled back the way she'd come.

"They're here!" Her high voice floated back to us, calling at full volume. "The princess is here!"

I coughed as Bryony elbowed me in the side.

"It seems your arrival has been highly anticipated."

"By four-year-olds at least." I glanced at Faylee. "What exactly did you say about me?"

"Nothing more than the truth," she said calmly. "That I was bringing a guest to meet them, and that you were Princess Verene of Ardann. You'll have to excuse the poor girl's enthusiasm. Kallorway doesn't have any princesses of their own, you see, so the whole idea is terribly exciting."

Bryony grinned. "Well she wouldn't be the first little girl to dream of princesses. And somehow I imagine not having any of their own only helps keep the dream idyllic. Princesses might not seem so appealing if Darius had a sister as icy faced as himself."

I sent her a glare, and she subsided, although her eyes still laughed at me.

A stream of people soon appeared in the courtyard. If they shared any excitement about my presence, then they kept it under better control. Faylee made introductions, but they were so numerous that even with all my court experience, I soon couldn't keep any of them straight. The overwhelming impression, however, was of well-dressed people with intelligent but lined faces and the rough hands of those who knew what it was to work for a living.

We were soon ushered around under an enormous portico which jutted into the garden from the back of the house. Both Captain Layna and Captain Vincent trailed us, never straying more than a few lengths from me, but the locals seemed to accept their presence, paying them no heed at all.

Tables had been set up, laden with any number of delicacies, some of which I recognized from the ball at the Academy the year before. Bryony's eyes lit up at the sight of them, and she had soon wriggled out of the endless introductions with consummate skill. I watched her go wistfully but forgave her when she reappeared with a small plate for me.

When the introductions were finally complete, and everyone had been given the opportunity to examine the foreign princess, fiddlers struck up a merry tune. The children, who had been running freely through the portico and gardens, squealed with delight and began to dance. The adults watched on fondly, although the matron who had been introduced as lady of the house regarded their exuberant antics with some concern.

"I hope you don't consider us too uncultured, Your Highness. But it's Midwinter, and no one has the heart to deny the children some fun."

"Not in the least," I assured her. "It does my heart good to watch them. I almost wish I was a child again myself so I could join in."

That earned me a radiant smile, and the conversation moved from the previous discussion of the weather and the state of the road from the Academy into more serious topics. I tried to keep my questioning as subtle as possible, but a common thread soon emerged.

None of the merchants openly spoke against their king, but one word was repeated more than any other: change.

They understood times had changed in Ardann.

One never knew when change was coming.

Change is always just around the corner.

No one could comment, even obliquely, on a negative situation, without someone else chiming in to say that last phrase. When I mentioned Darius—an easy enough topic to bring up given he was my year mate—curious, calculating looks sprang into many eyes. They knew the coming change had a name, and they were clearly desperate to know what sort of king Darius intended to be.

If they had hoped I would have answers for them, they were disappointed. I wouldn't risk Darius's plans by accidentally saying the wrong thing. And it struck me, now that I was here, that I knew Darius also wanted change, but I didn't actually know his intentions for his commonborn population. He had seemed on good terms with the servants at the Academy, but we had never directly discussed the topic. How could I blame my aunt for overlooking this aspect of Kallorwegian society, when I had apparently done the same?

When it came time to leave, however, the farewell smile on my face was genuine. Last night I had feared I would find nothing to like in Kallmon, but already I had been proved wrong.

CHAPTER 17

Faylee returned us to the castle, bidding me a fond farewell and all of us Midwinter greetings. We returned them with our thanks.

"Did you get the answers you sought?" she asked me in an under voice. "There were representatives there from most of the major merchant families."

"I believe so," I said. "Thank you again."

She patted me fondly on the cheek and disappeared back into her carriage. I watched her drive away, until Captain Vincent's gruff voice interrupted my musings.

"May I suggest we move inside, Your Highness? Best not to be loitering outside in the open unnecessarily."

I sighed and complied. I suspected the scenes waiting for me inside the castle would be a great deal less enjoyable than the one I had just left behind.

My fears proved correct. A reception was held in my honor that night, and the entire next day was taken up with visits from various courtiers—none of whom would be lured into any comments on either of their monarchs. Ashlyn brought her mother to see me in the late afternoon, and she was more direct and forthcoming than most. But her focus was her own discipline and what potential I saw for future collaboration between the Ardannian wind workers and her people.

I was grateful to have spent two weeks with the wind worker class because it gave me something to talk about with her, and her eyes lit up as we discussed some of the experiments the class had conducted with Bryony and Tyron. Despite Hugh and Raelynn's derisive comments about Ashlyn's family and their rush to seize power after the war, I could see that Duchess Ashten truly loved wind working.

The full hour she spent with me indicated that while Cassius himself might still hate me, his faction remained interested in an alliance with Ardann. I could only hope that boded well for Darius—especially if he was right and Cassius had abandoned the caution which had allowed him to hold his faction together for two decades.

While Darius was constantly on my mind, I hadn't seen him since our arrival at the castle. I had looked for him at the reception, but he never made an appearance, although Jareth was there with smiles for all.

I kept waiting to hear if he had made his move. The shock waves would no doubt spread rapidly through the castle and city when the time came, so I doubted I could miss it. But with every hour that passed without word, my foreboding grew.

"I suppose I'll have a chance to meet the rest of the Mage Council at the ball tomorrow night," I said to the duchess as she was making her farewells. It was the closest I dared come to alluding to Darius's plans.

"Unfortunately not," she said. "King Cassius and Queen Endellion must have enjoyed the more intimate celebrations last year because they declared this to be a special Academy ball, and only the family members of the trainees and instructors received invitations."

I stared at her, momentarily robbed of words. The king and

queen hadn't invited their own Mage Council to their Midwinter celebrations?

"Duke Rennon of the creators will be there, of course, since he has two nephews in your year," she said. "But then you would have met him last year."

I nodded, too numb to speak. Ashlyn gave me an odd look, and I managed to pull myself together enough to say the proper goodbyes. As soon as they left, I sank onto one of the sofas, however. Only two members of the Mage Council were at court —four counting Duke Francis and General Haddon, but that still didn't even make half. There was nothing Darius could do with six of their number missing. The whole trip had been for nothing.

I tried to remind myself it hadn't entirely been wasted—I had still met up with the commonborn merchants. But it was hard to muster any enthusiasm for the thought in the face of such a disappointing end to my tense wait. Darius's face filled my mind. He must be furious and far more bitterly disappointed than me. I wished I could see him, but I no longer had a door in my wall that would lead me straight to him. I had no idea where he might be hiding in this vast castle, and I wouldn't dare go looking for him. He had made it clear that we couldn't be seen to have any sort of friendship.

Thankfully, I was left in peace the next day. In Kallorway, as in Ardann, Midwinter day itself was for family. I spent the hours with Bryony and Layna, who were as good as family, although I missed my parents and brothers.

This year I had thought ahead and brought a gown from home. Last year I had worn red with gold embroidery. This year my entire gown was a shimmering gold, splitting down the middle to reveal a red underskirt. Sometimes I dreamed of having the freedom to wear any colors I liked, but on this occasion the dress suited my frame of mind. I had no sense of anticipation for the evening's event, and my black mood appreciated the bold, striking design of the dress. When I was young, I had hated that one of our family's colors was red, like blood, but it perfectly suited my mood now.

King Cassius had tried to reach out his long arm and kill me in my own bed. But I had survived, and now I came unafraid into the heart of his kingdom. He might have avoided his downfall on this occasion, but it was still coming for him.

The vast ballroom was the most elegant room I had seen in the Kallorwegian castle. But privately I congratulated Zora because despite the disadvantages of the Academy dining hall, she had done an even more impressive job the year before. The green garlands everywhere were still beautiful, though, as were the enormous red and gold blooms that had clearly been created through the efforts of a group of mages.

Since the guest list was largely the same as the year before, I escaped yet another endless stream of introductions. I had just as many dance partners, however, so I had little opportunity to look for Darius. But after two complete circles of the room in the company of Duke Rennon, I concluded he had yet to make an appearance. The first stirrings of concern grew in the pit of my stomach. Where was Darius?

Duke Rennon had chosen to wear a formal version of his orange creator robe, and it looked striking against the brown skin that he shared with his two nephews. But although he looked both serious and important, I couldn't keep my mind on his conversation. It insisted on racing, and with each new arrival my eyes jumped to the ballroom entrance. None of them were Darius, however.

Jareth caught me looking and came across the room in my direction. He cut in so elegantly that Duke Rennon gave way without protest, and much to my disgust, I found myself dancing with the younger Kallorwegian prince.

"Princess Verene, you look stunning."

I managed to force myself to smile and murmur thanks.

"I feel as if we have hardly had the chance to speak this year. You haven't resumed your experiments with your new ability?"

I stiffened. Although Jareth didn't know the full extent of my ability, I still regretted that he knew anything about it at all.

"I rarely train with Bryony now," I said, choosing my words carefully. "Her energy is in much demand among the discipline classes."

"Ah, yes, of course. Your loss is our gain. I look forward to seeing the three of you join our Royal Guard class after Midwinter."

"I'm not much assistance," I said. "But I'm sure Bryony and Tyron will be welcome."

"Don't underestimate yourself, Verene. I'm sure you have much to contribute, with or without power."

"You're too kind," I murmured, the words sticking in my throat.

We danced in silence for a moment until further words burst out of me. "Where is Darius? Have you seen him?"

"Ah." Jareth's easy smile didn't falter. "I fear my brother is in a foul mood this trip and hardly fit for polite company. But he knows he cannot entirely miss the Midwinter Ball. I imagine he will be along at any moment."

I met his eyes fully, trying to read whatever he wasn't saying. I had known Darius would be disappointed, but it seemed unlike him to so openly display his discomfiture by hiding away. My skepticism must have shown in my face because Jareth continued, a chuckle in his voice.

"Don't worry, neither our father nor our grandfather has had him chopped up and delivered to the river. He has been in various meetings since we arrived and has not had time for social functions, even if he had the inclination."

I looked away, frustrated that my concern had been so evident on my face. Jareth spun me around as the dance dictated, once again facing toward the entrance himself.

"Here he is now," he announced. "I told you he would be along soon."

I twisted my head and caught sight of Darius, standing in the doorway and surveying the ballroom with a cold expression. He wore the same black as he had the year before, alleviated only by a gold circlet on his head and gold and purple sashes across his chest. My breath caught despite myself. He wore the exact color of the flower from our composition class.

The music continued, but everywhere heads turned and the rustle and whisper of an interested crowd sounded. Cassius might be king still in Kallmon, but his son knew how to command the attention of a ballroom—even one full of powerful and important people.

Across the distance our eyes met, and something crackled between us, filling me with an energy I had previously lacked.

"I see I won't have any of your attention now." Jareth smiled, but something in his eyes didn't match the expression.

I looked again at Darius. He had moved from the door, but he watched us all the same. His expression looked dangerous and almost fierce, out of place in the elegant ballroom. I wished I knew what he thought of me dancing with his brother. I wished I could tell him I hadn't wanted to do it.

Our movements took us to the edge of the dance floor, and a pointed throat clearing made us both pause. Tyron stepped forward and bowed.

"If I may?" He held out his hand to me, directing a look at Jareth that was half inquiring, half impudent.

Jareth chuckled and stepped away from me. "Caught by my own trick."

I dipped the smallest curtsy in his direction and took Tyron's hand with gratitude.

"Thank you," I whispered as soon as we had rejoined the dancers.

He smiled down at me. "I never had the impression you liked

him much, although I'm not sure why. He seems a decent enough sort."

"He *seems* so, certainly."

Tyron looked at me with a quizzical expression. "Do you know something about the prince the rest of us don't?"

I sighed. "No. You're right. I just don't like his manner." I only wished I had something definitive, since then Darius would believe me.

Tyron's eyes moved to Darius, in conversation now with both Duchess Ashten and Duke Rennon.

"There's no accounting for the tastes of women," he said lightly.

I looked away, feeling flushed and tired of dancing suddenly.

"Would you like to rest for a while?" Tyron asked, sensitive to my moods.

"Yes," I said with relief. "I think I just need a drink and a chance to cool down. And thank you, again, for coming to my rescue." I smiled. "It was most gallant."

He led me off the dance floor and into a secluded corner before bowing extravagantly. "I aim to please."

"Perhaps you'd better go and see if Bryony needs rescuing too," I suggested. "The last time I saw her, she had a dance partner who was stepping on her feet."

"I also know how to take a hint," Tyron said. "And will take myself off with all haste."

I grimaced. "I just need a moment's quiet is all."

He smiled and slipped away, leaving me in blessed peace for a short span. But I remained flushed and strained, and my eyes strayed to the long windows that opened out onto the castle gardens. The air out there would be crisp and cold. I would only need a minute to regain my equilibrium.

I glanced around, but no one had spotted me yet. Standing up, I made a dash for the relative freedom of the outdoors.

I stepped out into a shockingly cold night, gasping at the

contrast with the overheated ballroom. I forced myself to breathe deeply, letting the frost sink into my core. After a moment I needed to move, though, or risk freezing in place. I strode along beside the stone balustrade that separated the paving where I stood from the gardens beyond. Moonlight shone down, illuminating the twisting paths and elaborate hedges of the garden. I thought I heard laughter, suggesting I wasn't the only one out here, but I could see no one.

I was about to return to the ballroom, too cold now for comfort, when a voice spoke out of the shadows behind me.

"Verene."

My heart stopped and then sped up. I no longer felt in the least cold.

I turned slowly. "Darius. Are you sure it's safe for us to be seen together?"

The words slipped out before I caught them. I hadn't even realized I was still hurt by his rejection on the castle steps at our arrival.

But as soon as I got a proper look at his face, any lingering hurt disappeared. He still looked fierce, but now he blazed, hotter than I had ever seen him before. The fire in his eyes seemed to be burning him alive, and it leaped across the cold air between us to set me ablaze as well.

"No, it's not safe at all. It is foolhardy beyond measure." The words came out quickly, his voice rough and full of emotion.

I swallowed, glancing around. "Darius, I—"

He stepped forward and took my hand, jerking me toward him. I went willingly, stopping only a handbreadth apart and looking up at his face. He gazed down at me for only a moment before growling and stepping away.

He didn't relinquish my hand, however, pulling me after him so fast I almost tripped down the shallow stone steps that gave access into the garden. He wove around a bed of roses and slipped behind a tall hedge.

As soon as we were out of sight, some of his taut energy relaxed, although he still stood straight, his grip on my hand firm.

"Sometimes I think I will explode from the pressure of holding it all in," he murmured. "And yet…"

"And yet you can't let it go, either," I said softly.

Feeling bold in the moonlight, I stepped forward and ran a gentle hand down the side of his face. He shuddered at my touch and briefly closed his eyes.

"You've worked so hard for this, Darius. And for so long. I can only imagine your disappointment. But you can't give up now. I know there's still hope."

"My father—" He stopped, biting off whatever curses he had been about to utter. Turning slightly away from me, he drew a deep breath, speaking in a calmer voice. "My father outwitted me. It was a bold move, not only excluding most of the Mage Council from the ball but actually sending them away."

"He sent them away?"

"Oh, not in so many words, of course." He sounded bitter. "He said he thought they deserved a year off from dancing attendance on him and should be free to enjoy a year with their families at their own estates."

I sighed. "A royal command couched in the gentlest of terms."

"I had thought my father beyond such subtlety. I wanted him to underestimate me, but I'm the one who underestimated him."

"This could still work in your favor, though. Some among them must be resentful at being sent away in such a fashion. It might make them more open to your cause."

"And yet I am trapped at the Academy." He ground out the words. "I have no hope of meeting with the full Mage Council there."

I bit my lip. "In summer you will return to Kallmon, and—"

"And my father will no doubt have a new stratagem prepared. He has been fending off this moment for years and has become a master at it."

I reached out with my free hand, holding his hand in both of mine.

"You think he knew of your plan, then? How could he? You told me you trust almost no one. You must know that I haven't told anyone but my aunt, and she would never betray you to Cassius." I took a deep breath, bracing myself for my next words. "But I'm assuming you told your brother. Jareth must have told your father—"

"Right there." Darius's harsh words cut me off, his finger pointing at a small pond with a fountain in the middle. "There is where my father held my head beneath the water, again and again. I was only eight, but he said if I wished one day to be king, I must first learn to be strong. I couldn't catch my breath, or fight him, and I was still eight long years away from controlling my power. I still see his face from that day in my dreams sometimes. He had a strange light in his eyes, and I have sometimes wondered just how far he would have gone if undisturbed." He gave a harsh laugh. "The cost of always being so controlled is that sometimes you lose your grip—just momentary flashes, but they can be deadly."

"But he was disturbed?" My voice shook.

Darius looked back down at me. "Yes, he was. By Jareth. He was even younger than me, only six at the time, but he threw himself at our father. He beat at him with his tiny fists and shouted for him to let me go. When Father did, he said that if anyone's head needed to be held under the water it should be his, since he wasn't the heir to anything."

Darius shook his head. "You should have seen him, Verene. So tiny but so determined and brave. He was the younger brother, but he didn't hesitate to leap in and protect me. He knew our father, and he had no way of knowing how he would respond." He drew an audible breath. "But his intervention broke my father's mood. He merely laughed and said he knew any son of his would be brave. And then he walked away and left us both there."

"He's a monster," I said, determination filling my voice. "And that's why you can't let yourself break, Darius. You have to defeat him. For the sake of your entire kingdom."

"I know." He closed his eyes and leaned down to rest his forehead against mine. "I've always known. Just like I've always known I can't have the things I really want."

He straightened, looking down at me with such a blazing expression that I struggled to breathe.

"It's just so hard sometimes," he whispered. "I'm more like my father than I would like to admit. I lose control sometimes too."

"No." I shook my head firmly. "You're nothing like your father. He's the one who forced you to have so much control, but once you have the throne, your life will be different, Darius. I truly believe that."

He looked away with a haunted expression. "I wish I could believe that too."

I reached forward and gripped his jacket with both hands. "Then let me believe it for the both of us."

"You're more patient with me than I deserve, Verene. I don't know why."

I laughed shakily. "Because my aunt might not be King Cassius, but she still wears a crown. I know something of the pressures and dangers that come from standing too close to such a position."

Something in his expression changed as he looked down at me.

"Is there something you're not telling me, Verene?"

I swallowed, unable to meet his eyes. He must have read the truth in my face, but I didn't speak.

"No," he said quickly, "forget I said that. I can't demand honesty from you when I keep everything to myself."

"I wish…" I gulped, my throat dry. "I wish we didn't have to have any barriers between us."

"Maybe one day," he said, his voice gentle. "In that perfect future you're believing for us both."

"I hope so," I whispered.

When I was with Darius, every moment had an intensity that the rest of my life lacked. Every part of me felt alive and burning with energy, and everything seemed possible. Nothing had prepared me for meeting him.

And yet I knew, without the smallest doubt, that Darius and I could never be anything more than this burning potential unless we could be open with one another. But I knew the reasons I still clung to my secrets, and I could only assume he had good reasons for his own.

I swallowed and stepped back, although my legs felt as if they would give way beneath me without the support of his warmth and strength. He swayed toward me, his eyes suddenly locked on my lips, and everything in me wanted to respond. But instead I made myself say the words I knew would break the moment.

"People change, Darius."

He straightened, his brow creasing. "Not Jareth, if that's who you mean. On that day, by the fountain, after our father left, we vowed that we would always protect each other. And we always have. And we swore that together we would pull my father down from his throne. We were six and eight, Verene. And we have never wavered from that purpose. Jareth would never betray me, just as I would never betray him."

I licked my lips. "Well someone has betrayed you. And it wasn't me."

He shook his head. "It's possible my father guessed. Or just acted out of an abundance of caution."

"I thought you said he'd abandoned caution."

Darius sighed. "I thought he had." His face hardened. "But whatever it was, it wasn't Jareth."

I said nothing, unsure why I found it so hard to believe him in this one matter, when I trusted him so implicitly in everything else. He must have read my doubt in my eyes because he turned away.

"We've been gone too long," he said, his face in shadows. "It's time we returned."

$\mathcal{W}$e returned to the Academy the day after Midwinter, the whole group seeming flat and tired. Darius and I didn't speak or interact, and Jareth avoided me too.

Even Layna seemed quiet. I had turned from my conversation with Darius outside the ballroom only to find her standing in the garden, just out of earshot, watching us. I turned away from whatever was in her eyes, not wanting to see it. And I didn't ask her what she meant to report to my aunt. I couldn't seem to muster enough energy to care.

Bryony could tell something had happened, but she also recognized I needed space. She made an extra effort to engage both Alvin and Tyron in conversation on the long carriage ride back, leaving me to sit in moody silence. When I thanked her, she waved my words aside. She had managed to make a shopping expedition on the day before Midwinter and seemed reasonably content with the whole trip.

"It doesn't compare to Corrin," she told me, when we finally arrived back at the Academy, "but I think Kallmon has potential."

I agreed with her assessment, although I knew it would never realize its potential while Cassius sat on the throne. Which led back to the same problem that had existed before we ever stepped into the carriage in the first place. The Academy stood between Darius and the crown he had to claim, and his future crown stood between him and me. The web had grown so tangled, I could no longer see a way through.

Duke Francis decreed we should have an extra rest day to recover from the journey, and then classes resumed as normal. Although there had been no attack on me during the trip, I continued to only observe the arena battles, and Mitchell made no protest at the arrangement.

In discipline class, we moved on to the healers, and I almost made a serious error, connecting with one of Raelynn's compositions for the first time when she was healing what seemed a straightforward cut. The cut itself was simple, but the layers of medical knowledge that flooded my mind when I took command of the working nearly made me lose the contents of my stomach. I barely retained control and was left shaking at the thought of what could have happened if I had lost it.

I was much more wary after that, connecting only with the trainees, and carefully choosing the compositions. After the healers, we moved on to the Royal Guard class which included both Dellion and Jareth. I didn't know if Darius had said something to Jareth about our conversation, or if Jareth had merely absorbed my attitude at the ball, but he didn't make any further attempts to be friendly.

I tried to look at him with fresh eyes after Darius's story about their childhood, but no matter what my mind said, some deeper, instinctive part of me insisted there was something off about the younger prince. Something in him couldn't be trusted.

Amalia took us to work with the law enforcement class when our two weeks with the Royal Guard trainees were completed. The class was heavily weighted toward first years, most likely a result of Darius choosing it the year before.

The instructor was nothing like how I had imagined a Kallorwegian law enforcement officer, and in our second week, I finally asked the question that had weighed on me since Kallmon.

"How can law enforcement support the people—the regular people—and uphold the laws when you don't have accessible buildings even in a big city like Kallmon?"

"The commonborns are the seekers' problem," a brash first year said, jumping in before the instructor could answer.

"No, indeed. The princess is right," the instructor corrected him in a gentle voice. "Important as the work of the seekers is, there is far more to enforcing the law than ensuring unsealed commonborns are kept away from the written word. There is many a criminal who has never dreamed of reading or writing. And law enforcement serves all citizens of Kallorway—mage or commonborn—regardless of rank. Indeed, we are the greatest of the disciplines because we are the only one to sit even above the king. All are subject to the law."

Although all disciplines talked of being the greatest, I refrained from rolling my eyes because he had a point.

"And yet the king makes the laws," I pressed, wanting to see his response.

"With the agreement of the Mage Council," said Darius. "No monarch acts alone. And a monarch can be guilty of treason against his kingdom just like any normal citizen."

The instructor nodded. "You are precisely right, Prince Darius. It is a pleasure to see both you and Princess Verene taking such a keen interest in our discipline. It is the bedrock of our society, and no ruler can take it too seriously."

"Then you think there should be law enforcement stations throughout the city and in the other major towns?" I asked, pushing the question boldly.

The instructor hesitated, glancing at Darius. "If the placement of our officers and commonborn guards were left in my hands, I believe I would arrange it so, yes. But one of the advantages of being an Academy instructor, is that I am no longer a member of law enforcement, and I am certainly not subject to the many tensions and pressures of the head of the discipline. Even the simplest of decisions are driven by a myriad of forces."

Darius's face didn't change, but something flickered in his eyes. When I recognized it as agreement with his instructor, I realized I was gradually learning to read him better.

But that night I knocked on the door to his suite anyway.

"Do you agree?" I demanded, without greeting. "About law enforcement and their responsibility to the commonborn citizens?"

A small smile curved his lips upward.

"Good evening to you, as well."

I just stared at him with a raised eyebrow.

"I agree," he said. "And I am more privy than the good instructor to exactly what sort of *pressures* are brought to bear on the Head of Law Enforcement not to expand the efforts of his guards. He is relatively young, and I know he would like to see reform in his discipline. He even sent some of his senior mages to Ardann, to study under your Duke Soren. But he was blocked from implementing any of their suggestions." He made a disgusted face. "My father would never agree to model anything in Kallorway after Ardann."

"And what of the law against sealed commonborns working compositions?" I asked. "How do you feel about that?"

"Pure folly and pride. What else is there to think?"

I grinned, my face relaxing. "Oh, good. I thought I had better check."

He raised an eyebrow. "What exactly is going on, Verene?"

"Maybe nothing." I shrugged. "Maybe something. It's just an idea I've been considering since the beginning of the year. But I had to be sure on your position before trying to progress any further." I hesitated. "If it actually comes to anything, I'll let you know."

I retreated before he could question me further. I didn't want to suggest something I might not be able to deliver.

I had already sought out Zora to thank her—ever so indirectly —for her information about the invitation. And while I might have imagined it, I thought disappointment had lurked in her eyes—as if she had hoped for greater fruit from the trip.

I was almost certain now that the commonborns of the kingdom would support Darius as king—I just had to work out how they could tip the tide in his favor.

Spring arrived, along with our move to the Armed Forces class. I enjoyed watching Amalia put Royce in his place—she seemed to have even less patience for him than she had for me. But I was starting to lose patience with myself. I couldn't think of a way to help Darius, and along with spring arrived talk of exams. I kept reminding myself we had weeks left still, but I could feel the end of the year closing in.

I had told Darius I would help him, and my aunt that he would have the throne by the time we finished second year, and I couldn't bear the thought of failing either of them. I even considered revealing my ability—except I could think of no way it could help. I had learned so much over the course of the year and honed my skills, but it remained a reactive ability. I needed someone else to work a composition before I could do anything at all.

I was so consumed with these thoughts one morning as I hurried toward my breakfast that I nearly collided with a servant girl. She gasped and dropped a curtsy.

"I'm sorry, Your Highness, ever so sorry."

"No, indeed, I should have been watching where I was going." I tried to move on, but she gasped again.

"Begging your pardon, Your Highness, but I was actually coming in search of you. Zora asked me to let you know that she's wishful to see you."

"Right now, you mean?" I asked in some alarm. Had some

disaster occurred? I could think of no such event that would inspire Zora to send for me, however.

"Oh no, Your Highness." The girl bobbed yet another curtsy. "At least, I don't think so. She didn't say anything about there being a hurry. She just asked me to deliver the message. I often deliver messages for her."

"In that case, I shall find her during the rest day tomorrow," I said. "You may tell her so."

"Thank you, Your Highness." The girl hurried away, leaving me alone in the entrance hall of the Academy, except for Jareth.

As soon as I noticed him, he dropped his gaze, moving for the dining hall. I frowned and followed more slowly. I didn't like seeing Jareth lurking around listening to my conversations, but I could think of no particular harm in the message.

By the time the evening meal arrived, I was regretting saying I would seek Zora out the next day. My curiosity had risen as the hours wore on, and Bryony and I had run through every possible speculation as to what she might want.

"Perhaps she's the leader of a secret rebellion of common-borns," Bryony whispered as we left the dining hall that evening. "And she means to mobilize them in support of Darius."

I shook my head. "I don't think you should say things like that aloud, Bree. What if someone overheard you?"

She rolled her eyes. "It wasn't a serious suggestion."

I snorted. "I picked that up."

"And besides," she added, "we were talking so long, I think we were the last ones in there. Who's going to overhear me?"

We said goodbye at the bottom of the stairs, Bryony leaping ahead of me. She had set herself the challenge of running up the many flights of stairs to her room each evening, defying any exhaustion she felt from the day's classes. I still preferred to ascend at a more sedate pace, however.

I moved even more slowly than usual, my mind still taken up with my plans to meet Zora the next day. I had resolved to seek her out straight after breakfast, an easier task since I had now discovered where her office lay in the labyrinth of back hallways.

I wasn't thinking about my feet at all as I reached for the next step, and I missed it entirely. I had time only for a moment of horror as I tried to catch myself and failed. Off balance, my other foot also slipped, and I went down hard.

Panic overwhelmed me as I struggled to breathe, the wind knocked out of me even as I continued to slide back down the stairs I had already climbed. Stones flashed all around me as my terrified mind struggled to orient myself. I tensed, waiting for an even harder contact with the stone floor at the bottom of the stairs, but it never came.

Instead I continued to slide, scraping along the flat floor of the entrance hall toward the great doors, one of which now stood open. A new kind of fear hit me. How had I not felt the power tugging at me and dragging me along? I hadn't slipped at all.

My hands scrabbled uselessly at the slick floor. My body moved faster and faster as I struggled to gain enough breath to speak. A moment later and I burst out into the evening air.

The light had almost entirely faded, but I could still see the shadowy figure I now sped toward across the ground. He wore a cloak pulled low over his face and carried a naked sword.

I gasped in a desperate breath just as I heard a tearing sound and felt a new sensation hit me. My body bucked and writhed, still caught in the grip of the pulling power but now also leaking energy.

A second shadowy figure stood on my peripheral vision, holding a composition instead of a sword. Two attackers. How had they made it into the Academy grounds?

But my chest had recovered from the initial blow, and I had no time for such ponderings. Sucking in a breath, I choked out, "Take control."

In my desperation and fear, I hadn't formed the composition

in my mind with my usual precision, but my instincts kicked in, directing it toward the working that sucked away my energy.

I had grown enough in my ability over the past months that I could recognize it as a working from the same mage who had attacked me on my way to the Academy, although both of the shadowy figures looked male. Perhaps both attackers had been supplied with compositions by someone else then.

Last time, I had merely thrown the working back blindly at my attacker, but now I took proper control, sending it after both of them. Doing so meant dividing the energy of the working in half, so it was unlikely to put them at risk of being completely drained, but I hoped it would slow them both enough to give me a chance.

Both figures shuddered as the energy hit them, responding by each pulling out a new composition. I braced myself, but though they both ripped them, nothing came for me. Too late, I realized they had been ready for my move and had refreshed their own energy. And in my moment of confusion, I had missed the chance to intercept either of the workings.

Still I slid over the hard ground, moving toward the figure with the drawn sword. There was no way I could draw my own weapon while in such a position. I needed to stop my forward momentum and get my feet under me.

"Take control," I gasped a second time and connected with the power that dragged me along.

It felt different from any power composition I had controlled before. While the power had shape, it didn't have the same limits as a normal working—it wasn't confined in the same way. As quick as thought, my mind raced along the shape of it, moving closer toward the waiting attacker.

With a ripple of shock, I realized what was different about this working. It was an open composition. Rather than confining a finite amount of power into the parchment of the composition, forever separating it from the mage who wrote it, this mage had unleashed a composition that connected back with him once it was worked, continuing to draw on his energy to give the working more and more power. But it didn't have unlimited power because every mage had their limits—which was what made open compositions so dangerous.

This particular composition didn't need that much power, though. So why had he composed it to be open? Unless someone who didn't properly understand how my ability worked had thought to try it as a way to circumvent me.

"Pull that stone," I wheezed out, pointing toward a large chunk of stone which seemed to have broken off one of the outbuildings and now lay pushed to the side of the courtyard.

The power immediately let go of me, and I rolled through the dirt several times before coming to a stop as it seized on the stone instead and sent it hurtling toward my attacker. But the composition remained open, and my mind followed in the wake of the power, reaching instinctively for the mage at the end of the tether.

I came tantalizingly close before another tearing sound cut off the sensation of power altogether, severing the connection between us. The stone's momentum carried it the final short distance, but it didn't have the force I'd envisioned when it collided with the cloaked figure's chest. He still gave a loud grunt, his own breath now gone.

I pushed my bruised body up onto all fours, scrambling to get to my feet so I could draw my sword and meet my attackers on more equal footing. But pounding steps sounded, and when I pulled my head up, the cloaked figure was already fleeing. I stared after him for a moment, wondering if I had enough breath to pursue, when I remembered the second man.

Spinning, I scanned the moonlit grounds only to see a familiar face hurrying toward me.

Jareth.

CHAPTER 19

"*Y*ou!" I drew back as he reached for me.

"Verene! What happened? Are you hurt?"

I frowned, trying to make sense of the unexpected words. I looked back over my shoulder, but the cloaked figure had already disappeared into the darkness. Jareth frowned in the same direction.

"I thought I saw someone running...Should I go after them?" He looked at me, concern filling his face. "But I can't leave you alone. You're hurt. I need to get you to Raelynn."

I shook my head. "No. No healing. Leave me be."

After the tumultuous last few minutes, I couldn't seem to make sense of his presence. Jareth had been the second attacker, just as I always feared!

And yet...he wasn't fleeing like the other man, and he wasn't talking as if he had just attacked me. I glanced at him doubtfully. He wasn't wearing a cloak.

"It's a good thing I was so close," he was saying. "I think my arrival frightened them off, whoever they were."

I furrowed my brow. Had he exited the Academy at the end of the fight? I hadn't seen him do so, but I hadn't seen him discard a cloak, either. My attention had been on the other attacker.

"I'm going back to my rooms." I pushed away his helping hand when he tried to steady me.

"I'll walk you there," he said quickly. "Although I really think you should go to Raelynn."

"No, I'm going to my room." I wanted to be out of his company and somewhere I felt safe as fast as possible.

"If you're sure..." He easily fell into step beside me, although I was going at the fastest pace I could manage. My chest still protested the abuse it had just received, and my breaths came shallow and fast.

I took each stair slowly and warily, but none of them betrayed me, slipping from under my feet as they had done under the influence of the composition. When I reached the door of my suite, Jareth made one last half-hearted attempt to convince me to see Raelynn. I cut him off unceremoniously by closing the door in his face.

Inside the room, I stood with my back against the door, my eyes closed as I struggled to control my breathing. With so many months since the last attack, I had let down my guard. And this time my attackers had been prepared for me to turn their compositions against them. They knew at least something of my ability. But not everything. It was as if they had been testing me, trying a range of different compositions to see how I would respond, ready to cut them off or replenish themselves when I reversed them.

In the calm of my room I considered what had happened. Two attackers had managed to access the Academy. They had known just when to find me alone and how to get me out of sight. And they had hit me with an attack that robbed me of breath, preventing me from immediately responding. Whoever had planned this had known some of my ability but not all. And perhaps the biggest coincidence of all—one of the very short list of people who had been told of my ability had been there. It all came back to Jareth.

I stormed across to the tapestry, wrenching open the door without knocking. Darius, who had been sitting at the desk in his sitting room, took one look at me and sprang to his feet.

"Verene!" He rushed over and gripped my shoulders, examining me carefully from head to toe. "What happened? Where are you hurt? We need to send for Raelynn."

I glanced down, taking in the utter mess that had started the day as my white robe. I must look terrible. But I pushed the thought aside.

"I was attacked. Here in the Academy."

"Again!" His whole face blazed, and he reached for his sword as if my attacker might be following behind me.

"It was Jareth," I blurted out, still suffering from too much shock to think of a softer way to frame it.

Darius's hands fell, and his face contorted with bewilderment. "My brother attacked you?"

I hesitated, truthfulness compelling me to clarify. "I didn't see either of my attackers' faces during the actual attack. But he was there straight after. One of them ran away, and when I turned around, he was there."

Darius frowned. "That sounds like he came along just in time to save you."

My eyes narrowed. "I saved myself."

I swayed, and he caught me beneath my elbow.

"Come in and sit down if you won't go to a healer. Explain it all to me from the beginning. I don't understand."

"I barely understand it myself," I admitted, following him to the sofa he indicated and sinking onto it with a sigh of relief. "But I'll try."

I outlined what had happened in the attack, mentioning the way I had turned back the drain on my energy since he already knew of that part of my ability, and focusing on how my attackers had been prepared for it. I glossed over how I had escaped from the power composition, making it sound as if I had thrown the rock rather than reattached my attacker's power to it.

"And just as I was getting ready to draw my sword, he ran," I finished. "It was almost like he wasn't fully committed to the fight. Not like the previous assassins."

"Almost like he was testing your abilities," Darius said thoughtfully, coming to the same conclusion I had just done.

I nodded. "And then Jareth was there. Right there. I haven't even told my own family about my ability, but you told him, and there he was."

"You haven't told your family?" Darius asked, diverted. "After all this time?"

I looked away. "I thought they might stop me from returning," I whispered.

Silence fell for a moment before Darius stood and strode once up the room before returning to stand in front of me.

"This is obviously a completely unacceptable situation, even if it wasn't a true attack on your life," he said. "And I can understand why it unnerved you to find Jareth there, right on hand at such a moment. But I'm afraid that's my fault, not his."

"Your fault?" I frowned at him.

"You must have noticed Jareth hanging around you," he said, "but it's not because he's plotting against you. I asked him to help me watch over you, to help keep you safe. And it sounds like tonight he did just that."

"You asked *Jareth* to watch me?" I cried, incensed. "You know how I feel about him."

He sat beside me, guilt twisting his face. "I'm sorry, Verene, but I care more about your safety than anything else. And while you're here in my kingdom, your safety is my responsibility, but—"

He broke off to rake a hand through his hair before more

words burst out of him, pouring out like water from a breaking dam.

"I wish I could watch over you every moment myself, but I can't. Not when I'm the reason you're in danger in the first place. You don't know how it's been tearing me up all year. All I want is to stay near you and make sure you're safe, and yet if I did so, I would only place you in more danger."

"What are you talking about?" I stared at him, bewildered. "You're not the one endangering me."

He groaned. "But I am, Verene. It's been my fault since the beginning. I told you that I lose control sometimes, but no one has ever made me lose control like you do. I can't afford to ever let my true emotions show, but around you it's too hard to contain them. I admitted at the beginning of the year that I was scared, and I was—I have been all year. I'm terrified of something happening to you, and I'm terrified of the way I can't trust myself around you. Just being near you makes it harder for me to keep my true self under control, but every time I make a mistake and let my feelings show, you end up hurt."

He reached for my hand before changing his mind and snatching his own back. "Ever since I broke my own rule and danced with you at the Midwinter Ball last year, you've been in danger. Nothing could so infuriate my father and whip up unreasoning anger and hatred than seeing his heir dancing and smiling with the daughter of the couple he blames for every one of his problems. My father would rather see the both of us dead than let you gain any hold over me."

He laughed, a raspy sound more of desperation than humor. "I can't imagine what he would do if he ever guessed the truth—if he even suspected how important you are to me and how I have entrusted you with everything. All year I've forced myself to be cold and rude in the hope that it would calm his anger toward you. I thought it was working, but..."

I gaped at him. "You said you needed to be seen to be neutral."

He nodded quickly. "That's also true, it just wasn't the whole truth. I was too cowardly to admit to you that I was to blame for all of those attacks."

I frowned. "Stop saying that. You're *not* to blame. Your father carries the full blame."

"But none of this would have happened if I hadn't lost control and let down my guard."

I reached out and grasped his hand myself, holding it in a firm grip when he tried to pull away.

"You can't see how much he's distorted your thinking. Occasionally letting others see your emotions isn't the same as lashing out violently against your own son or seeking to assassinate someone because you hate their parents. It isn't a fault to let down your guard every now and then or to let your true feelings show."

His lips twisted. "I thought if I could just keep away from you for this year—just long enough to rip the crown from his head—then it would all be over. I needed my control now more than ever and that meant staying away from you as much as I could. I'd already proven I couldn't trust myself around you. And so I asked Jareth to step in when he could and help keep you safe."

"But if Jareth isn't involved, how did my attackers know about my ability?" I asked, wishing I could explain more fully about how they had seemed to know only half the picture—just like Jareth himself.

"You did defend yourself during the attack in the village," he said. "Maybe the energy mage worked out what had happened."

I bit my lip. It was a stretch to suppose they had guessed something so impossible…but then my family was known for the impossible. I had thought for once I had real proof against Jareth, but again Darius had turned my suspicions aside.

I sighed and stood, surveying the mess of my robes again.

"I need to clean up."

Darius also rose. "Of course. Are you sure you're unharmed, though? I could work a healing composition myself."

I shook my head. "I need rest more than anything. I'm sure I'll bruise, but bruises will heal on their own. I just want my bed."

He shadowed me back to the door to my room.

"Verene, I wish…you don't know how I wish things were different."

"I understand," I whispered. "I do too. And perhaps one day they will be."

I slipped through the door and closed it firmly behind me.

The next morning I woke regretting my refusal of a healing composition. Everything ached, and a spectacular bruise was already spreading across most of my chest and one side. At least it was a rest day.

I eased myself into my loosest clothes, taking so long that I missed breakfast. I expected Bryony to come charging into my suite at any moment, demanding to know the reason for my absence. She didn't appear, however, and it occurred to me she probably thought I'd grown so impatient I went to see Zora immediately instead of waiting until after the meal.

The thought made me bolt upright. Zora! The attack and my subsequent injuries had driven all thought of her summons out of my mind.

I shuffled out of my room, a little of the pain and stiffness diminishing with the gentle activity. I could walk normally by the time I reached the stairs, although I was wincing before I reached my third flight.

When I finally arrived at Zora's office, I sank into one of the wooden chairs in front of her desk with a sigh of relief.

She looked me up and down, frowning.

"You don't look entirely well, Your Highness."

"I don't feel entirely well," I admitted. "But I'll recover." When she looked concerned, I added, "Just some soreness."

"Soreness?" She stood abruptly and strode around to join me on my side of the desk. "What exactly does that mean, Princess? What has happened to you?"

"I…" My mind scrambled, unable to think of a cover story in the face of such unexpected directness.

"Perhaps it would help you to answer honestly if I say something first," she said. "I have been the head servant of the Academy for many years now, and I know more of what happens within its walls than the duke himself. I know that last year, you suffered an unusual number of accidents, including a broken ankle that was highly unlikely to have been caused by a friendly practice bout."

"I—"

She held up her hand to stop me as she continued.

"You then suffered a second incredibly unlikely accident. And unlike that fool of a captain, I don't believe for a second that you and the prince were out in the dark on some sort of tryst." She gave me an amused look. "You would hardly need to stoop to such tactics, would you?"

I flushed, but she hurried on.

"And then there was whatever happened in your rooms just before exams. Add to that the attack on your carriage in the village this year, and I ask you again: Why are you so sore, Princess Verene?"

She fastened a look on me of such intensity that I wouldn't have prevaricated, even if I could have thought of a convincing story. I had already decided whose side I thought Zora was on, and it was time to trust my instincts.

"I was attacked last night in the entrance hall of the Academy by two cloaked assailants," I said. "However, I managed to scare them away before they could do more than bruise me. Unfortunately I discovered this morning that the bruising was a little more substantial than I realized. I was planning to make Raelynn my next stop after you."

"No. Absolutely not." Her resolute words took me by surprise. "On no account can you be healed. At least not yet."

"I beg your pardon?" I stared at her.

"That fool of a maid was supposed to deliver my message to you at your suite, not out in public. I wondered if it would cause trouble if someone overheard that the two of us have been meeting, but it seems their efforts may just play into our hands, after all."

My mouth fell further open. "You think the attack on me last night was in response to our planned meeting?" My mind flew to Jareth, the only other person in the hall when the maid delivered Zora's message.

"I think it is at least a possibility," she said briskly, crossing back around to retake her seat. "I am not a fool myself, Princess, and it has been apparent for some time that someone is mighty determined to ensure you don't make any useful connections in Kallorway. And while I'll admit that I'm not at the same level as someone like the prince, I am not without sway or authority."

"No." I leaned forward. "I agree completely. In fact, I was hoping that might be what you wanted to talk to me about today."

She nodded. "It was. I had decided the time had come to tell you some things, and it seems the timing may be even more fortuitous than I'd hoped."

I scooted to the edge of my seat, my eagerness driving away all thought of my lingering pain.

"So the servants do support Prince Darius? They wish to see the end of Cassius?"

"We live in something of a bubble here at the Academy," she said, "supported by the goodwill of the duke. But while his careful neutrality has shielded us for decades, we are not untouched by the outside world. The attack in the village proved that. It could have gone very differently, and none of my servants are unaware of that fact or the vulnerability of the loved ones they left behind. The duke suspects Cassius is behind the attack, but he is a cautious man. Even with hard proof, he would find it difficult to throw away his neutrality."

"The duke knows it was the king?" I asked. "He's never said a word."

"Of course not. Didn't I just mention he's cautious? And perhaps it's because of that, and his beloved neutrality, that he has so much influence. Many of the mages at court came through the Academy under his tenure. They respect him. He could be a powerful ally for the young prince."

"I agree. But how do we convince him?"

"I have been working on that problem for years now," she said, "chipping away at him. But I have lacked the final push to motivate him to action. You, however, Princess, might be the key."

My mind felt almost as dazed as my body. "You've been working to convince him for years? He listens to you, then?" It had seemed apparent the duke treated the Academy servants well and respected Zora, but I hadn't suspected her of having so much freedom with him.

"That is what I was going to tell you," she said, her voice matter-of-fact. "I am not just the head servant at the Academy. I am also, secretly, the duke's wife."

CHAPTER 20

I fell back in my chair, too shocked to do more than gape at her.

"Yes," she said, calmly responding as if I had spoken my shock. "I am married to the duke. He is married to a commonborn. Thus why our union has been a secret all these years. Most of the loyal servants know, or suspect, but they would never breathe a word to anyone."

"I...I don't quite know what to say," I said weakly.

"If you give it a moment, the shock will dissipate." Amusement sounded in her voice. She continued talking, kindly giving me a moment to recover myself. "As you can imagine, Francis has great sympathy for commonborns. But if there is one thing he loves more than any other, it is the Academy itself. He believes that for him, personally, his primary responsibility is the Academy—and that his neutrality is the best way of keeping it safe in the turbulent politics of the kingdom."

"But you feel differently?"

"I believe neutrality has served us well in the past. But I also believe the time has come to act. The prince needs as many as possible to rally to his cause, and it is clear since your arrival that allegiances are shifting. It is finally time to pick a side and make a stand."

"And you think my bruises can help with that?" I still couldn't quite make my mind accept everything I was hearing.

"I am almost sure of it." She stood. "In fact, we should lose no time in going to see Francis."

"We're going to see the duke right now?" I asked, feeling foolish but not seeming able to stop the inane questions.

"There is rarely a time like the present." She gave me another amused look as I scrambled to my feet.

I trailed through the servants' corridors behind her. I seemed to have lost any remaining capacity to be surprised and therefore felt not the smallest astonishment when she opened a concealed door in a wall and stepped directly into the duke's office.

Checking that his main door was closed, she smiled at him.

"Good morning, my dear."

"Zora!" He surged to his feet, looking from his wife to me.

"Don't fret," she said. "I have told the princess about our relationship."

"You've told Princess Verene that...that we're..." He gestured wordlessly between them, anger rising on his face.

"Certainly I have done so," she said, calm in the face of his ire. "And with good reason."

He sank back into his chair and sighed. "I am sure you have good reason. You always do. However, I wish you had consulted with me first. We had agreed that we would not tell—"

"Never mind that," she said briskly. "Something of greater significance has arisen."

He broke off, eyeing her with interest now, his disapproval apparently forgotten. I looked between them in fascination, but as Zora started talking, I was distracted from thoughts of their astonishing marriage.

"Despite your years of neutrality," she said, "the Academy itself has been violated."

He sat up straight. "The Academy? What do you mean?" His calculating gaze crossed to me.

"Princess Verene—who is not only a trainee here but under your especial protection—has been attacked within our walls."

He drew in a sharp breath, his eyes once again fastening on me.

"I was attacked last night in the entrance hall as I returned to my suite after the evening meal," I said. "They used a composition to drag me outside into the grounds."

I pulled down the neckline of my gown to expose a dramatic blue and purple bruise just below my collarbone.

"Stop." He held up a hand. "I must call Hugh and Raelynn."

His wife raised an eyebrow. "Must you?"

"They have been with me since the beginning and have been loyal through all." He gave her a significant look. "If the Academy is to change, they have a right to hear it directly."

He pulled a composition from a drawer in his desk and ripped it neatly in half. We all sat in silence for a number of minutes until his door opened without a knock and the librarian hurried in, followed by the healer.

"Your Grace? We came as fast as we could." His eyes took in the rest of the room, and he faltered. "Zora. Your Highness. I…"

"Princess Verene knows about Zora and me," Duke Francis said. "So you may speak freely. She has just been telling me of a vile attack perpetrated in our own Academy walls. After everything we have been through together, I felt you had a right to hear it from the princess herself."

"An attack?" Raelynn gasped. "But you should have come straight to me. You poor dear." She hurried forward, already ripping a diagnosis composition.

"Well?" the duke asked. "How bad are her injuries?"

"Widespread, but thankfully not serious." She gave me a sympathetic look. "I'm guessing they're rather painful, however. The bruising is severe."

I nodded, greedily eyeing the healing bag slung across her shoulder. She chuckled and withdrew a pain relief composition. I sighed as the cool mist sank into my skin.

"This time my attackers were scared away before they could do any significant damage," I said. "But at the end of last year, the assassin who broke into my bedchamber ended up dead himself. His master had bound him in such a way that once he named the person who hired him, his life drained away."

"An assassin in your bedchamber?" Raelynn looked like she was about to collapse, and Hugh rushed forward to help her into a nearby chair.

Even Zora looked faintly taken aback at my contribution to the conversation. Duke Francis, however, never lost focus.

"And did he name that master, then?"

"He did. Cassius. The man, not the king, if such a distinction really matters."

Hugh gasped, but the duke sat back, steepling his fingers. "It is a meaningless distinction. We are bound as people by the responsibilities we take on toward others just as tightly as we are bound by the role itself. So after all my years of service, all my years of neutrality, it has come to this. The king sends assassins into the Academy itself."

"It was one thing to remain neutral when there was a careful balance of power to be maintained," Zora said. "But change is coming, whether we like it or not. And we must seize the moment to shape that change to the benefit of all."

The duke fixed me with narrowed eyes. "Why have I not heard of this attack last year?"

"Of any of the attacks," Zora murmured. "There were others in the grounds."

"If we are to speak openly and honestly, Your Grace," I said, looking him directly in the eye, "I didn't tell you because I wasn't sure who I could trust. I didn't know what side you were on."

The duke sucked in a breath as if he had received a physical blow.

"Everything we have worked toward, gone in an instant," Hugh said, distress in every line of his body.

"But there is a different future possible." I kept my attention focused on the duke. "A future where you don't need neutrality because there are no sides and factions. A future where Kallorway is united behind a young, strong king who works for the good of all the people."

"Prince Darius." The duke's gaze didn't waver from my face.

I nodded. "Prince Darius isn't looking to create a new faction —he seeks to end factions altogether, to heal the rift tearing Kallorway apart. He will be a king for all his people." I glanced sideways at Zora. "And he intends to give sealed commonborns the rights they should always have possessed."

"Compositions." Her grin was fierce, her face alight.

I nodded.

Zora turned to the duke. "The time has come. You know it has. We must stand by the prince."

"And what is it exactly we can do for him?" the duke asked.

"You have influence—" Zora began, but I cut her off.

"Actually there is something specific you can do," I said. "Something only you can do. Something that might make all the difference."

Four pairs of eyes pinned me in place.

"As Academy Head, you're a member of the Mage Council. Call an immediate, emergency meeting of the Council here, at the Academy. Give the prince the chance to have his say, and when the time comes, lend him your support and your vote. I believe that if you are willing to do that, then Kallorway will never be the same."

"Call the Mage Council," Zora breathed. "Brilliant." She fixed her husband with her bright gaze. "And so little to ask, really."

He let out a long, slow breath, seeming to visibly deflate. "Very well. I will call them. Tell the prince to prepare himself."

"How long...?"

"They will ride through the night if necessary. Expect the full Council by afternoon tomorrow."

My eyes widened, triumph making it hard to stay in my chair. "So soon."

The duke gave me a reproving look. "I am calling an emergency session. Not one of us would tarry in such a situation."

"Of course not." I stood. "I must—"

"Not so fast, young lady," Raelynn said, reviving enough to jump from her chair. "I've only relieved your pain, not healed you."

I bit my lip, glancing at the door.

"It will only take me a minute." She rummaged through her case.

"I'm sorry, Hugh," the duke said quietly behind me. "I promised you a haven from politics and the court."

"And you have delivered on that promise for more years than I care to count," the librarian said solemnly. "Raelynn and I will stand with you now."

"Of course we will," the healer said sharply. "The very idea of sending assassins into the Academy after our trainees!"

As soon as she found the right composition, I hurried from the room, leaving the four old friends in privacy. They were the old guard, offering their support to the new, and they needed time to come to grips with the changing situation.

But someone else needed time to prepare as well, and all my attention was on him now.

I burst into my suite, almost tripping in my haste to pull aside the tapestry and open the door between us. Darius was standing at the window, but he turned sharply at my precipitate arrival.

His eyes latched onto my cheek, and his face softened. "You went to Raelynn after all?"

"What?" My hand flew to my cheek. I must have had a graze there that I hadn't even noticed. "Never mind that. I've been with the duke. He's called an emergency meeting of the Mage Council here at the Academy. They'll be starting their journeys even now. And he's going to support you."

Darius stared at me, his brow slowly creasing. "An emergency meeting here? But Duke Francis is always neutral. He has always been so since before my birth."

"We made a mistake about him," I said. "We didn't understand *why* he was neutral. His sense of responsibility to this Academy is absolute, we should never have kept the attacks secret from him. Zora was the one to see that. Once he understood that your father had been sending assassins into the Academy grounds, the rest came easily."

"Zora? How does she come into this?"

"That is the most incredible part of all." I hesitated suddenly, realizing their secret wasn't mine to tell. But I knew Darius wouldn't rest unless he understood exactly what had brought about the change in the duke.

"If the duke helps you win your throne," I said slowly, "you would never do anything to hurt him personally, would you?"

Darius frowned. "Of course I would not. And that's regardless of his assistance."

I nodded. "Then I think you'd better sit down."

The first members of the Mage Council arrived that afternoon. Rumors began circulating through the Academy within hours, but I heard none that approached the truth.

Bryony cornered me in my suite, and I told her as much as I could without revealing the duke and Zora's secret. I trusted my friend's discretion, but it wasn't my secret to tell unless there was dire need.

She was astonished enough without that revelation, a great deal of her ire directed toward the attack on me. She wholeheartedly agreed that Jareth's presence had been highly suspicious, despite Darius's excuses for him, and she looked ready to storm his suite.

"I just wish we could have kept the gathering Council from him." I sighed. "But Darius will have told him, of course. For an emergency session, the messages go direct to the ten discipline heads, and they know better than to explain the summons to anyone. But I'm afraid Jareth will tell his father, and then the king will arrive and ruin everything. Or Jareth will find some other way to destroy Darius's chance."

"You need to be there," Bryony declared. "If anyone tries to use a composition to interfere, you can turn it aside. You're more powerful than any shield."

I bit my lip. "But how could I possibly arrange that? Not even Darius could get me into that meeting."

"We'll think of something," Bryony said.

But in the end, it was Zora who held the answer.

I skipped classes the next day without a second thought, pacing up and down in my suite and listening to Darius doing the same in the room next door. I thought the tension of the initial wait was bad enough, but it was nothing to the feeling when he finally left the room, closing the corridor door behind him.

I wasn't left to wait alone for long, however. Zora appeared at my door and beckoned for me to follow her. I did so in silence, hardly daring to breathe, afraid of giving in to false hope. Perhaps she just meant to console me with tea while we both waited to hear the outcome.

She led me into the back passages, winding through increasingly dusty and unused spaces until she gestured me into a narrow cupboard. I peered into the space, bare except for a single chair. But when I began to ask her where we were, she gestured for silence. I gave the room a second look and saw a pair of holes at the height of a sitting person.

I turned back to thank her, but she was already gone. Without hesitation, I entered the narrow room, closing the concealed door behind me. Had this space always existed, or had the duke had it installed so his secret wife could be privy to his important meetings? I imagined the true council room at the palace was protected against such intrusions, but this was probably the first Council meeting the Academy had ever hosted.

In normal circumstances, I would never have hidden in such a way to spy on the deliberations of a Mage Council—Kallorwegian or Ardannian. But my aunt had sent me here to be an intelligencer of sorts, and Bryony's words kept ringing through my head. I might be needed to protect Darius and the Council itself. I was still wrestling over where my true loyalties lay, but here was an opportunity to serve them both at once.

*a*t first the only thing to be heard was grumblings from the heads who had ridden through the night, along with questions directed at Duke Francis. He refused to answer, however, saying they would all hear what he had to say when the Council was officially begun.

Finally Duchess Ashten arrived, apologizing for keeping everyone waiting. She took the only remaining seat, and nine pairs of expectant eyes fixed themselves on Duke Francis.

I knew the cost of this action for him, but there was no sign of it in his unperturbed features. Having decided on the right course, he pursued it as steadfastly as he had pursued neutrality all these years.

"Come then, Francis," Duke Rennon called. "You can have no more reason to delay telling us the meaning of this. You can imagine how astonished we were that you of all people would call such a meeting."

"I did call it," the Academy Head said, "but not on my own behalf."

"Not on your own behalf?" The youngest man present leaned forward with a creased brow. He wore a full red robe and must have been the young law enforcement duke I had heard about from Darius—the one open to new ways. "But you know these meetings are closed, Francis. Especially an emergency session. Only a member of the Council can call one."

"And a member of the Council did," Duke Francis replied calmly. "It was my choice to call the meeting. But you are forgetting that there are two other people who have a traditional right to speak at such a gathering, though they are not officially members of the Council, as such."

"I suppose you mean the king," Duchess Ashten said. "There's no need to be so formal about it all, Francis." She surveyed the room again as if she could possibly have missed Cassius hiding in some corner. "But I see His Majesty is absent."

"He means the heir," the young duke breathed, a look bordering on excitement lighting his face. "The other member with the right to speak is the heir. The law is clear on the matter."

An older lady in healers' purple frowned. "But an heir may speak only if he—or she—wishes to challenge the monarch."

Her words cut off abruptly, and absolute silence fell.

"So it has come at last," said a portly gentleman in a silver robe that matched that of Duke Francis. The University Head, then. "Young Prince Darius means to force his father's hand."

"I knew there was a reason we were all banished at Midwinter," a younger woman in a green growers' robe said in a sour voice. "Most inconvenient it was too to be sent packing in such a manner."

Her tone made me want to crow. The growers were aligned with the crown. For her to talk of Cassius in such a way must be a good sign for Darius.

Slowly silence fell as the attention of the group turned to its oldest member. General Haddon had so far been notably silent. The others all weighed him with their eyes. Had he known of this move of his grandson? Did he support it?

"Well, bring him in, then," the general said after an extended moment. "Let us hear what he has to say."

His manner didn't make his feelings on the matter obvious, but his words still signaled a release of tension in the room. Some of the tension drained out of my own shoulders as well. It appeared Darius had succeeded in taking his grandfather, at least, by surprise. Whatever his private feelings, the old general wasn't ready to take a public stand against his grandson. Whatever happened now, Darius would have his say.

Francis opened a door, saying something I couldn't hear into the next room, and Darius appeared. He stood tall, and the ice had finally lifted from his eyes, letting everyone see the fire that burned beneath. I wanted to cheer.

But before the prince could speak, the other door into the council room burst open as well. The various cries of outrage died as everyone got a look at the person interrupting them so boldly.

King Cassius looked furious, his eyes raking the gathered Council and then finishing on his son.

"What is the meaning of this?" he cried. "Why wasn't I informed the Council was meeting?"

"It appears," Duke Francis said, "that you were informed."

The king and the duke faced off, the fury in the king's face doing nothing against the calm implacability of the Academy Head.

"But not by any of you," the king at last snapped, his gaze once again sweeping the room.

"The laws on such emergency meetings are clear," the Head of Law Enforcement said. "It is up to the member who called the meeting to inform the monarch—or not. And in this case, the meeting has been called to allow a hearing for the heir. Which means the monarch cannot be present."

"Cannot?" The king's voice dripped anger. "You are trying to exclude me from the Mage Council?"

"Not me," the young duke said, showing more bravery than I expected. "It is the law that does so."

"And which of you intends to uphold the law?" Cassius asked, threat in every syllable he uttered.

"Thank you, Father," Darius said, his voice strong and calm. He made a striking contrast to his father—young and handsome but with steel in his face and fire in his eyes. "You are amply demonstrating why I was forced into seeking this meeting."

He turned to the Head of Law Enforcement. "And thank you, Duke Gilbert, for your passion for our kingdom's laws. But I waive my right to a hearing without my father present. I have nothing to say to you all that I will not say to him."

"Thank you, Your Highness." Gilbert nodded at the prince before turning to Duke Francis. "Perhaps two more chairs would be in order?"

There was a momentary pause as the Academy Head called for more seating, while the king's glower deepened. He had achieved what he wanted, but it had been granted him due to the graciousness of his son, and the victory no doubt tasted of sour defeat.

My attention kept circling back to the young Duke Gilbert. With his passion for the law and his interest in improving his discipline, I felt sure he would support Darius. And with his relative youth, he had a vitality some of the older Council members lacked.

Power hung around him in layers, most of which I assumed were his personal shields. The temptation to take control of just one of them, merely to test the layers of his expertise, pulled at me. If he was as strong as he was diligent, he would make a powerful ally for Darius.

The meeting had stalled, everyone waiting in terse silence for the extra chairs to arrive, and I felt ready to explode from the tension. It darted through my mind that it wouldn't do any harm for me to quickly sample one of Duke Gilbert's personal shields.

Not if I was careful to leave the instructions exactly as he had written them.

I didn't stop to think further, knowing I had only the briefest window before the meeting started again. Getting a taste of his composition might give me some insight into his mind.

"Take control," I whispered, my energy reaching for one of the layers around the duke.

I connected with it instantly, the shape of a standard shield unfurling in my mind. It held incredible power, though. Unless he came under attack, he wouldn't need to refresh it for days. And the precision was beyond anything I had experienced before, even from the Academy instructors. There was a reason he had ascended to such a senior position so young.

Fascinated, I pressed deeper, wanting to get more of a sense of him. If only the duke had written his shield as an open composition like my recent attacker. Not that the duke would be likely to do something so foolhardy. But I remembered the tantalizing feel of the way it had connected the power to my attacker's own energy.

Even as I thought it, the energy of the duke seemed to burn more brightly than the other balls of energy in the room. The composition had a taste of the duke himself—there was no other way to adequately describe it—and I realized now that his energy felt the same way. They were connected after all, if not quite in the same way that an open composition would have connected them. All I needed to do was connect with it.

I barely noticed myself murmuring the word, "Connect," aloud.

But I did notice when my whole awareness dove into the duke's pool of energy. For a moment I couldn't think or move or feel. Everything was chaos and whirling knowledge beyond my understanding. And then it coalesced into a single, clear composition. It glimmered before me, clear as anything I had ever seen worked by one of my year mates, although it was infinitely more complex. None of it made sense to me, and yet it all made perfect sense.

Duke Gilbert was thinking of a composition that would seal the room against eavesdroppers and interference of any kind. I could discern no actual thoughts, just the knowledge needed to create the working. From the discomfort in his face and bearing as he watched Cassius, I suspected the duke was wishing he had composed and worked one in advance. I could imagine the king's unexpected arrival would have brought such protections forcibly to mind.

I was suddenly reminded of one of the rules that bound the Ardannian Council—no members were permitted to work a composition during an active meeting. Normally they met in their council room at the palace where permanent protections rendered the sort of composition filling Duke Gilbert's mind unnecessary. And the same was likely true of the Kallorwegian Council.

Given the focus of the duke's energy and the expression on his face, my earlier thinking hardened into certainty. He had been reminded that this room lacked the normal protections of a proper council room. But there was nothing he could do about it now.

But I could act for him.

The thought came unbidden, clear as anything, although some part of my brain tried to assert that it made no sense whatsoever. My hands were already moving, however.

I could write the composition on the duke's behalf, using his expertise and his energy and his ability. It would be easy.

I pulled a folded sheet of parchment and a pen from inside my robe where I always kept them, ready to take notes in class. Placing the parchment on my knee, I carefully wrote out the binding words, feeling the building power already struggling to break free. It calmed as soon as I finished them, the pressure no longer growing. Now I could relax and write more slowly. I traced out the words, layering them with the necessary meaning, the power flowing through Duke Gilbert's energy.

When I finally wrote, *End binding*, I wasted no time ripping the parchment in two. Enormous power rushed out from my working, enveloping both the room and my hiding hole. I had made only a single adjustment to the composition the duke had been picturing—expanding it to include me. I nodded with satisfaction. Now no one would be able to interfere with the meeting in physical form or with any sort of composition.

"End," I whispered, slamming back into my chair as my connection to the duke cut off abruptly.

I breathed deep, ragged breaths, trying to clear my mind. Already the knowledge that had allowed me to write the composition was fading, disappearing far faster than I could grasp hold of it. I drew out another piece of parchment and rapidly scrawled the beginning of a composition. Nothing happened.

What had I just done? I trembled all over, but it wasn't from exhaustion. My energy felt no more depleted than when I sat down, despite the power of the strange working I had just achieved. Tentatively I let my senses stretch to the room beyond the wall. The duke's energy levels were noticeably lower than they had been earlier. In the dreamlike state of the moment I had been convinced I was using his energy to compose, and it must have been true. Yet another impossibility.

I didn't have the luxury to ponder it, however. The chairs had arrived, and the servants departed. Darius began to speak.

"You have all heard my father promise that he will give me the throne," he said.

"When you're ready," Cassius snarled.

Darius ignored him. "And you have all seen him bend over backward to prevent me reaching full and recognized mastery of my powers. But I am now nearly halfway through my training, despite his best efforts to hold me back. And I was content to let things rest until I had graduated. But my father's actions lately have compelled me to act."

"You mean the lure of a crown has done so," his father sneered.

Darius regarded him coldly. "I have no interest in the crown beyond how I might use it to serve my kingdom. Naturally such a concept is foreign to you."

He turned back to the Council.

"My father has allowed his emotions to so color his decision making that he places our entire kingdom in peril. He has let his hatred of Prince Lucas and Princess Elena of Ardann grow beyond reason, and he has sought, multiple times now, to assassinate their daughter, Princess Verene of Ardann."

A murmur passed around the seated Council members.

"Yes, you take a keen interest in the young princess," Cassius said with disgust.

"I take an interest in anything that affects the well-being of Kallorway," snapped Darius. "And Kallorway cannot afford for a princess of Ardann to be murdered in our Academy while under our care and protection."

He met the eyes of the various heads, one by one. "Ever since the war, Ardann has grown strong while Kallorway has grown weak. And it is entirely through our own fault. We cannot now risk the wrath of Queen Lucienne. Instead we must seek an alliance— one we are fortunate she wishes to extend. And yet my father blocks that alliance for no reason beyond his personal hatred."

Duchess Ashten stirred, exchanging glances with the Head of the Growers.

"I could give you example after example of the ways in which my father is slowly destroying this kingdom, but I don't believe I need to do so. You have all seen it with your own eyes. And you have all heard his own mouth promising that he will step aside for me, his son and heir."

"One day," Cassius growled. "But it is not this day."

"I seek to unite Kallorway," Darius said. "I seek to make us strong, as we once were—equal, and greater even, than Ardann. And I seek to do so not so we can wage war on our neighbors and spill our own blood in the process. I would see us grow strong for the good of our people. I do not believe such a future is possible under the rule of my father, and I do not believe he will ever willingly give up his crown. It is you, the Mage Council, who must hold him to his promised word. I am his rightful heir. I call on you to give me the crown."

As Darius spoke, Cassius grew increasingly restless, casting frequent glances at the door. And yet I couldn't imagine he wished to flee the meeting. Was he expecting some sort of external aid? Someone to work a composition strong enough to disrupt and delay any vote? It made sense. After all, someone at the Academy had alerted him to the gathering of the Council.

I wished I were still connected to the composition I had worked. But as soon as I had written, *End binding*, I had closed it off, and it had become as separate from me as it now was from Duke Gilbert. If someone was testing its limits in an effort to break through, I would feel nothing.

But the more restless the king became, the more convinced I was that someone was attempting something, blocked by my shield. The king had come into the meeting expecting back up, and his back up had not arrived.

The University Head was requesting proof of the prince's claims about the assassins, and Darius was describing the attack on me the year before and his interrogation of the prisoner. Several of the heads exchanged impressed looks when the prince referred to composing investigation compositions and truth compositions as if they were nothing.

"Those are advanced workings," Duke Gilbert said. "I've heard you chose law enforcement as your discipline of study."

Darius nodded at him. "I believe any ruler must know their own laws and how to uphold them."

"Well said, young prince." The Head of the Seekers nodded acknowledgment of Darius's beliefs.

"You cannot depose me," Cassius said, fury and fear making his voice rise.

"Actually, we're the only ones who can," Duke Gilbert said. "And only in favor of your heir. Personally I feel we are ready to proceed to a vote."

"Not so fast," Duchess Ashten said, and I held my breath. Her discipline had long supported the king. "We must first agree on the exact terms to be put to the vote. Are you proposing that Prince Darius be immediately crowned as king? While still at the Academy? Such a thing is unheard of."

"It is preposterous," Cassius spluttered.

My eyes found General Haddon. He had worked his whole life to see his own flesh and blood on the throne in place of Cassius, and yet rumors said he wanted no king without complete loyalty to him. He must be furious that Darius had not warned him of his intentions. But he held it in much better than Cassius, giving no sign of such feelings on his face. Darius must have been right about his father, because I felt sure that once the king could have matched the general for careful circumspection. He showed no such restraint now, however, every word out of his mouth only reinforcing Darius's case. It had been a master stroke to allow his father to remain in the room.

"Certainly there can be no official coronation before he graduates," the elderly Head of the Healers said. "But it seems clear he already has the intelligence, maturity, and control for the role. He can be named king-elect immediately, and Cassius may remain as king-regent until the young prince's graduation."

"And what exactly does that mean?" the Head of the Growers asked, her brow furrowed. "Regents usually rule in everything but name, holding the throne for young children. What is the role of a king-regent if we also have an adult king-elect?"

"It means that Cassius shall remain on the throne in Kallmon," Duke Gilbert explained, "but every one of his decisions must be ratified by either the king-elect or the Mage Council. And he shall have no authority to delay or prevent the coronation of the king-elect at the nominated time."

"That sounds reasonable," the University Head said.

He turned to General Haddon, and the rest of the Council followed his lead. The general had been remarkably silent throughout the meeting. Ostensibly, it should be the king's supporters who were the greatest danger to Darius, but they had always supported the crown in anticipation of Darius's ascension. The general and his supporters were the greater unknown. But they had hated Cassius for decades, and Darius was the general's own grandson. Haddon would need a sufficiently compelling—or crafty—reason to oppose him, thus why Darius had tried so hard not to give his grandfather warning to prepare for his accelerated coup.

"Let us vote," the general said after an extended pause.

Chairs scraped and clothing rustled as everyone adjusted their positions slightly.

"Very well," Duke Francis said. "As the one who called the meeting, I will call the vote. All those in favor of transferring power to the crown prince under the terms outlined by Duke Gilbert please indicate now."

He looked around the room expectantly.

The first hand up belonged to Gilbert, and his action produced an avalanche among those who supported the crown. Their loyalty had always been predicated on the eventual ascension of Darius to the throne, and they no doubt thought their moment had come. But Darius wouldn't truly have succeeded in his purpose unless he gained the votes from both factions.

I held my breath as I watched General Haddon. Duke Francis

cleared his throat, and in response, the general's hand slowly rose. As soon as it did so, the rest of the hands went up. His faction remained loyal, then.

"It is unanimous," Duke Francis said in stentorian tones. "The Council hereby rules that Cassius of Kallorway be henceforth known as king-regent, while his eldest son, Darius of Kallorway, becomes king-elect, with his coronation set for his graduation from the Academy."

Darius abruptly sat down, and I let myself sink back against my chair. We had done it. We had secured Darius his throne. And yet my emotions still whirled.

Darius had won, there was no question about that. But it was not unalloyed victory. We would not be truly free from his father for another two years.

CHAPTER 22

*N*one of the members of the Mage Council lingered, and I couldn't blame them given the expression on Cassius's face. Within minutes, Darius and his father were alone in the room.

Darius immediately stood and crossed to stand over his father. Cassius responded by leaping up himself, but I noticed for the first time that he was shorter than his son.

During the meeting, Darius had maintained an air of calm control, a fitting contrast with his father's fury. But now that he was alone with his father, he let his own anger blaze from his face.

"You told the kingdom you would give me the throne, and now you have been held to your word."

Cassius tried to speak, but Darius continued over the top of him.

"We have had this conversation once before, when I reminded you of Princess Verene's importance to Ardann."

I stiffened at the mention of my name, pressing even closer to the wall as Darius continued speaking.

"At that time I made the foolish mistake of thinking you still had enough sense to care about the well-being of Kallorway—or at least enough self-interest to consider your followers' opinions on the matter. I was wrong, and so here we are, having a very different conversation."

"The Mage Council are fools the lot of them if they cannot see how that girl has you under her thumb," Cassius snarled.

Darius leaned forward, his hands clenching into fists and every muscle tensing. Even from my hiding place behind the wall I could sense the danger radiating from him.

"Last time, I explained to you that Verene's safety was important to Kallorway. But I no longer have to play your games, Father. I am the one in control now, and so I tell you openly that Verene is important to me. Nothing and no one is more important."

Cassius stepped back. He looked almost nervous, as if he hadn't seen this side of his son before. Cassius had raised his son to be strong and controlled, but apparently he hadn't anticipated the fire that burned beneath his mask or the contained power he had been keeping leashed.

Darius stepped forward, following him. "If Verene is harmed again—in even the smallest way—I will not hesitate to destroy you."

The silence that filled the room at that pronouncement was dark and choking.

"Do you understand, Father?" Darius's voice dropped almost too low for me to hear, and yet the threat it contained did not diminish. "I will destroy you in every possible way."

Cassius swallowed visibly. His eyes narrowed.

"All this fuss over a girl," he said, trying for nonchalance and failing. "I can assure you I have no further interest in her."

Darius didn't loose his father from his gaze, holding him for another long moment before shaking his head and turning for the door.

"You were always ungrateful," Cassius spat after him. "I

should never have wasted my time on you instead of your brother."

Darius paused by the door, a harsh laugh rolling from his lips.

"You think Jareth would be more grateful? It is you who are the fool, Father. You held a kingdom in your hands, and you lost it. The sooner you accept that, the better your remaining years will be."

"And how many years might that be?" Cassius asked, regarding his son with narrowed eyes.

Darius shrugged, his voice uncaring. "That's up to you, Father, and the decisions you make next. Kallorway is mine to protect now. You can accept that and get out of my way, or you can become one of the threats I must guard the kingdom against." A dark note reentered his voice. "I wouldn't recommend the latter."

He pulled open the door and was gone.

My legs trembled despite the seat that still supported me. Darius had said I was more important to him than anything. Had he meant it? Everything in his manner had seemed sincere, but he had been talking to his father. Was it all just part of the act his father had always forced him to play?

Cassius stood still for a long moment, his eyes on the closed door, and his face ugly. Fury and bitterness warred for dominance, but slowly something else took hold. A dark determination that made me shiver. Cassius's own ability was sealed, and with a unanimous vote of the Mage Council, he had no discipline to support him. But my composition had blocked someone from coming to his aid. He still had an ally or allies. And if I was right, and it was Jareth, then we were still in deadly danger.

I waited, but Cassius left the room a moment later. With his exit, I felt the power that had ringed the room dissipate. My composition had completed its task.

I slipped out of the hidden cupboard, my breath coming fast, and my legs still shaky. My left hand clenched and unclenched repeatedly around the two halves of parchment hidden in my pocket.

My composition. I had completed a written composition—not taken control of someone else's working but initiated one myself. And I had used the strength, control, and expertise of someone else to accomplish it.

When I found myself at the door of my suite, I blinked in surprise. I couldn't even remember finding my way through the maze of back corridors. I had received too many shocks in the last few hours to be thinking clearly now.

Slipping into the room, I hurried straight to the desk and sat down. Picking up a pen, I laid it against a piece of blank parchment and then hesitated. The certainty I had felt while linked to Duke Gilbert was gone, and I struggled to call up the right words.

Withdrawing the crumpled composition from my pocket, I smoothed it out and carefully aligned the two halves. Using the words as a guide, I began to write.

I hadn't even made it through the binding words when I stopped. I didn't need to go further to know the experiment was a failure. No power built at the shaping of the words, straining to be released. It felt nothing like it had done in that hidden cupboard.

I sat back, taking several deep breaths. The events during the Council meeting had not unleashed some latent ability for written compositions. Instead it seemed I had stumbled on a much stranger ability.

The door to the corridor opened with force, but I didn't even turn around, still staring blankly at the parchment before me.

"There you are! Where have you been?" Bryony's voice asked breathlessly. "Have you heard the news? The Mage Council has voted Darius king-elect, and they're saying he's to be crowned immediately after graduation!"

I nodded numbly.

"Verene?" Her voice approached behind me. "What's going

on? Why do you look like that? This is good news! It's everything you've been trying to achieve. You're safe now!"

She reached the desk and leaned over my shoulder. Frowning, she picked up one half of the torn parchment.

"What's this?" When I didn't answer, she spun my chair around, giving my shoulders a gentle shake. "Verene? What's wrong?"

Her actions snapped me out of my state of shock, and I stared at her wide-eyed.

"Sorry, I just…It's all a bit much…" I drew a long breath, trying to regain my equilibrium. "Yes, I did know about Darius. I was there."

She raised an eyebrow. "You found a way into the meeting after all?"

I shook my head. "No, but it turns out the room they used had a hidden viewing spot. Zora showed it to me."

"Ooh!" She looked delighted. "How brilliantly sneaky. So it's all true then?"

I nodded.

She glanced down at the parchment in her hand. "So were you needed to protect them? Did someone try to interfere?"

I bit my lip. "I think so. And I don't think the Council was expecting it. Not here in the Academy, I suppose."

"Then it's a good thing they had a guardian like you watching over them."

"Bree, I…" I swallowed and tried again. "Bree, I composed that." I pointed at the parchment she had just returned to the desk.

She frowned at it. "I don't understand. You mean that's the composition you took control of? How did you end up with the pieces?"

"No." I shook my head. "I wrote that. I composed it."

She looked at me anxiously as if she thought I had lost my mind under all the pressure.

"Verene…"

"Sit down." I pointed at one of the sofas. "I'll tell you everything, but it might be a shock. It was for me."

She obediently positioned herself on the sofa, and I let everything that had happened pour out of me. Her eyes grew rounder and rounder, and several times she looked like she was refraining from jumping to her feet.

"So you actually composed that," she said when I finished, pointing at my desk.

I nodded.

She seemed to be struggling for words.

I gave her a pleading look. "It doesn't make any sense. Does it?"

"Not in the normal definition of sense, no." She laughed abruptly, delight breaking across her face. "But when were you ever normal, Verene?"

Leaping to her feet, she danced across the room to grab my hands and pull me up as well.

"You can compose! For yourself!"

"Not exactly for myself," I said, my lips twisting. "I stole his power, Bree! All his training, even his energy—the essence of him. I just reached in and stole it."

She frowned. "You say that as if you took something permanent from him. Did he lose some of his knowledge because you borrowed it?"

"No, I don't think so." I bit my lip. "But he did lose some of his energy—I could feel his reserves were lower."

She wrinkled her nose, dismissing my concern.

"He'll get it back soon enough. It might be an unusual situation, but you're hardly the first two mages to share energy."

I should have known that an energy mage with the ability to gift energy would consider my actions less of a violation than they seemed to me.

She looked at me, assessing my expression before speaking in a quieter, more earnest voice.

"I'm not saying you should start using this ability at every moment. Caution is clearly called for. But the very fact that you're worried is why I'm not. What you did wasn't something frivolous, and it wasn't for yourself. You acted to protect the Council. And from what you said, the duke would have written the composition himself if he could have. For all we know, you might have saved someone with that working, Verene."

I swallowed. "I wish I had your certainty."

"You'll get it. You're just still in shock." A gleam entered her eyes. "But we need to practice! Try if you can connect with me."

"Right now?" I stared at her.

"Of course! Why not? You said the actual composing didn't drain any of your energy, and it can't have cost you much to connect with the duke. At least it never seems to cost you much energy when you connect with active workings."

"No, I don't think it cost me much," I said slowly.

"Well, come on then! What are you waiting for? I'm dying of curiosity to see what it feels like."

Despite myself, my mind flew back to the moments of connecting with the duke, curiosity gaining the upper hand.

"I'm not sure it feels like anything at all. He didn't seem to notice, anyway."

She held out her arms wide, as if offering herself as a sacrifice. "Come on! Try it."

I licked my lips, trying to remember my exact words and the sensation that had accompanied them. Being alone in my suite made it easier to focus on Bryony's energy than it had been in the council room, and it helped that she was so familiar to me. I had monitored her energy levels a thousand times.

With the duke, I had taken control of one of his workings first. But it hadn't been connected to him like the open working of my attacker. I hadn't needed my connection to the working to provide a direct pathway to the duke. It had merely given me a sense of him that had made his energy easier to identify and connect with. Did I need that with someone as familiar as Bryony? Having felt the sensation once before, I only had to focus on her energy to feel the pull to connect with it.

"Connect," I murmured, as I had done with the duke.

Instantly I was inside Bryony's energy. It hit me differently from the way it had with the duke. Being prepared no doubt helped, but it was more than that. The duke's energy had connected me with his vast ability and expertise, and I had been overwhelmed by something so far beyond my understanding. It was different with Bree, though.

I had been with her through all of her training. Theoretically, at least, I understood her ability almost as well as she did. And energy mage abilities were far simpler, comprising a single type of working. On top of that, her overall knowledge was far shallower than that of the Head of Law Enforcement.

"Is it working?" she asked. "I can't feel anything, but you have a funny expression on your face."

I nodded slowly. "It's working."

"What does it feel like?" She leaned forward, her face eager. "Can you read my thoughts? What am I thinking right now?"

"What? No, of course I can't read your thoughts! I'm in your energy, Bree, not your mind."

She looked almost disappointed, although I felt nothing but relief. I didn't want to read anyone's mind.

"Can you feel my ability then?" she asked.

"Yes, I can. It's all there before me, so much clearer than it was with the duke. It's less overwhelming."

"Thanks," she said dryly.

I gave her a look. "You're talented, Bree, but you're also eighteen and not exactly a discipline head."

"Maybe one day they'll have an energy discipline, and I could be the head of that."

"I would vote for you," I said distractedly. "If either of us were actually Kallorwegian, that is."

"So, can you do an energy working?" she asked. "Can you speak it, or would you need to write it down?"

I frowned. "I could try speaking it. I've seen the words you write often enough." Even if I hadn't already been familiar with them, my access to her energy made them leap into my mind.

I spoke aloud, my words faltering and stopping halfway through the composition. "It's not doing anything." My hand clenched involuntarily, as if it gripped a pen. "I think I need to write it."

She pushed me back toward the desk. "Go on. Try it."

I sat down and pulled out a fresh piece of parchment. Biting my lip, I hesitated for only a moment before I began to write. Immediately I could feel some of her energy pour into the composition. I modified my intended words, keeping the drain on her light, and finished quickly.

When I wrote the last words, I looked up at her expectantly. She had a wrinkled nose and thoughtful expression.

"I felt that."

"What did it feel like?" I asked.

She shrugged. "Like a drain of energy. I don't mean that I felt your working, as such. I just felt the energy pulling out of me. But it's different for me because the working itself is one to drain energy, and I'm much more tuned to energy in general than a power mage is. I can well imagine they might not feel a thing. Although if you did a strong enough working, they'd likely feel the exhaustion afterward."

"Here." I thrust the completed composition into her hand. "Take it back."

She didn't argue, ripping the composition and letting her energy flood back to its rightful owner.

My usual senses would have felt the sudden increase in her levels, but being connected to her, I could feel it much more strongly. The sensation reminded me I should pull away now we had completed the experiment.

I opened my mouth to speak the necessary word and hesitated. Her ability to gift energy had been easy to access, the full scope of it so familiar to me. But something else lurked behind it. Something far less familiar—to both her and me. As soon as I fastened onto it with my mind, my awareness expanded.

Gifting energy wasn't Bryony's only ability. I tried not to think about her second, secret one because the thought of it had always made me nervous, afraid for her and her future. I could see it clearly now, though.

It had been partially hidden at first because she herself had never used it, never trained it or honed it or studied it. In fact, I suspected she tried as hard as me not to think of it at all. But she obviously knew how it worked because I saw exactly how she could permanently shear off a portion of her energy, and how she could shape that energy to bring life to the most hopeless of cases.

With certainty, I knew I could compose such a composition right now, the words coming as easily as they had done for the first working. If I put my pen against a fresh parchment, I could permanently steal some of her energy.

"End," I gasped, cutting our connection.

"What is it?" Bryony looked at me with concern. "You look white."

"I could access both of your abilities, Bree." My voice shook. "And I could have used the other one just as easily as I…"

She swallowed, staring at me before shaking herself.

"But you didn't, and you never would."

"No. I never would. I can promise you that. But still…Bree, I could have."

~

Later in bed, I couldn't stop thinking about it. Ever-loyal Bryony might be willing to brush off my concern, but it wedged in my mind. Bryony's ability was powerful enough, but how much more powerful for someone to be able to steal it from her without her permission.

Earlier in the year, I had nearly lost myself in the joy of delving into the workings of others. I had almost been consumed by my ability. And now I had discovered an even more powerful ability—and an even more direct connection into the power and expertise of others. How could I trust myself with it? If I started connecting with other mages directly, how soon before I lost myself?

I could come up with no satisfactory answers to those questions. I attended classes as usual, putting my full focus on studying for exams and refraining from even connecting with compositions. I was afraid that if I did, I wouldn't be able to resist following the next step to connect with the mages themselves.

Bryony kept suggesting we practice again, reminding me she could work the composition I created to immediately return the energy I had taken from her, but I was resolute in my refusal. Since she had study of her own to do, she didn't push too hard.

My thoughts about my new ability might not be positive, but I was glad to have them to distract me. Darius had disappeared directly after the Council meeting and had not yet returned. When I visited Duke Francis in his office, he explained that he had granted the new king-elect a leave of absence from the Academy to deal with matters in the capital and with the various discipline heads.

"He's in great demand, as you can imagine," the duke told me. "The next two years will not be easy for him as he balances his substantial new responsibilities with his role here as a trainee." He gave me a look that was startlingly close to amusement. "It is fortunate that he is such a good student and so advanced in his skills."

I held back a snort. After two years of private tutoring before his entry to the Academy, Darius had always been in greater danger of expiring from boredom than failing his exams—no matter how many classes he missed.

"He will be back before long," the duke said with dismissal in his voice. "The year is drawing to a close and exams will soon be upon us."

I had withdrawn after that, although I longed to press him on exactly what *before long* meant.

And as the days dragged on, the question burned stronger and stronger in my mind. When would Darius be back? After everything that had happened, and the conversation I had overheard between him and his father, I could barely contain my desperation to see him.

Jareth seemed equally restless, his eyes resting on me more often than they had before. What did he think of his brother's new status, and of his subsequent absence? And what did he know of my involvement in the unfolding events? I avoided him, not curious enough about the answers to risk conversation with the younger prince. I still considered him the most likely Academy resident to be Cassius's secret ally.

The final days of the year raced past, until one day I looked up in the dining hall to see a familiar tall figure striding toward the second year table.

CHAPTER 23

$\mathcal{E}$xclamations and conversations broke out across the hall as everyone turned to the new arrival. Several of the fourth years stood and bowed to their new king-elect, and the rest of the trainees scrambled to rise and follow their lead. I gave him a shallow curtsy, beaming from the unexpected rush of emotion at seeing him again.

Darius smiled around at the standing trainees.

"Thank you all," he said. "Your support means a lot. But I still have two more years as a trainee, so please—for all our sakes—you can go back to treating me as you did before."

A smattering of chuckles sounded across the room, and the trainees returned to their seats. I watched him approach our table, stopped a number of times by senior trainees who wished to congratulate him in person.

He looked so achingly familiar and yet, at the same time, so strangely different. He could afford to tell the trainees to treat him as they had before because he had always been the crown prince, superior and aloof and receiving respect on all fronts. But this Darius looked relaxed and at ease, smiling and laughing even, as he accepted the well-wishes of his generation.

My own fear still lingered. I had seen his father's face after Darius left that council room, and I knew he had a hidden ally still. But despite the sudden increase in responsibility, Darius looked free in a way he never had before. My heart rejoiced and feared for him at the same time.

I expected him to come to me, but he didn't slow as he approached the spot where I sat with Bryony and Tyron. As he passed, however, he met my eyes, the expression on his face making me flush.

Later, his eyes seemed to say, and I instantly realized he was right. Whatever conversation was coming between us, it wasn't one we could have in public.

I raced back to my suite after the meal, only to pace up and down as I realized he was likely to be delayed by the other trainees. At last a knock sounded on the tapestry door, however, and I flew over to fling it open.

At sight of him, I swept into a deep curtsy. "Your Majesty."

"Not for another two years," he reminded me. "I haven't been crowned yet."

"But you will be."

He laughed and swept me into his arms, spinning me around before placing me carefully back on my feet.

"All thanks to you, Verene."

I shook my head. "Don't be ridiculous. I just got attacked. I can't take credit for that. Zora is the one who spent years softening the duke, and Duke Francis himself is the one who called the Council meeting."

I placed my hand on the side of his face. "And you're the one who spent years building your position, winning allies, and proving your capability. You won your own crown, Darius."

"And yet, none of it would have happened if you hadn't been brave enough to come here to our Academy."

"Was it bravery?" My eyes dropped from his. "Or foolhardy determination?"

So much had happened since I arrived two years ago that it was hard to think of the naive girl I'd been then without a measure of sorrow. I had always hated not having an ability, and yet everything had seemed so clear to past-Verene.

"Never doubt your bravery." Darius's soft voice matched the gentle touch of his hand on my chin, lifting my face back to his. "It was a fortunate day for Kallorway—and for me—when you crossed our borders."

I flushed but couldn't escape the pull of his eyes. His head moved slowly downward, and I pushed up to meet him. Our lips met with the softest of sighs.

Despite myself, I had spent far too many hours remembering our previous kiss, and the way its fire had consumed me. This embrace was different. This time his lips promised the enduring heat of embers, burning slow and long, but no less consuming all the same.

Then his arms swept around me and tightened, pulling me against him as he deepened the kiss. I responded, rising onto my toes, only for him to pull back and groan.

"Prince Darius." The voice that had interrupted us came again.

I stepped out of his arms, looking frantically around for our audience, but could see no one. Slowly my attention focused on a ball of power in the middle of the room.

"A communication composition?" I asked.

He groaned again. "They won't leave me alone."

"Prince Darius?"

"Prince?" I asked with a smile, trying to suppress my disappointment at the interruption. "Don't they know you're king-elect now?"

"They appear to be well aware," he said dryly, "since they now seem to have need of consulting me day and night. But it's a bit of a mouthful. Most people seem to prefer to continue using my old title for now."

I shook my head. "You'd better go. That working is burning power."

He still looked reluctant, so I gave him a light push through the door. "We can finish our conversation later."

Fire leaped into his eyes. "Is that a promise?"

I flushed. "If you like. Now go!"

He disappeared through the door with a last backward glance, and I closed it firmly behind him. My fingers crept to my lips which still tingled from his touch.

I had meant it when I said conversation. There was much for us to talk about. I didn't know which official or discipline head had been calling him, but they had made a timely interruption. I could not afford to forget that this lighter, more open Darius was now responsible for an entire kingdom. He might still bear the title prince, but he was king-elect of Kallorway. And I was a princess of Ardann, with a secret too big for either kingdom. We were hardly free to follow wherever our emotions might lead us.

He fought in combat class the next morning as usual, although we weren't paired. And he turned up to composition class as well, bringing sheaves of parchment with him—reports of some kind by the look of it. Our instructors addressed him with added respect, and none called him to task for his distraction. We didn't speak, other than polite greetings, although his eyes apologized for his preoccupation. But I could only imagine the weight of work he now had before him.

I wasn't the only one who failed to hold his attention. Jareth, sitting beside him, sent several poisonous glances at the reports that so absorbed his brother. Several times he spoke, making Darius chuckle, but each time, Darius returned promptly to his reports. When his brother's eyes weren't on him, Jareth's expression turned sour, and when he looked up to see me watching him, his eyes flashed momentary anger before he smoothed the emotion away.

Darius wanted to change Kallorway which meant he was

consumed with a task big enough to absorb all his time and attention. And even when he had not yet had the distraction of a crown, he had refused to consider that he might be harboring a traitor in his inmost circle. If I was right, and Jareth was working against him, then Darius was even less likely to see it now. But I couldn't sit back and see all his efforts constantly thwarted. I would have to act to protect him myself.

I came to the conclusion during discipline class and was immediately filled with the desire to take action. Our small energy class had completed our final placement with the trainees studying to be seekers and were back in our original classroom. As soon as the bell sounded for the end of the lesson, I hurried out into the corridor, scanning the trainees who began to fill the hall from the other rooms.

The moment I spotted Jareth, I hurried in his direction.

"Verene," he said in a tone of faint surprise when I appeared next to him.

"Jareth." I nodded in greeting. "I would like to have a word with you, if you're willing."

He gestured with wide open eyes. "By all means."

I shook my head. "Not now. In private. Could you come to my sitting room after the evening meal?"

He raised an eyebrow. "Consider me intrigued. I shall be there most certainly."

"Good."

I hurried away before he could ask me any questions, dropping back to walk beside Bryony. She also regarded me with a raised eyebrow.

"What was that about? Were you just voluntarily talking to Jareth?"

"I invited him to visit me this evening."

"You what?" she squawked before lowering her voice. "Whatever for? Does Darius know?"

"Not unless Jareth tells him. I'm hoping he won't."

"You're hoping he won't..." She said the words slowly. "What exactly are you planning, Verene?"

"I'm going to prove to Darius once and for all that Jareth can't be trusted."

"And how exactly are you going to do that?" She sounded skeptical.

"I'm going to dangle the same bait I accidentally left out before and see if he bites twice."

"Bait?" She gave me a disapproving look. "Do you mean yourself?"

"Ultimately. But to start I just mean the compositions I use to protect my door. I'm going to give him the chance to read them again and then see what happens. If I'm right, he'll send another assassin, like he did last year. And this time, Darius won't be able to deny it."

"Then I'm sleeping in your room," she said resolutely. "And don't try to fight me on this."

I smiled. "I was actually hoping you'd say that. I want to catch Jareth out, but I don't have a death wish."

She nodded approvingly. "And this time, after we've caught the assassin he sends, we'll make sure you're ready to intercept any deadly compositions that try to cut short the interrogation."

I nodded. "I won't make the same mistake twice."

Bryony insisted on being in my suite for the initial meeting with Jareth as well, although she agreed to remain out of sight in my bedchamber. When his light knock sounded on the corridor door, I opened it unhurriedly and gestured him inside, displaying a hint of awkward uncertainty.

"I must say your invitation took me by surprise, Princess," Jareth said. "You seem to have been avoiding me of late."

"You're right, I have."

He looked surprised by my open admission.

"But Darius has assured me I've been harboring the wrong impression about you," I continued. "And given his triumphant return, I thought the time had come to mend matters. So I have something for you."

"I assure you that isn't necessary," he said with his usual light smile that didn't quite reach his eyes.

"Please humor me," I said. "It's just a token." I looked around the sitting room. "Just give me a moment. I must have left it in my chamber."

I left him alone in my sitting room, shutting my bedchamber door behind me. Bryony stood waiting, holding out a small sprig of green leaves with two small white tulips at their center. I took them from her and stood waiting for a moment, my head cocked.

"How long do you need to leave him?" Bryony whispered.

"As long as I can without seeming suspicious." I grimaced. "So your guess is as good as mine."

After another extended moment, I reopened the door, doing it as noisily and slowly as I could. Jareth had moved, now standing by one of the windows, right beside my desk. I carefully refrained from looking at the desk, although I wanted to analyze it for any sign of disturbance. This time I had left the top of the desk clear, but the stack of door compositions had been carefully placed in the top drawer.

I crossed over to the window and held out the small posy with a tentative smile.

"It's a little silly," I said. "But in Ardann, white tulips are used for apologies and fresh starts. I'm hoping we can have a fresh start."

He took the sprig from my hands with a gallant bow.

"How could I refuse such a gesture?" He straightened, a smile on his face. "Darius will be pleased."

"I hope so." I let my tension push a slight flush up my cheeks.

Hopefully he would think I was making the effort for Darius's sake. And hopefully the thought would enrage him.

"I will leave you in peace for now," Jareth said. "But I look forward to a new chapter between us."

"Thank you," I said, politely seeing him to my door.

As soon as it had closed behind him, however, I rushed back to the desk. I pulled open the top drawer and stared at its contents.

"Well?" Bryony asked from behind me.

I spun, triumph in my eyes. "They're definitely disturbed. He read them."

"So we won't be sleeping tonight then?"

I chuckled. "You should probably sound at least a little nervous."

"Never," Bryony scoffed. "The two of us can take on any assassin." She gave a smug smile. "Especially you. They won't have any idea what they're walking into."

CHAPTER 24

*B*ryony had somehow managed to raid the kitchen again and had a midnight feast ready for us long before midnight. But I could barely eat or drink, my nerves stretched taut.

I insisted we position ourselves on the bed with the door to the sitting room closed, as if I had already retired for the night. The hours stretched on, however, with no sound or sign of life.

"What if he's not coming tonight?" I asked Bryony. "Maybe he needs some time to source an assassin."

She yawned. "Then it's a good thing it's a rest day tomorrow. We can sleep all day and wait up again all night tomorrow night. But I suspect he'll want to move quickly. Exams are next week, and then you'll be gone back to Ardann."

As the hours wore on, her yawns grew closer together and longer until I suggested she lie down, just for a few moments.

"Of course not." She widened her eyes dramatically, making me giggle.

"You're not going to convince me you're not half asleep that way. It makes sense for us to take shifts, anyway. Otherwise we might both end up falling asleep at just the wrong moment."

She grumbled but admitted I was right, making me promise to wake her at the first hint of any movement—or in a couple of hours, whichever came first. I agreed, although now that I had carried my point, I was a little worried I wouldn't be able to stay awake without her company.

I needn't have worried, however. Despite the creeping tiredness, I couldn't have slept even if I wanted to do so. Bryony had dropped into slumber almost instantly, barely moving except for the occasional twitch, but too many thoughts whirled through my head for such peace.

I had been so determined to reveal Jareth's true colors for so long that I hadn't given much thought to how Darius would react. But now that the moment had potentially come, I found myself wishing someone else—anyone else—could be responsible for revealing the truth to him. I hated the thought of being the one to deliver such devastating news.

The minutes ticked on, Bryony's assigned two hours nearing a close, when I finally heard what I thought might be movement. I nearly roused her but hesitated at her peaceful face. I had been waiting here in tense expectation for hours now. And it wasn't the first time I had thought I heard something that turned out to be nothing.

I carefully slid off the bed and padded silently over to my bedchamber door. Placing my ear against it, I listened.

There. The scraping sound came again. Excitement raced through me, flinging me into full wakefulness. Someone had opened my door and entered my sitting room.

Of course, now I was too far away to shake Bryony awake, and I didn't want to call to her and alert the assassin. Should I run back to the bed, or was I better positioned here by the door? I hesitated. I might not need her assistance if it was a single assassin, and any scuffle would wake her anyway.

A muffled sound came again, like another door opening, but the one in front of me stayed still and silent. I frowned.

Surely the assassin wasn't retreating again already. I was certain I'd made no noise coming to the door. Had I somehow given myself away? I couldn't think how.

I pictured my sitting room in my mind, trying to think what else it could have been. It had definitely sounded like a door closing, although it had been slightly muffled.

A jolt of horror passed through me.

I had tried to lay a trap with myself as bait, but what if I had miscalculated? All this time, I had been the target of Cassius's hatred and anger, but everything had changed now. He no longer held the throne—not really—and it was his son who had wrested it from him.

I had suspected Jareth of betrayal, but it seemed my mind had shied away from the possibility that it could run so deep. I had made the terrible mistake of not considering that I might no longer be the target—and that access to my room also provided access to Darius's suite. Whatever protection he had on the door behind the tapestry was different from what he had on his main door—I knew that because I had barged through it myself more than once.

The assassin had never been coming for me, and I had just given him access to his true target. Ripping open my door, I abandoned all thought of subtlety and silence.

My sitting room sat dark and empty, giving no sign that anyone had sought passage through it. I almost fell in my rush across the room, tripping over a side table and bouncing off the side of a sofa.

I fumbled with the tapestry, my haste making me clumsy. But at last I managed to push it out of the way and pull open the door. The sitting room on the other side also sat dark and empty, and for a single moment I doubted myself.

Then I saw the open door on the far side of the room and heard the muted sounds of a scuffle. I ran.

I paused in the door of Darius's bedchamber, my eyes

straining to see in the dim light. It would have been pitch black except that someone had pulled open a curtain, letting soft falls of moonlight in.

Two figures grappled beside the bed. One had his back to me, his right arm held above his head by Darius, preventing the long knife gripped in the assassin's hand from finding its target.

The two swayed back and forth, grunting with effort. The strain of holding back the blade seemed to be preventing Darius from retrieving a composition that might keep him safe from it. At least that was the only explanation I could think of for why he hadn't already hedged himself in so many shields he couldn't be touched.

The assassin must have come with an arsenal of compositions himself if he had already broken through the protections Darius always wore.

I took two steps forward into the room, my foot colliding with something sharp and hard. Looking down, I caught the glint of moonlight on steel and snatched up the knife that lay there. Apparently the assassin had managed to kick Darius's own blade away.

Gripping a weapon, I moved more confidently, hurrying toward the two men.

Darius caught sight of me over his attacker's shoulder, shock twisting his face. He faltered slightly, one foot slipping, and the assassin pressed forward.

"Darius!" I cried, just as the attacker's knife plunged downward.

I threw myself across the remaining distance, screaming my rage. But I couldn't reach them before the blade slid into Darius's chest with a sickening squelch. He grunted, staggering backward, the hilt protruding from his wound.

His attacker spun, turning to face me now that Darius was incapacitated.

I gasped and almost dropped my own weapon. I had expected

to see the face of a stranger, but instead it was Jareth himself who had just stabbed his brother. Darius looked past Jareth, meeting my eyes, the shock even stronger than before. But now I understood its true cause—it hadn't been there because of my arrival.

"Verene," Darius gasped before crashing to his knees. His eyes flickered to his brother, now advancing on me, and he managed to whisper, "Jareth, no."

But even now I could read the disbelief and hesitation in his voice. Jareth had used his brother's trust and love to break past his defenses. Darius had been hampered because even now he didn't want to hurt Jareth.

Anger flared inside me, overwhelming all sense, and I launched myself at Jareth. My mind thrummed, waiting for him to unleash a composition in either offense or defense. Unlike Darius, I was ready and willing to send the attack straight back at Jareth.

But it seemed all his testing had made him cautious. He made no move to draw a composition, instead dropping into a crouch and pulling a second knife from his belt.

I didn't have the same skill with a shorter weapon as I did with a sword, and my height put me at a disadvantage, but I didn't hesitate. Lunging forward, I slashed with my blade. He danced out of reach before darting forward with an attack of his own.

I only just blocked him with my own knife, but the movement put us dangerously close together. He pressed forward, bringing his greater strength to bear, and I felt my arm give way.

A sudden blur of movement flashed in the corner of my eye, and Darius slammed into Jareth's side. The two of them staggered sideways, pushing Jareth away from me.

But the younger prince lost no time turning on his brother. Gripping the hilt of the knife still lodged in his chest, he pulled it out in a single fluid motion.

Darius cried out in pain as blood poured from his wound.

I nearly threw myself at Jareth again, despite the failure of my first attempt, but was halted by the realization of my own stupidity. I didn't need Jareth to work a composition for me to control. I could work one myself.

I had never gotten undressed for the night, so I had the full range of defensive compositions in my usual pockets. My hand flashed straight to one my father had provided me. It would have all the power I could need.

Jareth raised both his blades and moved toward Darius, who swayed on his feet as he tried to stem the flow of blood from his wound. I dropped my knife and ripped the parchment in half in one clean movement.

Power surged out, racing toward Jareth.

"Take control," I growled and instantly connected with it.

It had been so long since my father gave it to me I had forgotten the details of its purpose, remembering only that it was strong and would target any threat against me. It unfolded clearly in my mind, however, its purpose broad rather than targeted. It would disarm anyone within its range who held a weapon, and my father had poured enough strength into it to wrest the blades from several squads at once.

But I needed it for a single attacker only. The power here would be more than enough to destroy him completely. But even as I felt the strength of the power under my control, my eyes fell on Darius. I couldn't kill his brother.

"Bind Jareth," I whispered, and the power writhed and twisted. It had already been streaming toward the single attacker in the room, reaching for his knives, but it now sped even faster, crashing into him in an irresistible wave.

Both blades fell from his hands, and a moment later he collapsed to the floor, unable to move any of his limbs. As soon as he hit the carpet, Darius sank after him, the removal of the threat leaching away the last of his strength. He went to his knees first, and then toppled sideways to lie beside his brother.

I ran for them both, ignoring Jareth to fall to my knees beside Darius. But the sound of the younger prince's voice pulled my attention toward him.

"Darius! Darius!" The horror and anguish in his tone matched the expression on his face as he stared at his brother, bleeding out beside him.

I growled in disgust. It didn't matter how torn he might be about it now, he had still been the one to strike the blow against Darius. While Darius wouldn't strike against Jareth even to save himself.

"Silence," I muttered, viciously twisting the working so that it bound his voice as well as his body.

Excess energy still surged through me, so I shoved against him, rolling him over so he faced the wall, unable to see either me or Darius. Turning back to Darius, I met his eyes.

"Verene," he whispered, his voice so faint I could barely hear the word.

"Darius," I sobbed, pressing against his chest with both hands. He had already lost so much blood, and more kept pouring out, despite both our efforts. Soon he would have lost so much that no healing effort could save him.

"Surely you keep a healing composition ready," I gasped. "Where is it?"

His hand fluttered in the direction of his bed. I gasped another sob. Unlike me, he no longer wore his robe, and he must only keep a minimal number of compositions in his nightshirt. They were probably all chosen to keep him from being hurt in the first place—if only he had been attacked by anyone other than his own brother.

I didn't have time to go searching through his robe and bed for a healing composition. It would take me too much time to find the right one anyway. If only mine weren't all keyed to heal only me.

Wait! I jolted upright. For the second time my terror and grief were clouding my thinking. The original working might be designed for me, but I could twist it—I would gladly sacrifice it to the attempt, even if it didn't work.

I had never tried to take control of two workings at once, but the one binding Jareth no longer needed my attention. My hand flew straight to the pocket that held my healing compositions, once again reaching for the strongest one.

I ripped it, whispering, "Take control," as soon as I felt the swell of power.

It pushed toward me, determined to heal whatever minor scrapes or bruises it could find.

"Darius," I ground out through my teeth.

The power resisted, wanting to come to me. I had been embedded strongly into every layer of the working, both the words and the intent focused on me. But it was still a healing composition.

I latched on to the part of the power that had been shaped for healing and strengthened it, directing it toward Darius's desperate wound. It wavered and then buckled, reaching for him.

I gasped and sat back as it sank into his chest. The bleeding slowed and stopped as the wound knit itself back together. He gasped and spasmed, but his eyes didn't open.

Tears ran down my cheeks as I watched his pale face. I was too late. Healing compositions had only ever been able to do so much, and he had expended his final energy rescuing me, only exacerbating his blood loss.

He needed energy, and he needed it immediately. If only...

My desperate mind reached out for Bryony, now four rooms away from where Darius was fighting for his last breaths. Surely she was too far for me to—

But the familiar feel of her energy called to me, even across the distance. I could feel it there at the edge of my limits.

"Connect," I gasped out and dove into it.

My blood-stained fingers scrabbled inside my robe for my parchment and pen, streaking the surface red as I pulled it free. My mind fastened on to what I needed, the words of a healing composition unfurling inside my mind as easy as breathing. I put my pen to the paper and began to form the first word.

With a choked cry, I snatched the tip away from the parchment, my fingers trembling. Responding to instinct, I had nearly stolen a healing composition from Bryony, permanently robbing her of some of her energy in the process.

Gulping, I forced different words to form in my mind. My handwriting was sloppy and rushed, and I had to force my hand to stay steady enough to keep it legible. Thankfully I didn't need many words.

I ripped the parchment, the energy I had just taken from Bryony rushing toward Darius and filling him with a jolt. He gasped, gasped again, and then his breathing strengthened.

"End," I whispered, cutting off my connection to Bryony. I didn't want to be linked to temptation.

But as I watched, his breathing remained strong and steady, and the color slowly returned to his face. With the help of the extra energy, the healing power still lingering in his body was replacing enough of his lost blood to keep him alive. He would live.

I let out a long trembling breath and sat back, covering my face with my hands. It had been close, too close. And in more ways than one.

I had been scared of my new ability, but it had just saved Darius's life. I couldn't hate a power that had done that. But it had also nearly stolen something incalculably precious from Bryony.

But I couldn't blame my power for that either—that had been me. I had refused to acknowledge or train my new ability, and so when I had reached for it in panic, I hadn't had the experience I needed to use it properly. I had been afraid of misusing my ability, and those fears had nearly come true.

I had to make sure it never happened again, which meant I had to accept this new power and master it.

Even in my moment of greatest panic, watching Darius dying before me, I had managed to pull myself back in time. I hadn't taken Bryony's healing energy without her permission. I could trust myself to stay in control of this ability and not abuse it.

"Verene." This time when Darius spoke, his voice sounded steady and clear. "What happened?"

He pulled himself up into a sitting position, looking around at the streaks of red all over us both and then at his brother, lying awkwardly with his face rolled away.

"I bound Jareth," I said. "And I healed you."

I grabbed the torn scraps of parchment around me, shoving them deep into my pockets to hide the fact that the words they contained didn't quite match the feats they had performed. Darius had been too close to unconsciousness to see me using my ability, so I would let him assume I had come equipped with the right compositions.

Darius shook his head. "You shouldn't have put yourself at risk like that. You're not hurt?"

"I couldn't let you die." I gulped. "And it was my fault. I laid a trap for Jareth, but I thought he would come after me not you."

Darius's eyes moved back to his brother, his face displaying an echo of its earlier shock before it went hard, the old ice returning.

"I don't understand," he said.

Talking quickly, I explained my belief that his father still had an ally at the Academy, and the plan I had made to expose Jareth if it was indeed him.

"I thought he'd send another assassin," I said. "And I had a plan to ensure we managed a full interrogation this time. I never dreamed he would come himself."

"Verene!" Bryony's voice called from the other side of Darius's sitting room. "Are you in there? Something woke me up, and you were gone…" I could hear in her voice she was refraining from saying it was my theft of energy that had woken her. She couldn't see us where we sat, and she must be unsure who I was with.

"We're in the bedchamber," I called back. "Come through."

"I can't," she shouted. "There's some sort of…barrier."

"That's my shield," Darius said. "It won't let her through without…" He raised his voice. "Allow Bryony to enter."

"Oh!" Bryony must have been pressing against the apparently empty doorframe because it sounded like she was now stumbling forward into the room.

"It let me through," I said softly.

"Yes." He wouldn't meet my eyes.

"And him." I gestured behind me at Jareth's still-bound body.

"You're the only two," he said, his voice stiff.

"The only two." I bit my lip, a horrible thought floating into my mind. "What about your main door? Would that allow Jareth through?"

Slowly, Darius nodded, something terrible in his eyes. "Only Jareth."

"So he had no need to access your suite through my rooms," I whispered. "Not unless he intended to frame me. All he would need was a way to mask his own identity so that any investigation compositions merely showed someone entering from my room and stabbing you in your sleep."

I raised a shaking hand to my mouth. "And only one person has access through both my outside door and the door behind the tapestry. Me. Jareth would be heir, and Ardann would be blamed for killing Kallorway's king-elect. It would have been chaos."

"What would have been chaos?" Bryony asked from the doorway, ending her words in a gasp as she took in the scene before her. "Are you…?"

"We're both all right," I said hurriedly. "Now." My eyes conveyed a silent message, and she nodded.

"Even Jareth is unharmed," I said begrudgingly.

"Jareth?" She gasped again and strode over to see his face. "He actually came himself? But what are you all doing in here?"

I quickly explained my realization of what had happened, and my panicked reaction.

"I should have woken you," I said. "I wasn't thinking."

"Yes, you should have," she said severely. "I would have happily stabbed Jareth for you."

I glanced quickly at Darius, catching the pained expression that crossed his face before his features hardened into steel.

"No one will be stabbing Jareth," he said. "I have already sent for Captain Vincent. He will take charge of my brother and remove him immediately from the Academy."

"Where will he take him?" I asked, tentative in the face of Darius's emotional shutdown.

"He will take him back to the capital where he can be safely contained for now." His voice was flat and didn't invite questions.

"He sounded sorry," I whispered, my words catching me by surprise. "When you were dying."

Darius shook his head, a look of disbelief crossing his face. "While I lay dying by his hand. My own brother. You were right all along, Verene, and I should have listened."

"I wish I wasn't," I said, hating the way my voice trembled. But I wanted the happy Darius back, the one who had returned from the capital.

"The captain will be here any moment," Darius said. "And I think it would be better if you ladies weren't here. I survived, which means there will be no need for investigation compositions or any mention of your door. As far as the captain is concerned, my brother entered from the external corridor because I was too much of a fool to protect myself against him."

"Darius, no." I put my hand on his arm. "You aren't a fool."

He stepped away. "Apparently I am. You should go now. Hurry."

Mutely I stood, and Bryony gripped my arm, leading me back out into Darius's sitting room. I tried to glance back at Darius, but she pulled me along too fast, propelling me into the safety of my own suite.

CHAPTER 25

Bryony forgave me for my theft of her energy instantly when I told her the full story. She was merely delighted that it had changed my mind about fully exploring my new ability.

"You stopped yourself," she said. "And that's what matters."

She didn't even push me when I told her I couldn't focus to practice here at the Academy in the three days remaining of the year.

"Over the summer," I told her. "I'll find a way to practice at home."

All rest day I waited for Darius to appear in my sitting room, or for rumors to sweep the Academy about Jareth, but everything proceeded as usual. I did hear someone mention that Captain Vincent had left in a carriage, but no one seemed to consider this remarkable. The only piece of news going around was that Captain Vincent had received a promotion and was now captain of the king-elect's personal guard. Everyone seemed to assume he had royal business in the capital—possibly recruiting top members of the Royal Guard to his team.

I couldn't understand why Darius was keeping the truth a

secret, but neither was I going to say anything. Even if I had wished to do so, talking about it would have revealed my presence at the scene. And on reflection I more than agreed with Darius—it was better for both Ardann and Kallorway if no one knew I was present at an assassination attempt on the king-elect.

Exams passed in a haze. I barely remembered completing them, but my study must have paid off because I passed. The combat exam was a group exercise in the arena, but Bryony had already volunteered to do an exhibition bout with me for mine, and it felt much like our daily practices.

My performance suffered from my distraction, though. Darius had turned up for the exam, and it was the first time I had seen him since Jareth's attack. Thankfully Bryony went easy on me, ensuring I put in a creditable performance.

Darius didn't speak to me directly. In fact, he spoke to no one, his face utterly closed. He appeared for the beginning of each exam and disappeared as soon as it finished. My eyes were drawn to him again and again, but each time I saw him it caused me pain. How much hurt hid beneath that careful mask? The one person who had always been there for him had betrayed him in the ultimate manner, and I couldn't imagine how it must feel.

When I returned to my suite at the end of the evening meal— once again not having seen him in the dining hall—I went straight to the door behind the tapestry and knocked. For a long minute I thought he intended to ignore me, despite the fact I could feel his energy burning behind the door. But finally the handle turned and the door swung slowly open.

My heart contracted at the sight of his face, gaunt somehow, although it had only been two days.

"I suppose you wish to say farewell," he said curtly. "You leave in the morning?"

"Yes, I do, but..." I paused before a rush of words came bursting out of me. "Darius, I can't imagine how you're feeling.

I'm so sorry. But I can't bear to see you like this. I can't bear to just leave and—"

He cut me off in a harsh voice. "You have to leave, and the sooner, the better."

"What are you saying?" I wished my voice didn't sound so small. "Darius, some of the things you've said...I thought...I had the impression that you cared about me."

He gave a bitter laugh. "Care about you? You're the only one left in the world I care about, Verene. And that's why you have to leave."

I stepped toward him, raising a hand, and he pulled sharply away.

"I don't understand."

"I thought I could change Kallorway." His voice was rough and deep with pain. "I thought I could change the court."

"You can. I really do believe that."

"Maybe," he said, but his voice held no hope. "Maybe one day. But the court my father created managed to corrupt even Jareth." He shook his head, pain haunting his eyes. "I didn't think it was possible, but somehow they got to him. And if they can twist him..."

He straightened, a shadow descending over his face and voice. "You need to leave, Verene. You have to get as far away from the Kallorwegian court as you can and never return. I don't know how long it will take to leach Kallorway of its poison, but I can never bring someone I love into this court again."

I sucked in a breath, feeling as if I had just been winded. Love. Darius had said he loved me in the same breath as he said I had to leave him and never return. It was too much to take in.

"I will go," I said, my voice trembling, "because it's the end of the year, and I must. But I will return for third year." I hesitated. "Unless as king-elect you mean to bar me entry?"

"As king-elect, I must consider the good of my kingdom. I

cannot afford a diplomatic rupture with Ardann right now. I have promised my people an alliance and future peace, and I mean to deliver. But as myself, I'm begging you—please complete your studies at your own Academy. Flee Kallorway while you still can."

"No, I won't give up on you." I said the words fiercely, although it shook me to the core to hear Darius of all people begging.

"That's the problem, Verene," he said, his voice a tortured whisper. "You're too good for this place and for me."

I shook my head. "I don't believe that."

"I wish I could convince you," he whispered.

A moment passed, both of us frozen in our own rooms, the open door between us. Then he straightened, his face turning stiff.

"Farewell, Princess Verene. Enjoy your summer."

I tried to think of an answer, but he had already shut the door in my face.

I slept little that night, everything that had happened in the last few days tumbling around and around my brain, too jumbled for me to make straight. Darius had said he loved me, and I knew that despite everything I loved him back. But it was the sort of tangled, impossible love that seemed hopeless.

I had sworn I would be back, and that I wouldn't give up on Darius, and I meant those promises. But at the same time, I knew Darius wasn't the first one to try to protect me from the Kallorwegian crown. I had made the decision to protect myself before ever he tried to make it for me—when I chose to conceal the truth of my abilities from him.

What hope did I have of convincing him I was safe in his court and at his side if I didn't believe it myself? And yet, I could no longer imagine returning to my old life in Ardann, as he claimed he wished me to do.

Ida arrived in the morning, efficiently packing my belongings and those of my clothes I indicated I wished to take. In a mood of defiance, I left even more behind than I had the year before.

I thanked her profusely for her year's service, and she seemed a little bemused by my enthusiasm. But although she might never know of it, I remembered the small part she had played in securing Darius his throne. She had passed on word of my questioning to Zora, prompting the head servant to be open with me and setting in motion a chain of events I could never have predicted.

Bryony turned up as Ida was leaving, already tearful before she even began her farewell. Her parents had insisted she return home for the summer, a position I could understand, although Bryony herself had made many pointed comments about small villages and their lack of shopping.

"Maybe you can come and visit for a week or two at some point," I suggested, causing her to brighten considerably.

She gave me a long hug, pausing when she pulled back to fix me with a fierce look.

"You are coming back, aren't you?"

"Yes," I said firmly. "I'll be here for the first class, don't worry. Kallorway is on the brink of something new, and I don't mean to walk away now."

"I still can't believe Jareth…" Her voice trailed off as if she couldn't bring herself to speak his crimes aloud.

"I've never wished so badly I was wrong about something." I rubbed at the side of my head. "And yet, at the same time, I can't help but feel relieved that he's safely locked away."

Bryony nodded fervent agreement before pausing. "And your new ability? You still mean to practice with it?"

I nodded again. "Over the summer if I possibly can. Or next year if I can't. I refuse to be caught out like that again. And next year I'm going back in the arena. I can't afford to run away from stressful, dangerous situations—those are exactly the settings where I need to learn to control my power."

"You do seem to encounter an unusually large number of such situations in real life," Bryony said.

"Hopefully that's all at an end now. But I still want to be prepared."

I stepped forward and gave her a second hug.

"Thanks for always being there for me, Bree." My voice came out muffled and thick.

"You mean thanks for not being a Jareth?" A hint of amusement tinged her voice. "I could say the same thing to you. Unless you're harboring any murderous tendencies you've failed to mention before."

"None whatsoever," I assured her.

"Then, in that case, I'll do everything I can to convince my parents to let me visit at some point over the summer. Maybe I can come at the end of the break and make Corrin a stop on my way back here."

"I hope you can. The summer won't be the same without you."

She ran off after that, exclaiming that her carriage was already waiting. I made a slower exit from my room, running into Dellion in the corridor.

"So you're off for the summer, then."

She hadn't said it as a question, but I nodded anyway.

"Will you be going to your grandfather's estate again?" I asked, watching her face carefully for her reaction.

I still had no idea what the general really thought of Darius's change in status, let alone what Dellion might have heard about Jareth.

"This year is…different," she said, giving nothing away. "I'm not sure what the summer will look like."

"Well," I said, "I suppose whatever happens, I'll see you back here in the autumn."

She sighed. "Unfortunately, I'm sure you're right."

I chuckled, too used to her now to take offense. "Farewell and happy break to you, too, Dellion."

The shadow of a smile crossed her face. "Farewell, Princess Verene."

I had nearly made it out of the entrance hall when another voice called my title, pounding footsteps racing after me. I turned to confront a breathless maid. After a moment I placed her as the one who had delivered Zora's message to me previously. For a moment she just stood there, panting, before thrusting a sealed note toward me.

"Here, I was asked to give you this."

"Thank you," I said, wondering why Zora couldn't have just come and talked to me if she had something she needed to say.

The maid bobbed a quick curtsy and dashed off again, leaving me shaking my head in bewilderment. Layna called to me from the front courtyard, so I tucked the note into a pocket and went down the steps to join her.

"Will you miss the Academy?" I asked her. "Or are you glad to be heading home?"

She frowned up at the gray building. "Is it strange to say both?"

"If it is, then we're both strange." I paused. "I hear Captain Vincent has changed roles. Does that mean we'll be getting a new Captain of the Academy Guard?"

She shook her head. "It was felt that for the duration of the king-elect's time at the Academy, the two roles are so closely aligned that Vincent can continue in both of them. After Prince Darius graduates, however, they'll have to find someone new for the Academy."

"That makes sense, I suppose."

"Are you ready to go?" Her horse pranced beneath her, as if sharing her eagerness to be moving.

With a last lingering look at the Academy building, I nodded and climbed into the waiting carriage.

We had made it all the way across the border and back into Ardann, my mind full of the people I was leaving and the people I was returning toward, when I remembered the note the maid had given me.

Pulling it out, I broke the seal and glanced at the contents inside. When my eyes fell on the signed name at the bottom, I stiffened.

I read it and read it again in disbelief.

It wasn't a note from Zora at all. If the signature was to be believed, it was a note from Jareth.

I returned to the top and read what he had written.

Verene—

I hope this note finds its way to you. Something terrible is wrong, although I cannot understand what it is. I need your help, but not for my own sake. I need your help to save Darius. It's the only reason I dare ask since I know I deserve no such assistance for myself. But for Darius and Kallorway, I implore you. Please help me. Please return next year and find out what is happening here.

Jareth

I read it five times, but no new words appeared to give it greater sense. My first reaction was to order the carriage to turn around and race back so I could reassure myself that Darius remained unharmed. But I suppressed the impulse. Showing him this letter would only hurt him further after everything Jareth had done.

He gave no specifics of any credible threat, and I had no reason to believe he cared for his brother's well-being. Why did he beg me to save Darius when he was the one who had tried to kill him?

And that was even assuming the letter had actually come from Jareth. How had he managed to write it and give it to the maid? None of it made any sense.

And yet, now that I had read the note, neither could I entirely dismiss it. If Jareth's intention had been to unsettle me, then he had succeeded.

The tiniest of thoughts wormed into the back of my mind. I pictured Jareth's voice and face when he cried his brother's name as Darius lay dying. And I remembered the sensation I had always had that there was something strange about Jareth—something wrong on some level that defied conscious analysis.

What if there really was something going on beyond surface appearances? What if some other threat truly did exist? The very fact that Jareth had found a way to get this note to me suggested he might not be as securely locked up as I had believed.

Again, that was if the note even came from him, although I couldn't imagine who else would have written it or what reason they could have to forge such a letter.

And, perhaps more importantly than all, what if—impossible as it seemed—there was some explanation for Jareth's actions? I knew I was grasping at anything, however unlikely, because I wanted to see the light return to Darius's eyes, but the thought had taken root now. I couldn't ignore this note.

I watched the walls of Bronton approach. Soon I would be back home among family, and I would have access to vastly more resources. I would ask for a law enforcement composition, the kind that could confirm if a letter was written by the signed name.

Once I knew if this was truly a note from Jareth, I could consider my next move. I had already decided on returning to Kallorway, now I would just return forewarned. If there was some threat we had yet to perceive, then Darius, Bryony, and I would find it together. If there was some excuse for Jareth's actions—however slight—then I would help Darius to see it. And if this was just some mind game from Jareth, then I would put an end to that, too.

I wasn't alone, and despite what he seemed determined to think, Darius wasn't either. Second year hadn't turned out how either of us expected, but we had still won a great victory. Darius would have his crown, and Ardann would have an alliance.

I pushed aside the grim sense of foreboding that lurked at the back of my mind. I had a new ability, more powerful than I had yet let myself fully contemplate. And while I couldn't bring myself to commit it to the service of any one kingdom, I wouldn't hesitate to use it to save my friends. If there was a threat lurking, waiting to pounce, then I would face it head on and defeat it. I was no longer powerless, and I defied anyone to hurt the people I loved.

Read about Verene's third year at the Kallorwegian Academy in Crown of Strength.

If you missed it, you can also read about the adventures of Verene's mother, Elena, when she attends the Ardannian Academy as a commonborn and becomes the Spoken Mage, starting in Voice of Power.

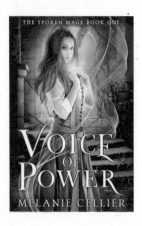

To be informed of future releases, as well as Hidden Mage bonus shorts, please sign up to my mailing list at www.melaniecellier.com.

And if you enjoyed Crown of Danger, please spread the word and help other readers find it! You could start by leaving a review on Amazon (or Goodreads or Facebook or any other social media site). Your review would be very much appreciated and would make a big difference!

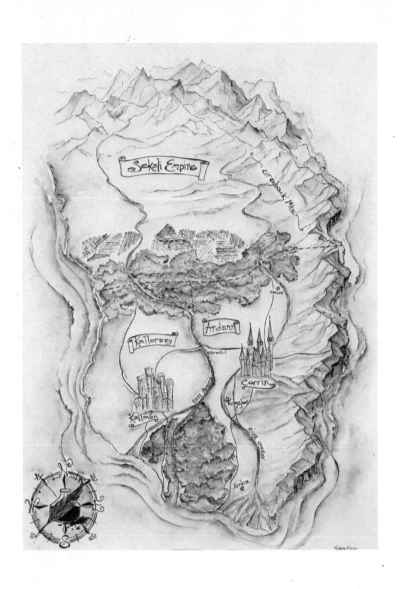

ACKNOWLEDGMENTS

Verene's second year at the Academy expanded the world of Kallorway somewhat, but I look forward to exploring it further in her third year. While I enjoy writing my standalone fairytales, it's always nice to write a book where I'm coming back to familiar, established characters and settings. And it's fun to weave in plot threads, knowing I'll have the chance to explore them in future books, and to journey with characters through a longer arc of growth and change.

But at the same time, 2020 has brought plenty of challenges, and I'm sure I wouldn't be able to keep writing and publishing through them all if it wasn't for my supportive family and team.

My beta readers were a wonderful source of encouragement with this book, in particular, Rachel, Greg, Ber, Katie, Priya, and my mum. And my editors—Mary, Deborah, and my dad—went above and beyond to stay flexible and work with my timeline. It's only because of your support that I can turn raw words into a published book in the midst of the current tumult of my life.

The further I get into this publishing career, the more I realize how valuable it is to find skilled and reliable professionals to work with, so as well as my editors, I want to give an extra big thank you to my cover designer, Karri, who has never let me down in any way.

And to my friends and family, your patience with me is appreciated so much, and I look forward to a new season in 2021. I intend to never again combine a pregnancy and house move with an intense, aspirational writing schedule!

And finally to God. Thank you for being reliable even when I am not, and faithful and loving when I need it most.

ABOUT THE AUTHOR

 Melanie Cellier grew up on a staple diet of books, books and more books. And although she got older, she never stopped loving children's and young adult novels.

She always wanted to write one herself, but it took three careers and three different continents before she actually managed it.

She now feels incredibly fortunate to spend her time writing from her home in Adelaide, Australia where she keeps an eye out for koalas in her backyard. Her staple diet hasn't changed much, although she's added choc mint Rooibos tea and Chicken Crimpies to the list.

She writes young adult fantasy including books in her *Spoken Mage* world, and her three *Four Kingdoms and Beyond* series which are made up of linked stand-alone stories that retell classic fairy tales.

Made in United States
Troutdale, OR
11/24/2023

14906520R00170